D0558867

DEEP FREEZE

BOOKS BY MICHAEL C. GRUMLEY

THE MONUMENT TRILOGY
The Last Monument
The Desert of Glass

THE BREAKTHROUGH SERIES
Breakthrough
Leap
Catalyst
Ripple
Mosaic
Echo

DEEP FREEZE

MICHAEL C. GRUMLEY

TOR PUBLISHING GROUP

NEW YORK

This is a work of fiction. All of the characters, organizations, and events portrayed in this novel are either products of the author's imagination or are used fictitiously.

DEEP FREEZE

Copyright © 2023 by Michael C. Grumley

All rights reserved.

A Forge Book
Published by Tom Doherty Associates / Tor Publishing Group
120 Broadway
New York, NY 10271

www.tor-forge.com

Forge® is a registered trademark of Macmillan Publishing Group, LLC.

The Library of Congress Cataloging-in-Publication Data is available upon request.

ISBN 978-1-250-89868-5 (hardcover)
ISBN 978-1-250-89869-2 (ebook)

Our books may be purchased in bulk for promotional, educational, or business use. Please contact your local bookseller or the Macmillan Corporate and Premium Sales Department at 1-800-221-7945, extension 5442, or by email at MacmillanSpecialMarkets@macmillan.com.

First Edition: 2024

Printed in the United States of America

0 9 8 7 6 5 4 3 2 1

To my mother, Autumn.
One of the most beautiful souls I know.

DEEP FREEZE

DEEP
FREEZE

1

The slide of the gun was pulled back and released in one quick motion, giving its distinctive metallic sound as it snapped back and automatically chambered the first bullet.

Outside the car, another snowfall was heavily dotting the car's windshield and hood as well as the ground around them; a pothole-ridden parking lot, partially illuminated by the bright interior lights of a convenience store.

Scanning the area revealed an empty street, and on the far side, away from the road, a small one-story veterans' hall—dark and empty, surrounded by an undisturbed snowy field. Behind them, a single streetlamp, two blocks away, provided a shower of light upon a tiny building, the town's only bus stop.

"Let's go!"

"Wait!" A nineteen-year-old sporting a dark ski mask stared through the back window toward the stop. A distant cloud of billowing heat rose from the tail end of the bus. Only the back half was visible on the other side of the small building. Between them, thousands of snowflakes drifted gently down from the darkened sky above, some passing through the glow from the distant streetlamp as they fell.

"What the hell are you waiting for?"

"The bus, man!"

"So what?"

"Wait till it leaves!"

"What? Hell no! Go now!"

"What if they see me?"

The driver, another teenager, glanced back and shook his head. "Ain't no one gonna see you at this distance. Just go!"

The first teenager hesitated, contemplating, before his adrenaline finally won out.

"Fine! Turn the car and get ready."

The warmth inside the store was welcoming. Beneath a ceiling of old fluorescent lights, most still working, the modest store packed a surprising amount of shelf space within its meager walls, despite some remaining empty.

Near the front, a television was affixed to the wall just below the ceiling, displaying the local news.

Behind the counter, the cashier smiled politely at the woman and small boy before him while bagging their items. Two bottles of water, a bag of potato chips, and a tiny box of painkillers.

The man, presumably the owner, repeated the amount displayed on the register and took the money without comment, briefly noting the second customer in line behind the woman, who was patiently watching the TV overhead, and carrying a small four-pack of beer.

The man in line looked quietly at the mayhem playing out across the large screen. Thousands had gathered in downtown Philadelphia to protest. Signs bobbed up and down while throngs of people chanted and marched forward in a surging wave of anger.

The picture moved, panning to another section of street, where perhaps a dozen had descended upon an empty police car, beating and smashing its side windows while others climbed on top to stomp and crush the vehicle's red and blue lights. A Molotov cocktail was thrown against the side of a nearby building and exploded into flame, causing the mob to roar and cheer.

The customer in line was the only one watching, silent and staring. Neither the owner nor the woman and her son bothered to look up.

It was almost a daily occurrence. Citizens rising up in anger. Yelling, marching, and destroying. This one appeared to be a crowd of city workers furious over labor conditions. The night before was in downtown New York.

His thoughts were interrupted by a chime when the outside door was suddenly pushed open, followed by a brief blast of frigid air. And with it, a young man with wide brown eyes staring through two large holes in his ski mask.

Behind the counter, the owner glanced up momentarily and then froze when a gun appeared in the hand of the teenager, who briskly scanned the store for anyone else, but found only the three in front of him.

Noting the look on the owner's face, the woman turned and gasped, clumsily stumbling backward in an effort to shield her son. The thug eyes narrowed and focused past her.

Mere seconds had passed when behind the thug a bottle was retrieved from its carton and smashed down over the hand gripping the gun, breaking the bone in an audible crack.

The masked teenager screamed and dropped the gun. In a panic, he scrambled backward and lost his balance, falling to the floor. The eyes behind the mask were wild and changed their focus from searching for the gun to searching for an exit. Whirling around to find the glass doors behind him, the teenager immediately pushed forward and lunged outside, on one good hand and both knees.

Over the icy concrete, he struggled to his feet and bolted clumsily for the waiting car. Flinging its door open, he jumped in, screaming.

Inside, the cashier retrieved a revolver from a shelf below the counter, then, after watching the car rocket from the parking lot, turned to his male customer with a stunned expression. The man was still holding the bottle in his hand, while the woman at the counter stood immobile, still clutching her son behind her.

Without a word, the man placed the beer bottle back into the cardboard holder and glanced at the gun on the floor. Bending over, he picked it up, then stepped past the trembling woman to place both items on the counter and retrieve his wallet.

He held out a bill to find the owner staring at him incredulously, before simply shaking his head and motioning for him to take the item.

The customer nodded in appreciation and picked the carton back up, leaving the gun on the counter. Without comment, he turned and pushed through the glass doors, back into the snowy night air.

The first bottle was empty by the time he reached the stop. With crunching snow beneath every step, he slid it back into the carton and opened another.

Upon reaching the idling bus, he gently tapped the base of his second bottle against the vehicle's tall glass door, which was promptly opened from the inside.

The driver frowned from his seat. "No open containers."

The man, sporting a heavy two-day shadow, stared at the driver and nodded. He scanned the area surrounding the tiny station and found a trash can. He approached it, finished the second beer, and discarded both empty bottles.

He returned and looked to the driver for approval, and the driver motioned him up the steps.

The last to reboard were the mother and son. The woman staring in silence as they retook their seats.

The man looked out his window, into the darkness at the shadowed outlines of their surroundings. One of the houses on the far side of the street was still illuminated by what looked to be a living room window. The rest of the buildings lay dark and appeared as muted shapes obscured beyond the increasingly dense snowfall.

He paid little attention. His thoughts were elsewhere. On his destination . . . when he was interrupted in his seat.

It was the woman. The mother. Of the boy, who was perhaps seven or eight and peering cautiously at them over his seat's headrest.

The woman was standing over him, appearing flustered. Unsure of what to say.

"I just," she stammered, "wanted to say thank you."

The man's expression was wholly unconcerned, but he nodded receptively while the driver put the bus into gear and slowly accelerated.

"No problem."

2

The trip through southern Minnesota was met by even harsher weather, blanketing the landscape in thick white snow, the only exception being the dark tire tracks directly in front of them, traversing the lonely two-lane highway before disappearing ahead into a flurry of white flakes, all brightly illuminated by the bus's headlights.

The driver steadily slowed as the visibility decreased, and he was barely able to see the headlights of oncoming traffic as they approached and sped past. Grumbling under his breath at their recklessness, the older man leaned forward with both hands firmly gripping the oversized steering wheel. His old eyes intent and undeterred.

Before long, several faint red lights appeared through the bitter gale, as a square, boxed pattern, and gradually revealing the multiple taillights of a large semitruck as the bus steadily closed in.

The driver glanced into his overhead mirror at his handful of passengers, all lulled to sleep by the bus's interior heat and the powerful vehicle's slow, methodic rumble.

Traffic began to move, and the bus began to accelerate again, passing a neon-green sign that read NARROW BRIDGE AHEAD.

Even from a distance, it was clear the driver of the oncoming vehicle was traveling too fast for the conditions. Too fast to notice the road abruptly narrowing at the aging girder bridge. Unaware or unconcerned that, unlike asphalt, metal bridges could not trap heat. Instead, the girders iced rapidly in extreme weather, pulling heat from what little asphalt there was and allowing snow to thicken over its surface. Just enough to prevent traction above a certain weight and speed.

It was the tires from the oncoming SUV that met those conditions under a sudden stomp of the brakes. Causing the vehicle to slide—suddenly and uncontrollably—across the narrow road's double yellow line and into the lane of the approaching semitruck directly ahead of the bus.

The truck's driver was as crisp as one could expect at three in the morning. Reacting reflexively, he attempted to remain in his lane by forcing the nose of the truck through the diminishing space left between the sliding SUV and the bridge's right-side railing.

Almost instantly, the semitruck's cargo trailer pitched violently, causing a slow-motion slide across the width of the entire bridge, and leaving no escape for the large bus immediately behind him.

In an instant, the bus driver was nearly standing on his brake, in an uncontrolled slide as he fell back into his seat and rapidly pumped his foot up and down upon the pedal, applying quick, repeated jolts of momentary traction. It was the proper braking procedure, but it was not enough.

At thirty-five miles per hour, the sheer weight and momentum of the passenger bus could not be stopped, and it plowed headlong into the cargo trailer. Smashing into it as though it were a brick wall, and the bus a slow and unstoppable train. The giant windshield was obliterated on impact, and the rear of the trailer shoved violently forward and through the bridge's protective side railing.

Inside the bus, the passengers screamed as they were jolted from their slumber into a scene of panic and chaos. Two near the front shrieked at the swirling carnage in front of them before an blast of bright sparks and shattered windshield imploded, raining a curtain of pebbles over the first several rows of seats in glittering destruction.

Then came the sound. Through the destroyed windshield came a thunderous bang as the bus continued its violent slide, followed by the screeching of heavy metal of thick girders as they twisted, snapped, and finally tore loose.

The giant vehicle stopped, and for a moment teetered over the edge.

All breathing stopped. Briefly.

Before the bus's two front wheels gave way and eased forward over the edge. Causing the undercarriage to scrape mercilessly over the bridge's asphalt and slowly extend out into open air. Sliding, gradually at first . . . then quickly, and then all at once, plummeting just over twenty feet to the frozen river below.

3

The screaming resumed. And continued throughout the fall. Through the bus's entire plunge and sudden impact, where it was met by an explosion of ice and water through the missing front windshield.

The driver, strapped in his seat, was pinned by the force of the icy water. And behind him, horrified passengers screamed at the wall of oncoming water before them.

The first half of the bus was filled in seconds by icy water swirling with glass, while just outside, a thick layer of ice from the frozen river could now be seen surrounding the vehicle. It scraped against the glass until several windows shattered inward, creating a second deluge into the bus's interior.

The roiling water reached the mother and son, who were both paralyzed and buckled where they sat, only beginning to fumble with their tangled belts when besieged by the river water.

Able to free herself, the mother turned to search for her son—desperate and frantic—only to see him immediately disappear from view.

She stood up screaming his name, and quickly found him in the arms of the man from the store, who now pulled the boy up and over the headrest as if he weighed nothing, thrusting him up the rising floorboard toward the back of the bus. He then grabbed the woman and did the same, pushing her forward in front of him and yelling over her shoulder at an older couple struggling at the rear of the bus.

"Get one of those windows open! Above the ice!"

The older man, perhaps in his sixties, stared back in panic. As if trying to understand.

"The window! Get it open! Now!"

The man's eyes focused and he jumped, using each headrest to pull himself up the narrow aisle until he reached the last row of seats and lunged over both seat cushions on the left-hand side to grab the two bright red metal handles. He yanked as hard as he could, then pushed.

Nothing.

He pushed again, harder. Watching as the ice outside crept insidiously from window to window. Closing in on the same window he was trying to open.

"Other side!"

The stranger behind the mother and son continued shouting as he pushed forward, even while they repeatedly slipped and fell back into him.

The older man now raced to the opposite side and yanked the window handles up. This time throwing his weight against the glass and sending the large pane flying out.

"Go!" the stranger ordered. "Get out and help pull them through!"

The older man didn't hesitate. He scrambled out and onto the river's frozen surface. Slipping at first, he managed to spin around and grab his wife's outstretched hands.

Inside, mother and son were still being pushed forward, scrambling up the slippery aisle, but no longer making progress. Prompting the man behind them to yell over the noise, "Climb over the seats! Over the seats!"

The icy water reached his legs and lower back with a paralyzing sting.

If there was any fortune at all, it was in the temporary rotation of the bus, allowing the last two windows on the right side to remain above the water level. But not for long, because he could feel the entire vessel continuing to sink downward. And it was accelerating.

The young boy made it over the last seat, scrambling to and out of the window with helping hands from the outside. The bus continued to sink, and the thick layer of ice continued rising toward the only open window.

"Hurry!" the man shouted, and suddenly heaved the woman forward with both hands, sending her over the last seat.

Outside, the older man and his wife wrapped hands tightly around the woman's and pulled.

The entire bus was almost underwater, with the ice finally reaching their escape window, allowing the couple to retrieve the woman by sliding her out belly-first onto the ice's surface.

It was then that a giant cavity of air escaped, and the bus suddenly plunged, and the open window was abruptly slammed back up and closed again.

"*No!*"

The older man scrambled from the outside to pull it open again, his fingers tracing around the frame, searching for a gap to pry free. Finding nothing, he waved to the stranger trapped inside. "Get back! *Get back!*"

The older man turned and cocked his leg and foot back as far as he could, sending a powerful kick into the center of the pane.

A small crack appeared.

He pulled back again, kicking harder. Another crack.

It was sinking too fast.

"*Damn it!*" he yelled, and kicked again. This time the crack broke open with a small hole. Again and again he kicked, enlarging the hole as the entire pane slowly began to disappear from view. His last kick missed, instead hitting the outer frame as the window finally sank below the frozen ice and water.

4

In a dark bedroom, a phone lying atop the nightstand buzzed loudly as it vibrated. It was answered on the third ring. Picked up with a sigh, it illuminated a portion of the bedroom from its screen.

"Who is it?"

"Burkhart."

"Burkhart?" Who the hell was Burkhart?

"Out of Minnesota."

It took several more seconds to place the name.

"Right. Right. What is it?"

"I think I found who you're looking for."

Beneath a mess of gray hair, two eyes widened. "Say again?"

"I said, I think I found who you've been looking for."

A pause. "Are you sure?"

"Not positive, but I *think* it's a match."

"Where?"

"About an hour south of Minneapolis. In a bus accident. Plunged off a bridge about two hours ago. He was trapped inside."

"You're kidding."

"Nope."

The man pushed himself up in bed, thinking before checking his watch. "I'll be there in three hours. Don't let anyone at him."

5

It didn't look at all like a research center.

With oversized windows and decades-old red brick and mortar, the large rectangular building in the old downtown area looked like it belonged more to a run-down university than a common city block.

Or maybe an old church.

Which it had been was a question Rachel Souza wondered many mornings as she approached. Stepping over some windblown trash, she left the oversized sidewalk and climbed the dozen steps leading to the front entrance.

Taking hold of the small badge dangling at the end of her lanyard, she casually pressed it against the dark magnetic plate on the wall. After several seconds, the door buzzed and unlocked with a loudclick. Inside, a small lobby greeted her, attended by a familiar uniformed figure behind a window. The security guard looked up and smiled at Souza, scrutinizing her only briefly before reaching down to buzz a second door open. This one wider and painted in a light gray earth tone to match the surrounding and somewhat featureless walls.

The first corridor was as bland and forgettable as the foyer, leading past three sets of permanently locked double doors before ending at a lone elevator. In the upper corner was mounted a single rectangular-shaped security camera.

She pressed her badge against the second plate and glanced at the symbols above the elevator, watching as a red light appeared in the shape of a down arrow.

Casually, she stepped back and waited, adjusting the black leather satchel hanging from her right shoulder.

At five foot six, she was dressed in jeans and a light collared long-sleeved blouse, her dark hair arranged neatly in a French braid hanging just below both shoulders.

When the doors finally parted, she stepped inside and turned, pressing the next button down before catching a reflection of herself in one of the narrow strips of beveled glass and grinning at herself in nervous excitement.

The first floor below ground was the lab. Or at least one of them. The room was lined on each side with long metal shelves and counters, which held several microscopes, both compound and inverted, along with multiple computer monitors. Above them, bottles and containers were neatly shelved and labeled, storing various tissues and cultures. And finally, a chest-high glass refrigerator at the end, filled with bricks of test tubes and dozens of petri dishes.

Without a word, she continued along one of the counters and dropped her satchel with a muted thunk, then proceeded to a nearby monitor.

Noting the time at the bottom corner of the screen, she used the mouse to switch views, bringing up another window that displayed several live video feeds.

One by one, she studied all the feeds, then straightened with a satisfied nod. It was a big day, and she had only a few hours to ensure that everything was ready.

Returning to her bag, Rachel retrieved a metal thermos and unscrewed the lid, then took a sip of coffee. Her morning octane.

She was both excited and nervous. Excited for everything leading up to the big event but nervous in the fear they had missed something. Something important. If they had, she couldn't imagine what it was. Of course, she was only one part of the project. A significant part, but the rest was still out of her hands, and she had precious little control over that. She had her specialty, just as the others had theirs. All she could do now was hope everyone had done their job and missed nothing.

"Nervous?"

Startled, she pulled the thermos away from her mouth, catching a few drops in the palm of her hand. Turning, she found her colleague Henry Yamada leaning against the open door.

With a shrug, he stepped inside. "Sorry. Been here since six."

"Why so early?"

"Double-checking everything. Just like you."

Rachel raised the thermos again and smiled behind it. "Your stuff is easy."

Yamada, in his thirties and one inch shorter, laughed. "Is that so?"

"I'm joking!" she said, still grinning. "Mostly."

"I'm going to pretend I didn't hear that, since I'm running on very little sleep anyway."

"If that's the case, I think we're all in trouble. How are things looking for you?"

"So far, so good." Lowering his hand, he rapped on the counter. "Knock wood. You gonna be there for the final test?"

"When is it?"

"Nine thirty."

"Meh."

He was surprised. "Really? I thought for sure you'd be there."

"That's more your thing than mine."

"But it's the very last check."

She contemplated before shrugging. "Yeah, okay. Maybe just in the background to watch. You think it's going to work?"

"What the hell, Rach?! You trying to jinx me? Don't say that; of course it's going to work!"

She chuckled and glanced back at the screen behind her. It took a lot not to fixate, so she hoped he was right. Yamada was one of the guys in charge of the Machine. A prototype unlike anything ever designed before. And if that didn't work, nothing would matter.

Several minutes later, Rachel stepped into her lab's second room as silently as possible.

As expected, they were all staring at her.

She eased the heavy door closed behind her and strolled forward, passing each cage in ascending order of size. Studying each one individually, slowly and carefully.

First were the mice. Three. Each in its own cage to avoid biological commingling. Cells and systems, even within a separate body, had a way of sensing and reacting to one another. Some in ways still not fully understood. So precautions were important.

Next were the rabbits. Two. Also separated. In cages several feet apart. Both resting calmly, through a series of tiny rapid breaths, with soft unblinking eyes as she smiled down at them.

"Good morning, Pixie. Good morning, Tinkerbell."

She wasn't supposed to name them, but she couldn't help it. A person could only study and care for an animal for so long without forming some level of connection.

The next cage was larger, housing Lester, a small Duroc pig. A common research breed, smart and easily trainable. Representing a significant step up in cognition and neurological complexity.

Next was Isabella, a fifteen-pound white terrier-Chihuahua mix who was already on her hind legs, wagging her tail excitedly and whining. Rachel grinned and leaned over to open the wired latch, and reached in to pet the dog's head. "Good morning, Bella. How are you?"

The short-haired dog jumped up and down, whimpering with excitement.

"Okay, okay. We'll get you out in a minute."

She straightened and continued moving to the final two cages. Both much larger and sturdier. The first housed a capuchin monkey named Dallas, gray in color and sitting calmly inside. He watched Rachel through a pair of unblinking, amber eyes.

And finally, the last. Otis. A larger chimpanzee bundled up in his blanket in a corner of the largest cage, dozing.

She watched the outline of his small hairy abdomen rising and falling with every breath. His head and blanket always reminded Rachel of her grandfather Otis, whom she remembered as old, bald, and perpetually napping, while she baked in the kitchen with her grandmother.

She had grown fond of all of the animals, especially Bella. Studying them for months, one by one, as each new subject was introduced. Increasing in size along with biological and neurological complexity. All still ostensibly happy and healthy, and, more importantly, normal in every observable measurement. It was now time to hand off these lucky few to the local animal parks for more permanent homes.

Because the truth was, these were the survivors.

6

The final test Henry Yamada was running was for calibration purposes. The last complete diagnostic check before the actual event, but in this case, much more complex.

The Machine was the result of the most sophisticated microengineering project in medical history. Long and cylindrical, it was mathematically shaped, based on meticulous calculations, and lined with high-density elastomers for maximum absorbency—polymers and rubberlike solids carefully designed to reduce electromagnetic radiation emitted by the 1,024 tiny transmitters spaced perfectly throughout the device's interior.

Surrounding each transmitter like a two-dimensional halo were small circular diode sensors that detected the faintest changes in microwave strength and modulation while passing through its intended target from every conceivable angle, and were able to adjust the signaling almost instantly to ensure near-perfect uniform exposure. They measured signal strength, vibration, and temperature in real time, all of which lay at the heart of the heating process, by causing molecules to vibrate very, very carefully.

After just a few minutes, the final test was successfully completed, if a bit anticlimactic. Rachel watched from an observation booth, standing behind the others.

Below them, inside the main laboratory itself, Yamada and two other technicians sat in front of a comprehensive digital panel hosting dozens of connected monitors and controls. They typed away on their keyboards, paused to validate another result, and continued on.

On the main screen, an infrared image of the Machine was displayed, glowing in various auras of yellow, orange, and red. A similar image was displayed on an adjacent screen, this one in 3D and overlaid with more than a thousand tiny green circles representing the internal transmitters and diode sensors.

After several long minutes and dozens of output tests, Yamada finally swiveled in his chair and faced the booth overhead, including the three people standing in front of Rachel.

Yamada looked at the figure in the front and center, Robert Masten, the man in charge, and gave a thumbs-up. He and his technicians then rose from their seats and circled the giant device as its cover automatically released and slid back, exposing its interior.

Through a plume of gentle steam, the three surrounded the opening and reached inside with handheld instruments. Over and over, inserting, waiting, and reading aloud each result.

When finished, they conferred and nodded again. Prompting Yamada to look back up at the glass window with a final thumbs-up.

On the opposite side of the floor-to-ceiling window, in his dark blue slacks and dress shirt with sleeves rolled up, Robert Masten leaned to the side and pressed the intercom button. "And?"

Yamada stepped back to the console and spoke through his microphone. "Everything looks good. All transmitters are firing perfectly. All within twelve degrees."

Masten turned to the woman on his right.

"Still well within range," she said.

The director then turned to the man on his left, who wore a stern expression through a neatly combed white hair and mustache, and was nodding in agreement.

Satisfied, Masten pressed the button again.

"Time for the final prep."

Rachel was still looking through the glass after the room had emptied, watching Yamada and his assistants conclude the test and finally, together, reach in and carefully extract the test subject. It was heavy; all three were required in order to lift the 120-pound slab of beef from inside the Machine. It was several feet long, and oozing droplets of liquid blood as they hefted it out.

Rachel had to remind herself that this final test was only meant to be an integrity check. The monstrous slab of dead cow was, of course, in no way representative of the final subject.

7

"Well?" Masten asked, easing back into his thick leather chair and panning around the table. His dark hair was graying at the edges and above a face that could have passed for that of a B-list celebrity. At least an older one. But he wasn't a model; he was a mogul. A decades-old prince of biotech and a hardened executive who knew the ins and outs of the industry as well as anyone. Perhaps better.

When no one spoke, he looked to the woman seated next to him. Nora Lagner, his chief technology officer and right-hand man, or rather right-hand *woman*.

"We're as ready as we'll ever be," she said.

Masten nodded and continued around the oval table, glancing past Henry Yamada and Rachel Souza to Dr. Perry Williams, the project's chief medical officer and the man in charge of the medical staff.

After a moment of careful thought, the older doctor finally nodded as well. "I'm inclined to agree."

"Just inclined?"

"Well, assuming we haven't overlooked anything."

"Like what?"

Williams gave a shrug of his shoulders. "If I knew that, it wouldn't be missed."

An amused Masten leaned forward and increased the volume on the triangular-shaped speakerphone in the middle of the table. "Anyone else?"

There was a brief silence before—one by one—six remote subject-matter experts replied on the speakerphone with a simple "Agreed."

But even as the others concurred, an air of hesitancy remained. A certain nervousness, especially in Williams. In many ways, the secrecy of the project was both a blessing and a curse. There was little interference to hamper their ambition, but there was enough real-world experience among them to know what could happen if they were wrong. In other words, what they were really up against, and of course, the odds of them pulling it off.

The sobering fact was that either way, people would know. Good or bad. They would eventually find out. It was inevitable. Frankly, it was a miracle the project hadn't leaked already, especially once the trials began. But Robert Masten had managed to keep it quiet from the outside world.

"Rachel?"

She looked to find Masten looking her way, noting briefly his stiff, pressed collar and pin-striped shirt. Well-dressed as always, with hair that even when messy managed to look good.

"Yes?"

"Are we good?" he asked.

"From my side, yes." She glanced at Williams, on her right. "Again, it will come down to the primary factors."

"The heart—"

"And lungs," added Williams. "Without oxygen, nothing else will matter. But we won't know how effective the protectants have been until we're almost finished."

Masten looked back at Rachel.

Once again, she nodded in agreement. Her boss, Williams, was an internist. A medical doctor specializing in the major organs of the body. The heart, lungs, diaphragm, kidneys, and liver. Or in this case, the preservation and survival of said organs. The body could live for a short time without a liver or kidney, up to several days, but without a heart or lungs, the survival window dropped to mere minutes. Yes, there were artificial ways to compensate. Temporarily. But without the four principal organs, complications would increase immediately and dramatically.

Which brought them to her.

Rachel Souza's training was in another critical area: the body's thousands of miles of arteries and blood vessels, known as the vascular system. She was not an expert on organs like Williams, but instead on the vital pathways linking them together. And though Williams was right, no amount of pumping or oxygenation to those organs was going to matter without the vascular system being liquid.

The biggest wild card was the protectants, chemical compounds designed to prevent excessive damage, which in the end would show just how successful the vitrification process had been. Just as Williams indicated.

"Doctor?" Masten asked again.

Rachel quickly nodded, stymieing her nervousness by turning to Henry Yamada. "As long as we can stay within range."

"And will we stay within range?"

Yamada cleared his throat and nodded as well. "There's no reason to think we won't."

"Good," said Masten. "Then we're ready to jump-start."

It was an attempt at levity. To which the older Williams added, "If the tube insertion is successful. Yes."

Rachel remained quiet. The most significant risk was that everything, every single step, had to happen within just a few minutes. Which was where her and Williams's real worries lay. That the electric shock would come too soon. Before the arteries were fluid enough. Because if they weren't, there would be no point. *You can't pump something frozen.*

But now that the day was finally here, Rachel could feel her confidence morphing into apprehension. It was all beginning to feel so . . . theoretical.

Yes, they knew how quickly blood would warm. *Should warm.* She and Yamada had tested it hundreds of times. Along with large sections of tissue. Heart, lung, liver, kidneys, stomach, all of them. And, of course, the brain. The science and the math told them the same thing over and over again; it *should* work.

But there was still a lot that could go wrong. And she and Williams both knew it. Unlike Lagner, Masten's CTO, who believed that every problem could be solved with enough technology. Biology was different. Much less precise and predictable. Because life often had a way of operating according to its own set of rules, presenting surprises when one least expected them. Even in the most routine and controlled procedures.

An hour later, Rachel knocked quietly on Williams's office door and heard his answer from within. The older doctor stood by the window on the far side of the room.

She passed his desk, covered in stacks of dark-colored X-rays and MRI images, organized and carefully labeled. Next to them towered a giant computer monitor spanning nearly half the entire desk, and in front of it, a keyboard, a desk phone, and several handheld medical devices.

Williams glanced over his shoulder when she approached, then turned back to the window.

"You okay?" she asked.

There was a long pause before he answered.

"This is it, Rachel. This is for all the marbles."

She turned an empty chair toward him, then sat. "I know."

"We have one shot."

She nodded but said nothing.

"After this, we may never get another chance. At least not in our lifetimes."

"It's going to work."

He sighed. "Is it?"

"Yes."

"How do you know?"

She managed a grin. "Just more hopeful, I guess."

"Hope is not a strategy."

She leaned back, watching him. "What is it that worries you the most?"

The older doctor exhaled, still staring through the glass. "The unknown, what else?"

"We've tried to think of everything. Every contingency."

"That's not what I mean." He finally moved from the window to the second upholstered chair, next to hers, lowering himself. "This has implications, Rachel. Serious implications."

"I know."

"Either way," he said. "Whether we succeed or fail. And I don't know which will be worse."

"What do you mean?"

"Win or lose, what we do today will ripple for a long time."

"But is that bad?"

"It depends on the outcome." He leaned back. "Let's just say judgment can be very unpredictable. Especially after the fact."

"We're the ones with the opportunity. Not them."

"Exactly. And why do you think that is?"

"We found the anomaly."

Williams smiled below his white mustache. "The 'anomaly.' I suppose that's a better word than 'luck.'"

"None of us know why, Perry. We can't find any rhyme or reason. We've tried. Maybe it is just the luck of the draw. Who knows? Maybe we find out, and maybe we don't. I'm not even sure it matters. If it works, it will be incredible, for everyone. Are there risks? Yes. But have we done everything we can to address them? Also yes. So what judgment are you worried about? The ethics?"

Williams's eyes stared past her. "At the very least. Yes, we've tried to contain all the risks we can think of, here in our lab. But the tide of public opinion is far more powerful and much less certain. Everything we do tomorrow will be dissected. Later. Every . . . single . . . thing. No matter how small the decision. No matter how insignificant it might seem in the moment. Every minute will be dissected, examined, and second-guessed for years to come. Even decades."

"Only if we fail." Rachel winked.

"*Especially* if we fail."

From his seat, Williams turned and glanced back through the window. His glasses reflected the sunlight. "It all comes down to this. A single stroke of luck."

"Or coincidence."

"Same thing."

She thought it over. "Well, whatever it is, on this I actually agree with Robert and Nora. Reluctantly, but I agree." When Williams raised an eyebrow, she finished, "We're as ready as we'll ever be."

He blinked absently. "Now or never, eh?"

"Now or never."

"And should we fail?"

"Then we tried our best."

Williams finally released a grin. "That's what I love about you, Rachel. Even when you know the odds, you still manage to be optimistic. It's an admirable trait."

"I really think we have a good chance of pulling this off."

"I hope you're right," he said. "Because if we don't . . . someone dies."

8

The long chrome examination table was wheeled in at precisely 6:00 A.M. The black body bag on top was made of thick plastic with a long zipper running its entire length—just over six feet. And sewn into each side, at two-foot intervals, were reinforced nylon straps for handles.

Bringing the bag alongside the Machine, Yamada reached out and pulled an overhead section of dangling fabric closer. A heavy-duty sling attached to four large chains suspended from a rail system. Across the table, Williams carefully unzipped the bag, pulling each side down to reveal a human body, unclothed and still, with skin tinted light blue.

Without a word, Williams, Masten, Yamada, and Rachel worked together to lift one side of the body while pulling half of the hanging sling beneath it. Then the opposite side, where the rest of the fabric was laid flat against the bare metal. They then gently lowered the figure back down on top of it.

Attaching the two remaining chains to the opposite side, Yamada gave a tug on each before moving to the wall. Where he nodded at the others and pressed a large green button to activate the overhead winch.

They carefully watched each corner before taking a small step back, prompting Yamada to begin. Ever so slowly, under the whirring of the winch, the sling lifted from the table, rising higher into the air. Once fully levitated, it was pulled along the railing over the Machine, where Yamada then switched buttons to begin lowering. He paused within a few inches of the opening, then continued, easing it inside, while the other three each gripped a chain to control the descent, so that the distance from the body to each side was carefully measured and adjusted before the sling was lowered the final few inches and the chains removed.

Together, Williams and Souza attached a total of fourteen sensors to various areas on the arms, torso, and legs, delicately connecting them to one side of the Machine's interior wall.

When finished, both straightened and nodded to the others, leaving Yamada—and Masten behind him—to move to the computer console and examine the digital readouts.

Still on the far side, Williams wheeled a large defibrillator into place and powered it on, waiting several long seconds for the audible confirmation. He then carefully arranged both electrode paddles into position. When finished, he double-checked the settings and stepped back.

Timing would be everything.

Masten glanced up at the large observation window above them, where Nora Lagner calmly watched from the other side.

"How are we looking?"

Yamada nodded. "Good." His eyes continued scanning, moving from screen to screen. "Running the self-check one last time. . . ."

Rachel watched him move back and forth along the console, transfixed. His two engineers were notably absent, intentionally left out of the final event. Not for security reasons, but in case something went wrong. If it did, plausible deniability would be important.

"All systems active," announced Yamada. "Verifying electrode feedback and closing the lid."

Now seated, Yamada began typing, then shot a look to Masten before loading the final sequence. All three were now standing behind him.

On one of the screens, a complex diagram of the circuitry and microfiber wiring was overlaid atop a three-dimensional image of the Machine. And over that, the thousand tiny circles, each icon representing one of the system's miniature microwave transmitters and sensors.

He turned and looked over his shoulder to Masten. "Ready?"

Masten inhaled. "Let's do it."

Yamada launched the countdown. "Here we go."

The process was something they had all witnessed before, multiple times. On animals. They watched the energy build until the clock on the

screen finally began incrementing and all the tiny circles suddenly illuminated into a sea of colorful blue dots.

There was no turning back now.

It didn't take long to see that something was wrong.

Less than thirty seconds in, several of the blue dots began flashing.
Back at the keyboard and quickly zooming in, Yamada traced their paths,
while examining the data being spit out along the right side of his screen.

"We have some inconsistencies."

"We can see that," said Masten. "Where?"

He zoomed out to show the sensors again, now flashing yellow, then
rotated the 3D image to display the affected areas.

He glanced at the timer, now approaching fifty seconds. Touching
each flashing circle presented dozens of tiny numbers along the length of
numerous faint lines. "Areas of the left kidney . . . parts of the liver . . .
and some patches in the stomach. Maybe one in the right ventricle."

"Shit. That's more than we saw in the others."

"We're also dealing with more mass."

Behind Yamada and Masten, Rachel stared at the timer as it reached
one minute.

"Some look like they're normalizing," called Yamada, pointing to
several icons whose colors had changed back from yellow to blue.

They knew what it meant. Each circle measured faint changes in the
strength of the microwave signals as they passed through one side of the
body and impacted the sensors on the other. A drop in signal allowed
Yamada's machine to judge how much of the signal was lost during the
act of heating molecules within the tissue.

But meat samples and small animals had different tissue and density
levels. Especially when it came to the size of each organ. They knew
how quickly human liver tissue heated, both on a slab and in a petri
dish. But an organ that was still attached could only be estimated, just
like everything else.

"Most areas are still within range."

Onscreen, more circles turned returned to blue as the Machine self-
adjusted. But other circles abruptly turned red.

One minute and thirty seconds.

Rachel looked to Williams, who was transfixed. They were more
than halfway through, and most were looking good—

Then groups of red circles appeared around the heart.

Yamada touched the flashing icons to display a string of numbers. He then skimmed the numerous temperature readings passing through three-dimensional bone, tissue, and blood.

"They're not warming fast enough," said Yamada. He turned to the timer as it passed two minutes and looked at the two men beside him.

"Thirty more seconds."

Robert Masten's eyes moved to Williams. "Perry?"

There was no answer.

"Perry?"

The older doctor glanced at the timer and back to the onscreen image. "More time."

"How much—" Yamada stopped when he saw another circle appear—this one black.

Everyone stopped breathing. A single black circle, inches below the left lung. Then another a few inches away. And then another.

9

There was nothing. Except pain. Instant and unbearable pain. Everywhere.
Then nothing.
Until it returned.
Agony. Impossible agony.
So intense that it muffled the barrage of noise in the background. Stifled and unrecognizable. Sporadic.
Then nothing.
When it came again, the noise was louder. Splintering through the pain. Like a collision.
Someone was yelling.

10

The silence was longer this time. Then the pain returned. Like a flood. Everywhere at once.

Then a jolt. Holding momentarily before collapsing into a sea of terror and panic.

There was no more air, only water! Rushing in as the bus sank beneath the ice. And the hands still pressing against the window before everything disappeared into a flood of paralyzing icy water washing over every inch of his extremities. The last of his oxygen seeped out from his lips in a tiny stream of bubbles, as his lungs screamed in protest.

His hands and fingers searched. Panicked and desperate. Hunting for something. Anything!

And then it was over. Darkness interrupted by neural-driven flashes from a brain in the process of shutting down.

Bright, glowing, fleeting. Hallucinations of random images and sounds. Unintelligible and senseless.

Before they, too, were swallowed by the blackness.

11

"ECG is normalizing! P and T waves within range! Beats per minute—one hundred nineteen. Definite tachycardia."

Dr. Williams collapsed onto a nearby stool, sweating profusely and trying to catch his breath, before finally shaking his head. "Tachycardia is the least of our worries."

Exhaling in fits, he watched the small monitor intently as, one by one, the numbers gradually began to improve.

After several long seconds, Rachel Souza announced with excitement, "We have a repeating pulse!"

Still panting, Williams reached up and wiped his forehead with a handkerchief, while directly in front of him, the rise and fall of the patient's chest could now be seen. Slight, but it was there. Up and down, while the skin steadily changed from blue to light pink.

It was a miracle.

Just getting the respiratory system restarted had proved to be the fight of their lives. Let alone a stable pulse—faint but stable.

The doctor stared at their patient for a long time before his eyes rose to meet Rachel's.

They'd almost lost him multiple times. And it wasn't over. A functioning respiratory system did not mean they were out of the woods. But it was a foothold.

Suddenly the body on the table convulsed. First moderately, then violently. Arching up and off the cold metal, then immediately slamming back down against it with a thunderous bang.

The patient's mouth suddenly gaped open, then closed.

"Hold him!" shouted Williams, jumping to his feet and grabbing one arm, while Rachel reached for the other. "Hold his legs! Hold his legs!" he called out to Yamada and Masten.

The convulsions worsened, with arms and legs straining against their nylon binds. The mouth still opening and closing while hands and fingers began clawing uncontrollably at the open air.

Still clutching an arm, Williams turned and looked for the table tray behind him. Reaching out to grasp the edge and pulling it forcefully toward him, he caught the syringe in midair as it rolled off the edge.

In a fluid motion, he brought it to his mouth and yanked the cap off with his teeth, before plunging the short needle into a man's bucking right thigh.

Overhead, in the observation room and behind the glass, Nora Lagner watched the group scramble to control the convulsions, until the body finally appeared to relax under the powerful sedative, and eventually grew still.

The entire procedure had clearly not gone as planned, but in all honesty, that would have been a surprise in and of itself. It had taken over thirty minutes, and in witnessing the event from above, it appeared multiple times as though they would fail, if not for the team's determination. All that, for what Williams had said would be the easy part.

As for Lagner, her feelings were different. Not just out of surprise but disbelief. *The Machine actually worked.*

12

". . . a lot of damaged tissue. Some in vital areas, some not. But we don't know how severe, yet."

"When will we know?" asked Masten.

Williams frowned thoughtfully. "We can only estimate at this point. Conventional diagnostics won't tell us much for a few days. So, until then, we're in uncharted territory."

Masten nodded from his chair at the head of the table. "What are the priorities?"

"Kidneys, then liver. Then GI. If we can verify those are working, at least well enough, then we can start talking neurological. But right now, it's just about keeping the heart pumping."

The director turned to Dr. Souza. "Anything to add?"

She shook her head. "Circulation is slow but functioning, so the thawing worked. But we should expect significant vascular damage as well."

Masten exhaled and leaned back. They had expected problems. And they got them. The greater size and girth of a human patient introduced complications with the microwave transmitters, preventing them from warming the cells and tissues evenly, leaving pockets of tissues and fluids still frozen that would have blocked the primary respiratory organs from being reinstated, and forcing them to run the warming process longer than planned. Too long, trading the risk of frozen tissue for burned.

Now they were left trying to assess the damage—and the permanency. The liver was the only organ capable of regenerating damaged tissue, and even then, only so much. Damage to the other organs was expected to be much more problematic.

But like Dr. Williams said, at least the subject was alive. For the moment.

13

It took two days for the convulsions to fully dissipate without seda-
tives, replaced by small, occasional tremors within the limbs and larger
muscle groups. But all told, most symptoms had moderated somewhat,
enough to consider the next step, neurologic examination: brain, spinal
cord, and both motor and sensory ganglia.

Rachel watched as Williams moved progressively through the steps
of unconscious-reflex testing. Pulling back the patient's eyelids and
turning the head to one side. They watched for the DOLL response,
a natural deviation opposite the direction of the head's rotation, part
of the vestibulo-ocular reflex, or VOR. Next came the oculovestibular
testing of the cupulae, which so far had indicated normal functioning
of cranial nerves III, IV, VI, and VIII.

The results were encouraging. Especially in conjunction with
breathing pattern, motor response, and pupil response, meaning that
from an unconscious state, everything *appeared* intact.

The real test would be in the Glasgow scoring. And for that, they
would need to achieve consciousness.

14

The flashes returned.

Of the water.

Surging in from all directions. Like a wall of icy death, Undeniable. Inevitable. Washing over everything and reaching the bus's arched interior roof in seconds.

Then came light. Everywhere.

First white. Then changing colors through a mosaic of bright and dark yellows . . . and then a steady orange. The color of the flames.

Flames all around him.

Followed again by noise.

It was a cacophony. A harsh jumble of sound, from every direction and from none. Abrasive and piercing, it mixed together in an unbearable barrage, unrecognizable and unintelligible.

Until . . . something.

In the background.

Beyond the discord.

Something faint, and vaguely familiar.

A pattern . . . of recognizable tones.

Recognizable. And repeating. It was human speech. That very slowly turned into words.

"Can . . . you . . . hear . . . me?"

15

There was movement in the eyes, beneath the lids. Back and forth, most likely indicating a reaction to pain.

The activity ceased, prompting Rachel to glance at Williams, who remained still, waiting.

More movement.

They met each other's eyes with the same look of excitement. *A level-two reaction.*

Rachel leaned in and continued. Repeating the same words slowly and calmly. "Can you hear me?"

Activity beneath the eyelids increased, driving her to speak again, to reach down to place her hand upon the exposed forearm.

Then again. "Can you hear me?"

Someone was there.

Beyond his vision. Beyond the wall of flames that had now receded back into bright white—a powerful glare—painful and inescapable.

The bombardment of sounds began to fade, dimming enough for him to hear the words again.

"Can . . . you . . . hear . . . me."

This time they were unmistakable.

16

When his eyes finally fluttered open, they were met by a flood of blinding light, and immediately closed.

"Kill the light!" shot Rachel, propelling Williams from his stool to turn off the overhead lamp. Even dimmed was too bright.

It took several minutes before the patient tried again. This time, reopening in a series of uncontrolled flutters, blinking repeatedly over a pair of highly dilated pupils.

"Now close them," she whispered. "If you can."

The eyelids shut.

Rachel looked at Williams breathlessly. *Glasgow three!*

"What's going on?"

Masten answered the younger Yamada without turning from the monitor. "GCS. Glasgow Coma Scale. Neurologic assessment for patients following severe trauma."

"Ah. And?"

This time Masten turned. "And a response to sound, or voice, is a good sign."

Like Lagner's, Yamada's background was in engineering. He had little to no understanding of the medical side of the operation beyond what he picked up in their meetings or what Rachel told him. But it was clear from her and Williams's expression onscreen, as well as Masten's explanation, that this was a significant step forward.

With the light still off, Rachel leaned forward and spoke again. "If you can hear me . . . try opening your eyes again."

Several seconds later, the fluttering returned. Uncontrolled, but interrupted by brief moments of straining open.

"It's okay," she said, tenderly stroking his forehead. "Take your time. Go slow."

She and Williams waited. Patiently. Expectantly. And were surprised when something else moved instead, a mild tremble in his right hand and then fingers.

Then it stopped.

Next, the left hand moved, more erratic at first, but a similar pattern.

They continued watching as the movement ceased and started again in the right foot. Then left. Small movements, as if the patient was searching out each extremity.

When all movement stopped, their attention returned to his face, where the eyes were trying once again to open.

The sounds continued to fade along with some of the pain, allowing him to focus on the words—the voice sounded like a woman. And close by.

He tried moving but couldn't tell if any of his limbs had responded, and he returned his attention to the words coming to him from the ether, followed by another attempt to open his eyes.

But when he finally managed to open them, he saw only white.

17

Both Rachel and Williams could see the blankness in his eyes. An utter lack of recognition of anything.

Repeated blinking continued for several minutes until it subsided and prompted Rachel to speak again. In a calm and soothing female voice, she said, "Can you close and open one more time?"

With some difficulty, they closed and reopened.

"Very good," she whispered, before adding, "Don't be afraid if you can't see anything. That's normal."

It wasn't the truth. They didn't know whether it was normal or not. It wasn't just the neural pathways involved. It was the signaling itself. And even more worrisome, the interpretive processing taking place in the brain.

"Don't worry if you can't move either," she whispered. "We'll start off slow. If you understand, close and reopen your eyes twice."

He did so. More fluid this time, resembling slow blinks.

"Excellent. Now close and open them just once."

He answered with a single blink.

"Good. We'll use once for no and twice for yes. Do you understand?"

Two slow blinks.

"Can you tell me if you are in pain?"

Two blinks.

"Okay. We can do something about that."

She nodded at Williams, who picked up a syringe and withdrew a measured amount of liquid from a tiny brown bottle. He then stood and smoothly injected it into the man's IV tubing

"That should help," Rachel said softly. "Now . . . are you seeing anything yet?"

One blink.

"Okay. That's completely fine. Can you try moving again?"

After a lengthy pause, the right hand briefly twitched.

Rachel grinned. "Good. Very, very good."

"Jesus, did we blind him?"

Nora Lagner frowned. "Maybe." She turned from Masten to Yamada.

"I didn't see signs of overheating in the occipital area or the eyes, but the MRIs will tell us for sure."

Masten didn't reply. He simply remained still, watching the video feed of the two doctors and their damaged patient.

18

Inside Williams's office, Masten and Lagner both stood in front of the desk with the doctor next to them. His giant monitor was swiveled around to face outward, while Williams used a digital pen to highlight areas of a pale blue MRI image.

"As expected, we have tissue damage here in the left kidney," he circled a patch of darkness, "here in the liver, in the gallbladder, and some along the stomach lining. We also have some damage in the heart's right atrium and more in the left lung."

Williams moved from section to section before zooming out for a wider view. "Some good news is that the rest of the damage is in non-organ tissues that, like the liver, *should* be able to heal."

Masten gave a grim nod. "So, what are we looking at functionally?"

"We're not sure yet. The heart is now pumping at about forty-five percent capacity, and lungs a bit better than that. But it's hard to know whether those levels are due to our heat damage or just the overall stress and recovery of his system."

"You're talking about temporary or permanent."

"Correct."

"And when will we know that?"

"Hard to say," said Williams, leaning back and folding his arms before briefly raising a finger to nudge his glasses back into place. "A couple weeks, perhaps longer." Observing the expressions on Masten and Lagner's faces, he then added, "Keep in mind that, in retrospect, this is good news."

"*Good* news?"

Williams spread his hands as he talked. "Let's not lose perspective here. The outcome could have been far worse."

"You sure about that?" Masten's reply was sarcastic. "You said yourself he's barely alive."

It was Williams's turn to frown. "He's improving. Just slowly."

Masten shot a look at Lagner. *Too slowly.*

It took several hours for his vision to return. Gradually, beginning with broad shadows, then patches and shapes, and finally, nondistinct but recognizable silhouettes. Which was how he was viewing Rachel Souza as she sat next to him.

The pain was returning, everywhere, as billions of cells attempted to recommunicate with one another, releasing a flood of microscopic calcium ions for signaling in a complex biological symphony. Including countless nerve cells, many screaming of severe damage throughout his nervous system, making concentration nearly impossible. All while trying in vain to operate his mouth.

For her part, Rachel remained patient after each sentence. Watching as he struggled to respond.

The blinking had been replaced by low, guttural sounds emanating from the back of the man's throat in the form of single or double groans.

"Take your time, your throat should feel a little sore. That's natural."

"Natural" was an understatement. Even though the use of the oxygen tube was brief, the procedure most likely injured some of his esophageal lining. It would heal, but painfully.

The good news was that there appeared to be minimal issues with the kidneys and no buildup in the lungs that might suggest pneumonia or the need of a ventilator. Two of the most common problems with recovering coma patients.

Of course, he had not been in a coma, but the symptoms were similar.

Most importantly, his cardiovascular system now appeared stable, and his respiratory function was good, with no signs of significant infection. And there were no signs of significant muscle or organ atrophy. Which was what made it possible for her and Williams alone to handle the nursing duties. As for consciousness, his Glasgow scoring so far was at least partially responsive on all levels: optic, verbal, and motor. The question was whether he would continue to improve from these remedial levels.

She watched him quietly, her eyes sympathetic, knowing how difficult it must be for him, and only being able to guess at what he was having to endure. Trying to give support and explanations where she could for what his body was struggling through. And, of course, medication when possible.

The man's body had become still again—resting—when Rachel was startled by a tap on her shoulder. She turned to find Henry Yamada standing behind her, dressed in mask, gloves, and white lab coat.

"Masten wants to talk to us," he whispered.

She nodded and turned back to her patient, watching his eyes glaze over beneath a set of drooping lids before she checked her watch. The latest dose should put him out for another few hours.

With that, she gently patted his arm and rose from her chair.

They arrived in the conference room to find the others waiting, as Henry and Rachel circled one end of the oval table and sat down. The only two still wearing their white lab coats.

"How is he today?"

Rachel answer began with a nod. "Good. Stable."

"Sounds like he may be speaking soon."

"Hopefully. I think his throat still has some healing to do."

"Good to hear," said Masten. He stared briefly across the table before taking a deep breath and exhaling. "The reason I wanted you all here . . . is to discuss next steps."

Rachel glanced at Williams, but his face remained impassive. Instead, he maintained eye contact with the director.

Next steps? she thought. They already had their list of procedures and tests to carry out over the next several days. What was he—

"What we need to talk about," continued Masten, "is our communication."

Her eyes widened with surprise. "We're making an announcement?"

"No," he said. "I mean *internal* communication."

Rachel frowned. "I don't—"

"Given that you two," he gestured at her and Williams, "are our two doctors on-site, you will continue to rotate shifts with him. At least for the time being. And because of that, it's important that we're all on the same page, in case any of us need to step in."

Rachel's expression grew curious, and she glanced back and forth around the table.

"We all need to be very much in step going forward."

Yamada raised an eyebrow. "With what exactly?"

Masten's gaze was as firm as his tone. "With what we tell *him.*"

19

Rachel was sitting on the floor, cross-legged, and playing with Bella when Yamada knocked and opened the door to her lab. She rubbed the dog's head playfully, causing the mutt's small white ears to flop back and forth, while she watched her colleague ease the door closed behind him. Pulling over a nearby stool, he sat beside her.

"So, is it just me, or was that a little weird?"

She moved her hand down to scratch just above Bella's wagging tail. "What do you mean?"

"Yeah. Like you don't know what I'm talking about."

"You mean what Masten said?"

"Exactly."

"It did feel a little odd."

Yamada swiveled anxiously atop the stool, glancing absently around the lab's tall metal shelving. Stopping on the other animals in their cages through the open doorway. "Why do you think he said that?"

Rachel thought for a moment. "Well, there's the obvious reason . . ."

"Which is?"

"Which is that from a clinical standpoint, we *are* trying to minimize all stressors to his system. Including psychological."

"I get that," he replied. "I do. And frankly, I'm not all that involved in this part of the project anyway. But . . ."

"But what?"

Yamada shrugged. "I don't know. Should we really be lying to the guy?"

"We're not *lying*."

"What would you call it?"

She struggled. "We're just—"

He tilted his head sarcastically. "Let me guess: 'We're just not telling him *yet*.'"

She stopped petting and stared at him. "More or less."

"And you're okay with that?"

"No," she admitted. "But right now, it's more important to keep him alive."

"Really?"

"Yes. Really."

"So then, we just don't tell him anything."

Rachel glared sarcastically. "We just need to be thoughtful with our answers."

"Thoughtful?"

"Or creative. Just . . . steer the conversation."

"Right. So, if he looks at me and asks what my name is, I just say, 'I like pineapple!'"

Rachel's eyes narrowed.

"Isn't that what you're saying? As long as we avoid lying, it's not a lie."

"You're twisting my words. Besides, it's just for a little while. Until he's stable. Until he's ready."

"And when exactly would that be?"

She continued staring up at him, this time longer, before relenting. "Fine. To be totally honest, I don't like it either. But they *are* valid reasons. Medical reasons. Whether I like it or not."

"Medical reasons for not telling him what the hell just happened to him. Maybe we shouldn't tell him his name either."

"I think he'll remember his name."

"And what if he remembers more than that? What if we end up feeding him a line that he already knows is not true?" Yamada shook his head. "Wouldn't that be worse?"

She gazed back down at the dog, who was still wagging her tail and watching Rachel affectionately through a pair of brown-hazel eyes. "I suppose it could get messy. We just have to be careful."

"That's what I'm saying. It starts with something small. Until someone asks the wrong question. Then what?"

Having resumed her petting, Rachel stopped again, examining Henry. "What exactly is bothering you so much?"

"I just told you."

"No, you didn't."

He twisted again on the stool, fidgeting. "I don't want to screw things up."

"What do you mean?"

"I'm afraid I'm gonna screw it up!" he blurted. "I'm not a good liar, Rach. I'm afraid I'm going to accidentally let something out!"

"Relax. You're not even going to be talking to him."

"I *might*. Like Masten said, what if I need to stand in? Or help with something."

"Then just don't say anything."

"Oh, right. '*Just don't say anything*,'" he mocked. "Hey, this is our engineer Henry Yamada, he's deaf."

"Mute," she corrected.

"Fine! Mute!"

Rachel grinned. "We'll say you were in an industrial accident."

"This isn't funny!"

"What are you afraid you're going to say?"

"I'm not that afraid of what I say," sputtered Yamada. "I'm afraid of what he might ask."

"For example . . ."

"For example . . ." he replied slowly, "*what exactly happened to him?*"

20

He could see them now, clearly, watching him with worry. Staring, but saying nothing. Dozens of them.

He slowly turned.

Not dozens, hundreds.

After a moment, he realized they were not looking at him, but past him. Surging forward. Moving toward and surrounding a large structure. Metal. Some kind of industrial building. Shouting, the crowd quickly enveloped it, massing at both ends. Beating windows and doors with bats and sticks. An ax flashed in the moonlight overhead and sent out a resounding clunk when it sank deep into the painted metal siding.

The rest were using their bare hands, shouting in a garbled flow of rancor. Suddenly, the crowd at one end spread out as the man holding the ax moved in front of the latch with an oversized lock securing it.

After several strikes, the lock's shackle gave, and it broke open. It was quickly removed, and the giant doors were pulled apart with an earsplitting screech from the mammoth steel hinges.

The shouting intensified, and the crowd surged forward, funneling into the dark opening.

The deafening noise was overwhelming, erupting even louder when the building was found to be empty. Reverberating back at him like a verbal clamor of death and destruction.

Suddenly, he heard that voice again. Through the carnage, just as the darkness around him began to lighten . . . words. Distinct. Gradually growing louder. And then the entire sentence.

"Can you hear me?"

Squinting from the gentle light of the room while his pupils shrank to adjust, he looked around until he found the woman's familiar silhouette, this time with slightly more detail: the general shape of her nose and chin, and dark hair pulled back from a blurry and more lightly colored face.

Struggling to suppress the noise, the sound of her voice resonated in his ears above the chaos. He managed to move his lips. Still unintelligible, but much closer to a word this time, including some inflection.

He watched the blurry outline of a smile form. "You look like you're feeling better."

Another shape appeared behind her. An older man with white hair and glasses. And a mustache.

The fuzzy image of the man leaned toward the woman and said something inaudible to her.

He recognized the second voice, too. The older man had spoken to him before. When he couldn't see.

"Are you in pain?"

A light groan followed, sounding like "*meh*."

"Good." Rachel smiled. "You should be able to talk soon. Hopefully, your throat is feeling better."

She glanced at Williams and continued.

"We want you to relax. You're safe." After a brief pause, she cautiously added, "You were in an accident. But you're okay. Just relax."

His seemed to ponder her words.

"You're doing very well," she repeated. "But the important thing is you're safe."

He didn't reply. Even with a grunt. Prompting both doctors to watch him curiously until the lips began to move again.

With some effort, the patient made an O shape with a long exhale. Whispering something that sounded like "*who*."

With a grin, Rachel said, "My name is Dr. Souza." Turning, she added, "And this is Dr. Williams."

The older man leaned in. "Call me Perry."

The man continued staring wordlessly until Rachel finally asked, "Do you know your name?"

He continued blinking. Repeatedly before he tried again. Fighting to move his mouth.

"Jjjaaaa."

Rachel leaned in.

"Jjjjaaaaaan."

This time, she and Perry smiled together.

"That's right." She nodded. "Your name . . . is John."

21

It felt like a dream. No—a nightmare. As though he were drugged, he tried to move parts of his body only to have them barely respond. But each attempt at speaking seemed to return some level of progress, along with feeling in his lips.

The two people in front of him were still blurry, but he could now see enough detail to note the woman being noticeably younger than the man, who was intently watching him through what appeared to be a set of large, square-rimmed eyeglasses.

"Can you see how many fingers I'm holding up?" asked the woman.

Instead of replying, John glanced down and found his right hand. With prolonged movements, he extended two fingers.

"Very good," said Dr. Souza, returning her attention to his face. "And you can hear me okay?"

The shouting in his head continued to fade. "Yeesss." After several seconds of looking about the room, he asked, "Wheeerre?"

"You're in a hospital," she replied. "And just regaining consciousness. So, let's take things slow?"

He nodded weakly.

"John, we want you to close your eyes and try to concentrate. We'd like to test some things."

He did as she said.

"Let's start with your right hand. Show us how many fingers you can move."

Rachel was jubilant. As was Williams, standing beside her in the elevator as it ascended to Basement 1.

He was recovering well. Not quite as quickly as they'd hoped, but not far off. His cogitative presence was almost normal now, lucid and communicative, and with improving levels of dexterity.

Moving limbs was one thing, but touching fingers, especially in sequence, was big. It required a complex neural-motor-mechanical process that most humans took for granted. *Dexterous manipulation* was far more complicated than people realized. The act of simply tapping a fingertip, or holding an egg, set off a complex pattern of muscle coordination from brain to hand that stimulated all seven muscles in each finger, demonstrating that some of the simplest physical tasks were actually quite complicated. And why biomechanical engineers still could not artificially replicate the same level of dexterity even after decades of trying.

But for medical doctors, the hands provided wonderfully simple tests in validating successful signaling on different neurophysical levels at once. An area that she and Williams had been concerned with should too many of those nerves be damaged in the thawing process.

Now it seemed—at least for the time being—that those particular neuropathways were working correctly. Leaving at least Rachel hopeful that the rest of the pathways might have fared similarly.

She turned to Williams, who was lost in his own thoughts, absently watching the buttons illuminate on the panel in front of him.

"He's still sleeping a lot."

The older man nodded. "Not surprising. The same thing happens to coma patients when they come out."

The elevator slowed and softly lurched to a stop before a bell chimed and the doors opened. Rachel stepped out and turned back briefly to Williams, who looked at his watch.

"It's nine thirty now," he said. "I'll be back in six hours or so to switch off. Say three thirty. You going to be okay here?"

She winked. "I have plenty of coffee. Besides, I don't think I could sleep right now if I wanted to."

With that, the older doctor smiled and let the elevator doors close between them.

Less than a minute later, Rachel entered her own lab and was greeted by a darkened room, illuminated by a single fluorescent tube affixed overhead to the far wall, casting a contained curtain of light over the glass refrigerator and nearby stainless-steel sink while leaving the rest of the lab in shadows.

On the opposite side of the room, near the door, was her desk, its smooth metal edges muted in the dim light. Her computer remained idle, displaying the screensaver's artificial fish floating, or rather "swimming," noiselessly across the dark face of the monitor.

Rachel gingerly tiptoed to her desk, trying to avoid waking the caged animals in the next room. Sitting down, she moved the mouse, and her screen burst to life in a bright glow.

After letting her eyes adjust, she expanded one of the files she'd been looking at, which was still open. The file displayed a colorful graph of the motor testing she and Williams had just completed and uploaded, along with the results.

Not bad for just five days in.

A thought occurred to her, and she began typing, bringing up the early test results of the other animals and adding them to the larger graph. They appeared as new plot points and lines across the screen. Not surprisingly, they produced similar patterns.

She scrutinized the comparisons for a long time before finally checking her watch and rising from her chair. Quietly, she stepped out of view from the sleeping animals to the large sink and, next to it, her coffee machine.

A few minutes later, she poured a third of the steaming coffee into a mug and returned the pot to the warmer. Sipping and contemplating.

They were finally out of danger. All vitals were stable, and they now just waited to ensure the entire GI tract was healthy. At which point they would try removing the IV. If all major organs appeared functional, even with the damaged areas observed, they would try to ambulate.

She couldn't stop thinking that with so many patches of damaged tissue, the whole thing was simply . . . miraculous. They had managed to accomplish something impossible. Something no one else ever had done in all of human history. Something she still couldn't tell anybody.

A look of deep satisfaction appeared on her face. Not from arrogance but from giddiness. Yet still wrapped in a veil of disbelief. Not just for what it meant but for what came next. Williams was right. The implications were enormous. Win or lose.

And thankfully, they'd won.

She took another sip of coffee and then padded back toward her desk. She noted the animals again as she passed, which prompted her to stop and enter their room.

All were sleeping on small beds or beneath blankets. The cages grew smaller and smaller in size until she reached the far end, checking on each in turn.

She suddenly froze.

Without her body moving, her eyes returned and stared for several seconds through the thin wire mesh at one of the three mice. In their own cages, all three were lying on their sides in their bedding of wood shavings.

But only two of the tiny bellies were moving.

22

Sitting on his couch with his wife sleeping against him beneath a colorfully knitted blanket, Henry Yamada felt the vibration of his phone. He muted the television and raised it to his ear.

"Rach?" he answered softly.

"Hey, Henry. Yeah, it's me. Sorry to bother you, but I need some help. Quickly."

Yamada's expression grew serious. "What's going on? Is *he* having a problem?"

"No, not him. It's one of the test animals. I'm doing a full analysis and genome sequence right now, but I need to get a copy of the Machine's logs on it, too."

"How detailed?"

"A full breakdown."

Yamada stared forward, thinking. "Okay, but I don't think you'll be able to read it."

"I know," she said apologetically. "Which leads me to my second favor."

Yamada moaned, "Craaap."

"Can you be here in thirty minutes?"

. "Yesss."

"Thanks, Henry. I owe you one."

From his couch, he looked down at his sleeping wife's head. "I'm not the one you're going to owe the favor to."

Just before midnight, they both leaned back in their chairs simultaneously, eyes glued to Yamada's giant computer monitor.

"So, nothing then."

He shook his head. "Not that I can see. No anomalies. With any of the three procedures—just in case we're not sure which mouse is which. Nothing that suggests any notable cellular damage." He turned to her. "Are you sure it's dead?"

She frowned sarcastically.

"Sorry." It was a serious matter. He knew that. One of their test animals suddenly dying on them was a serious concern. Although Rachel had already pointed out that mice lived only twelve to eighteen months. And this one was already nearing the upper range of that span.

Nevertheless, any anomaly, no matter how unrelated it might seem, had to be investigated. Thoroughly.

"So, no fluctuations with the Machine like we saw with our patient?"

"Nope," answered Yamada. "The body mass and density were trivial in comparison. Of course, there *were* other mice."

It was true. They'd gone through dozens of mice in the beginning.

"Let's see if the sequence reveals anything. But I appreciate you coming in to go through this with me."

"No problem. I was just watching the news."

She gave a bleak frown. "Ugh. Why would you do that to yourself?"

Yamada was studying the screen of computer code. "It's really not easy to parse this stuff. Even for me."

"I bet."

"So my brain feels doubly fried."

She grinned and leaned forward, beginning to stand up. Then she stopped in midmotion. "Why is that?"

"What?"

"Doubly fried?"

He chucked and used his computer mouse to close the window. "Second time today I've had to do this. I'm surprised I was even awake when you called."

Rachel's paused. "Second time?"

"Yeah. Had to go through a bunch of this stuff for Nora earlier today."

"Nora wanted this information, too?"

"She wanted a lot more than this. She wanted everything. Which took forever to put into something intelligible for her."

"She wanted everything? Is that normal?"

"Not at all."

"Why did she want it?"

He shrugged. "Don't know. She is *my* boss. I assumed she was going through it with the India team. To try to work out what happened."

Rachel looked at him curiously. "I thought that was your job."

"Well, it is. But they did most of the final design. I just put it together and got it to work," he said humorously.

"Huh." Rachel thought for another moment before letting it go. Finally standing. "Well, like I said, I owe you one. Or your wife, I guess."

Yamada stood alongside her and pushed his chair in. "Just don't expect me early tomorrow."

There was something about being at work when everyone else was gone that felt refreshing to Rachel. Motivating. Even in the middle of the night.

Maybe it was being completely undisturbed, or the silence that allowed her to truly concentrate, or maybe something else entirely. Whatever it was, it was deeply enjoyable to her. And conducive. Allowing her to focus on the dead mouse's genetic sequence, scanning for biological anomalies. As opposed to instrumentation issues like she and Henry had been searching for. But looking through and comparing section by section of data with those of the other mice produced nothing of note.

Sure, all animals had differing DNA, but nothing jumped out in any areas of primary concern. Allowing Rachel to relax and begin work on her third and final cup of coffee.

Now standing in the hall, she peered curiously through the door's small window and into the recovery room where their patient was quietly sleeping.

23

The gentle knock sent a startled Perry Williams halfway out of his chair, gasping as he turned to find Rachel standing in the doorway of his office.

"Good God!" he exclaimed, slapping a hand to his chest.

"I'm sorry. I didn't know you were back."

After a deep breath, the older man swiveled back around and nodded. "I was about to come relieve you. Was just reading up a little on our patient."

Behind him, Rachel could see their patient's headshot displayed on Williams's computer screen, along with several lines of physical description followed by paragraphs of background information.

"That doesn't seem like very much."

"It's not," he replied. "And what we do have is not terribly helpful either. At least not for our purposes."

Rachel squinted at the screen. "I remember he was born in the same city as my mom."

Williams checked. "Your mom was born in Flint, Michigan?"

"Yep. Not the same year, though." Still leaning against the doorframe, she added, "I wonder what he did in the army."

"It doesn't say."

"Can you read it aloud again?"

Williams began rambling through the text. "Six foot one, a hundred and ninety pounds, brown hair, blue eyes, born in Flint in 1980." He paused, scanning. "Enrolled in the army after high school. Served for about eight years, judging by his change of address. Had a job as a contractor in Ohio for several years before moving to Montana. The rest just covers where he was stationed in the army."

"How can we have so little on him?"

"Beats me." Williams scrolled down, revealing copies of two separate news articles. "We probably know more about his accident than his past. We also know more about him medically now than anything we would have gleaned from records."

"Well, we've done enough workups on him."

"Right."

Falling silent, she took a deep breath and exhaled. "Maybe he knows."

"Knows what?"

"Maybe he knows the secret of *why him*."

Williams pondered the question from his chair.

24

The flames were almost on top of him. With the heat so intense, he could feel the skin on his arms singeing.

It continued drawing closer. Slow. Inescapable. Until it surrounded him. Blotting everything out. Swallowed up by the massive flames, now reaching out for him like wild, violent tentacles.

And then they touched him.

He lurched violently, and the flames jumped back against a bright beige wall of the recovery room, where they licked frantically at the air. Then were suddenly sucked into the whiteness as if by a giant vacuum. All of it taking place behind the two figures appearing before him. Visibly startled by his sudden outburst.

Both put their hands on him. Gentle and consoling. "You're okay!" Dr. Souza said loudly, touching and squeezing his right arm.

Dr. Williams's hand was on his lower leg. Also squeezing firmly through the blanket. "You're okay, son. Everything is fine."

"John. Can you hear us?"

"Yes."

Feeling him relax, she looked into his eyes. "What happened? What did you see?"

"Flames."

"Flames, like a fire?"

He nodded.

"Were they close to you?"

"Yes."

She glanced at Williams. "It was just a dream, John. You're here with us, and everything is fine." She looked him over. Perhaps his body was having trouble regulating its internal temperature.

With both hands, she folded the thin blanket down to his waist, leaving the sheet over his chest. "Is that better?"

He didn't answer.

"John?"

His eyes were on the walls. Searching for what he'd seen until finally returning.

"Are you okay?"

"Yeah."

She and Williams waited until his breathing slowed while she checked her watch and retrieved a clipboard from the foot of the bed. She noted the time, 10:31 in the morning, before peering back down.

"Do you remember who I am, John?"

He stared at her before replying. "Rachel."

"That's right. My name is Rachel Souza." She motioned to Williams. "And do you remember him?"

"Perry."

Rachel grinned. "Very good." She made a quick notation. "John, do you know your last name?"

Another pause. This time longer.

"Reiff."

"Excellent. And do you remember what year you were born?"

He blinked, thinking. "Nineteen eighty. November," he then added. "Fifteenth."

"Wonderful." She made another notation and lowered the clipboard. "Let's repeat a few of the muscle tests we did yesterday, shall we? We'd like to measure your improvement."

He was still improving, with noticeably more energy, now following along, moving limbs and fingers when asked. Even bending each arm at the elbow and touching a finger to his face.

Following the tests, Rachel recorded the results and lowered the clipboard once again to her lap. "You're doing much better. Are you feeling any pain?"

"Some."

"And where are you feeling it?"

"Everywhere."

"Would you like us to give you something? It will probably make you drowsy again."

He shook his head. "It's not as bad as it was."

She smiled, noting that his sentences were becoming smoother. "Okay. If you change your mind, just let us know."

John Reiff looked up at the IV bag dangling above his head and left shoulder, then asked, "What's that?"

"It's an IV line."

"What's in it?"

"It's called a perenteral tube. It provides nutrition to your system in the form of proteins, carbohydrates, and electrolytes. Until you're ready to eat."

He continued studying the bag as if trying to make sense of something. Before looking back at Rachel. "How long have I been here?"

"You just regained consciousness a few days ago."

Another pause. "And where am I?"

"Minneapolis, Minnesota." It was another lie, but for his own good.

"What happened?"

"As I said before, you were in an accident. Do you remember anything about it?"

He thought for a moment, then shook his head.

It wasn't a surprise. Trauma patients usually had little to no recollection of their accidents. As if their memories were wiped clean of the minutes leading up to the event. In some cases, even hours or days.

"Let's not talk about that now. Let's try some simple cognitive tests."

Standing in front of the monitor, Robert Masten turned to Nora Lagner.

"What the hell was that?"

"What?"

"That outburst. When he woke up."

"I don't know. A bad dream?"

"Seemed like more than that."

"Maybe a hallucination, then?"

Masten returned his attention to the screen with a dour expression, watching Rachel and Perry continue their examination. "If there's something else going on, that's a problem."

"I'm sure it's normal."

"We're in uncharted waters here. There is no normal."

Lagner shrugged. "A lot of coma patients—"

"He was not *in* a coma," snapped Masten.

"I understand that. But it's the closest thing we have to compare."

"I disagree."

She folded her arms. "Just like any new technology, this man is essentially a prototype. And prototypes always bring surprises."

"He's not a program, Nora. Or a robot. He's a human being."

"I know that. I'm simply saying we must continue to expect surprises."

Masten's brooding face remained glued to the screen.

"We still have some time before we have to make a decision."

"Not much time," he answered. "And the decision is only half of it. There's also *them*."

There was no response from Lagner. She knew what he was referring to and whom. Souza and Williams. And potentially Yamada.

25

"Illusions and other cognitive episodes are normal," Williams assured them. Across the table once again, facing Masten and Lagner. "Especially considering what his brain has been through. There's obviously no standard for this scenario, but coma patients have similar outbursts, particularly following serious trauma."

Masten and Lagner listened, saying nothing.

"The good news is that most other measures look very positive. Reiff's mental and verbal processing, vocabulary, short-term memory, everything is pointing to a successful cognitive recovery. Which is huge. Even if he's having something more serious, even hallucinations, we can deal with that. Over time."

"How do we know?" asked Lagner.

"How do we know what?"

"How serious it is."

The doctor pursed his lips. "It will take time to assess."

"And the tissue damage?" Masten asked.

Williams leaned back in his leather chair with a squeak. "With no food in his body for five days now, his markers are way up as expected. Production of human growth hormone has increased by nearly five hundred percent, and the process of autophagy has begun. Replacing old cells with new ones along with the accelerated production of stem cells. Which we will soon be able to cultivate and regrow, then begin stem-cell therapy on the damaged organs."

"What about BDNF?"

"Brain-derived neurotrophic factor is also being produced in high amounts. Coupled with the HGH, the two should be stimulating new connections in the brain, which could help with these cognitive episodes over time."

It was their secret weapon. Or rather Williams's. Over the years, the medical industry had discovered amazing biological effects from the centuries-old practice known as fasting. Natural and highly rejuvenating processes triggered within the body that produced astonishing results. Especially when assisted by modern biochemical therapies. But in this case, with what had been done to Reiff, everything was an unknown, and that meant nothing was guaranteed to work. Yet Williams remained positive. John Reiff's body was responding as normally as any of them could have hoped. Normally enough that the restorative effects from keeping him off food for an extended period *should* have similar healing effects.

"When do we begin stem-cell therapy?"

"The first cultures can be ready in ten days," replied Williams. "Naturally, we'll target the most critical areas first, one at a time."

Robert Masten scratched at the table with a finger. "Let's stay on track and decide when we think he's ready for a full psych eval. Just keep steering away from the topics we discussed."

Williams's expression changed to a fixed stare. "About that . . ."

"What?"

"Tomorrow, we're attempting to ambulate."

"And?"

The doctor shrugged. "If we're successful, it's only a matter of time."

Masten saw where he was going. "How long do you think it will take him to walk?"

"I have no idea. But at this rate, it's possible he could be mobile within a few days."

The director inhaled and looked to Lagner, who remained silent. "Take him anywhere he wants inside the building," he replied. "Except Rachel's lab. And *don't* let him outside under any circumstances."

26

"Hey, big sister!"

"What are you up to, Abs?"

"Not much. Just hanging out."

"Yeah?" Rachel was leaning against the counter in her kitchen, waiting for a pot of water to boil with a small box of pasta nearby. She put her phone on speaker and used both hands to tear the box lid open. "How you feeling?"

"Not bad. Blood markers haven't changed much, which is good, so same ole same ole. Just getting ready to go for a walk with Dad. *Oh my God*," Abby suddenly said, "have you seen his new haircut?!"

Rachel stopped momentarily, raising both eyebrows. "Nooo."

Her sister laughed. "I *have* to send you a picture!" There was a short pause before her voice returned. "Take a look at this!"

Rachel's phone dinged, and she picked it back up, examining the picture. "Oh . . . my . . . God. Who in the world did that?"

"*Mom!*"

"No way!"

Abby continued laughing. "I didn't have the heart to tell her. And Dad keeps insisting he likes it!"

Rachel laughed, too, with a hand over her mouth.

"How are things with you? How's the hospital?"

Rachel's laugh faded. She had never told her family that she'd left the hospital. "Oh, you know. Same ole same ole."

"Still kicking ass and taking names?"

Rachel chuckled. "Something like that."

"Save any lives lately?"

"I'm trying."

An unexpected knock on the door gave Rachel a small start, prompting her to lean out of the kitchen. "Hey, sis, I gotta run. I'll call you back later."

Not expecting anyone, she slowly approached the front door with an air of apprehension. She almost jumped at the second round of rapping. With one hand on the knob and the other on the dead bolt, she asked through the door, "Who is it?"

"It's Perry."

Surprised, she immediately turned the lock and pulled the door open. Williams stood on the other side, his expression grim.

"Can I come in?"

"Of course," she said, and motioned him in.

Her boss and mentor entered and glanced absently around the sparse apartment before turning to face her. He began by answering the question she was about to ask. "He's asleep. I'll be back in twenty minutes."

"Is something wrong?"

"Maybe."

"What is it?"

"It's Masten," he said in a low voice. "And Lagner."

Rachel stared back in a mix of surprise and confusion. "What do you mean?"

"I think there's something else going on."

"Like what?"

"Another agenda in play."

"What does *that* mean?"

"They're not following protocol, Rachel."

She began to reply, but he interrupted, holding up his hand. "I know, I know, things are fluid, and things haven't exactly gone to plan. But that's not what I'm talking about."

She seemed to be waiting expectantly, shrugging as if to say, *Then what?*

Williams paused as if reconsidering what he was about to say. Then he shook his head and told her, "None of the remote staff are being updated."

"None? At all?"

"They've been in the dark on everything for the last few days. Masten said he will be the point of contact with them going forward. Which is not what we agreed on."

Rachel thought it over. "Why would he do that?"

"No idea," said Williams. "On the surface, it wasn't a big deal. An odd change but not critical. By then, our patient was out of immediate danger, so I assumed it was just an effort to streamline communication channels. To keep things simple. Reserving the larger discussions for our group calls."

"I suppose that makes sense."

"Exactly what I thought. But he just canceled tomorrow's call."

Rachel frowned. "Why?"

"Your guess is as good as mine."

"Who told you?"

"Soliz."

"Dr. Soliz?" She sounded surprised. "But he's our . . ."

"Neurologist," said Williams, finishing her sentence.

"That seems a little weird."

"More than a little. Especially since Masten and Lagner said they want a full psych eval as soon as Reiff is ready."

"Soliz wouldn't be the one to do that."

"No. He's not the psychiatrist. Dr. Bennett is. But medically, Soliz would have to give the green light when he thought the patient was ready."

Rachel continued thinking. "So, Masten said he wants an eval, but he's not letting it happen?"

"Precisely."

She ran a hand through her hair, puzzled. "That doesn't make sense."

"Nope. And that's not all. I just talked to Yamada. It seems Lagner has instructed him to begin disassembling the Machine."

"What?!"

Williams looked equally perplexed.

"When?"

"About twenty minutes ago."

Rachel was stunned. "Why on earth—"

"Don't remember writing that into our procedures, do you?"

"Uh, no! Why would Nora want it disassembled?"

"Because something else is happening," he said. "Something you and I are not part of. Which is why I'm here."

"They can't just unilaterally make these decisions without us."

"Of course they can," said Williams dryly. "And they are."

"It feels like—"

"Like we're being shut out."

"But shut out of what?" she stammered. "We don't know anything yet."

"Maybe that's the idea."

Her eyes narrowed. "Excuse me?"

"Maybe we're not supposed to know."

"Supposed to know what?"

"Anything."

She lowered her gaze while shaking her head from side to side. "Perry, this isn't making any sense."

"It does if you step back far enough."

"What is it they don't want us to know?"

"I don't know. It could be anything. Like talking to John Reiff."

"They don't want us talking to our own patient? That's absurd!" Her head continued shaking. "No. It has to be something else. Another explanation."

"I'm all ears."

Rachel glowered at him. "I didn't say I knew what it was." After pondering again, she held up a hand. "Maybe . . . it's not what we think. Maybe there's a simpler explanation here. Like they're just waiting longer to brief everyone. And they're going to reschedule the call."

"While disassembling the Machine?"

She tried to think of another logical answer. "Maybe Lagner wants to examine it? Or improve it?"

Williams remained fixed, saying nothing. Her optimism was still admirable. Like so many others in her generation. Young and innocent. Always holding faith and instinct back in favor of a hopeful outcome.

But Williams was older. He'd been around the block. More than once. More than a few times. And had been involved in more of these projects than he could count. All with great potential. Some small, some large. Whether independent projects like this one or government-funded, they all proved to be more or less the same. Enthusiastic and visionary at their birth, but always caught within the same inevitable webs of fighting, politics, and hidden agendas. Eventually leading them to their deaths. Because if there was one thing Williams had learned over his seventy-plus years on Planet Earth, it was that everyone *always* had their own agenda.

Personally, or professionally, everyone had their own priorities. Their own hidden goals. And Williams had been around long enough to see it all. Always repeating the same pattern over and over. Leaving him skeptical and jaded but somehow still hopeful. Hopeful that, somehow, he would find the right one. The right person or the right project that would eventually transcend the greed, and power, and the bureaucracy. Finally providing what he sought in his heart of hearts. The opportunity to make one last significant contribution to the world. To do something truly momentous for medicine. For everyone. Before his time on this planet was over.

But so far, his desire only left him cynical and old. Bitter at the machinations of industry that sadly and ironically had left him all too skilled at spotting the subtle signs of trouble, and guile. Of incompetence and corruption.

And now it looked to be happening again. Red flags were popping up, as his father used to say, *like a field of ground squirrels in the spring.* Leaving Williams resigned to find out what was happening and ultimately a way to extricate himself. And Rachel.

His greatest mistake this time was getting too attached to her. A young woman who reminded him far too much of his own daughter.

Williams finally spoke. "Do you remember what Reiff told us today?"

Her look was sarcastic. "John's conversations are pretty short."

"About his birthday."

"November fifteenth."

Williams nodded. "It was a short conversation. Just like his file."

Rachel tilted her head.

"Our file on Reiff is short and sweet. Unnaturally so, which is odd, but it *did* have his birthday in it."

"Meaning?"

"The file said his birthday is November *sixteenth*."

Once again, Rachel's eyes narrowed.

"The sixteenth," he repeated. "Not the fifteenth." As she remained gazing at her boss, he added, "Why do you think that is?"

"A typo?"

He nodded in agreement. "Clearly."

"So, it doesn't mean anything."

"Maybe." Williams relaxed against the empty wall and inhaled. "It may be nothing at all. But let me ask you this: When was the last time you remember a person's medical history being manually entered by someone?"

Her expression changed.

"Several pieces are beginning to not make sense here, Rachel. And something tells me our patient may be one of those pieces."

She folded her arms, struggling with the thought, before peering up at the ceiling. "This is all just so *weird*."

Williams wished he could disagree.

Slowly, finally, her mindset began to shift. "Okay. Let's say that Masten and Lagner *are* hiding something. That there *is* something we're not supposed to know. What do you think that is?"

Williams could only shrug. "I have no clue. But something tells me we should have another conversation with Mr. Reiff."

27

The face on the screen appeared emotionless and detached. Drawn and aged, with a background of a darkened room behind him, creating an eerie contrast to his pale, chiseled features. Staring through a pair of intense gray-blue eyes, beneath a short cropping of gray hair, through the video feed at Robert Masten and Nora Lagner.

The truth was Masten didn't know the man's real name. But he was their contact. And his knowledge and experience were indisputable, way beyond just competence.

Nor did they know his location.

"I have studied the latest video footage," he said in a slow, methodic tone. "Your patient is getting worse and showing signs of altered mental status."

Masten and Lagner remained quiet.

"He is not experiencing 'illusions' represented by misinterpretation of sensory input. But rather hallucinations, which are not based on input at all. They are fabrications."

"Fabrications from what?"

"Most often the misfiring of neural synapses."

Facing their monitor, Masten and Lagner glanced at one another but did not react.

"The problem is not psychological. It's biological," the man explained. "Most likely damage from your botched resuscitation."

"We don't see any evidence of damage in the brain," offered Lagner.

"Then look again."

Another nervous glance before Masten said, "If it is, it may be repairable."

"Unlikely. Neural plasticity provides for new and changing pathways in the brain. Not the repair of those already existing. Your doctors,

Williams and Soliz, will no doubt focus on adaptation of the patient's neural condition using antipsychotics. That is not what we are interested in."

"It's possible this is just a side effect of the resuscitation that will, in time—"

"It won't correct itself," the man said, cutting them off. "It is, in all likelihood, a permanent change to your patient's brain function and puts him on the schizophrenia spectrum. This is of no use to us." The face on the screen changed to another subject, addressing Lagner. "We've gone through your data, but we need more."

She eased forward. "I gave you everything."

The only movement in the man's face was his mouth. "I said we need *more*."

The call ended less than a minute later, leaving both staring at a blank monitor.

Things were not going as planned. Or even as hoped. They were losing control. Everything now riding on one thing: the mental health of their resuscitated patient.

Williams and Soliz were confident that if there was any neural damage, as long as it was limited in scope it could be dealt with. But their handler on the call made it extraordinarily clear. *They* were not interested in treatment. To them, there was a tremendous difference between a treatable brain and a healthy brain.

28

Entering the recovery room, Williams and Rachel were surprised to find John Reiff waiting for them. Already sitting with legs dangling over the edge of his bed. And both hands gripping the mattress for support.

"You're up!" exclaimed Rachel as she and Williams reached him to add extra support behind each shoulder.

"Don't get too excited," said Reiff, "this took a while."

His speech was excellent now.

She reached behind with her other hand to secure the back of Reiff's gown.

"How's your pain?"

"Manageable."

"Good," Williams said. He looked down at the man's dangling feet. Both had regained their color. An excellent sign. "Let's start by taking turns rotating your feet for range of motion."

Ambulation was a long and arduous process. And meticulous. Ensuring that a patient's muscles had not only the function and control necessary, but the strength to support the body's weight, even temporarily. And, of course, enough dexterity to balance and eventually step.

It took almost an hour before Reiff was standing. Against his bed, still supporting most of his 190-pound frame. And for a grand total of five minutes before Dr. Souza and Dr. Williams eased him back up onto the mattress and into a sitting position.

"Fantastic, John. Really fantastic."

He adjusted his position and groaned. "If you say so."

"I do," replied Souza. Now let's rest a little."

"John," said Dr. Williams, glancing briefly up at the room's video camera. "Can you tell us your full name again?"

If Reiff thought the question odd, he didn't show it.

"John Reiff."

"No middle name?"

"No."

"And your birthday again?"

"November fifteenth."

With clipboard in hand, Dr. Williams began writing. "And year?"

"Nineteen eighty."

"Do you remember where you were born?"

"Flint."

Dr. Williams nodded. "Nice area." When there was no response, he asked, "Do you have any family?"

"Not alive."

"Not even extended family?"

Reiff was examining the walls of his room. "They're very extended."

"Anyone we should call?"

"No."

Reiff peered at the plant in the corner of the room. Bushy and green atop a thick, lightly colored stem, with a mossy substance around its base. No discoloration on the leaves at all. *Artificial.*

His eyes then moved to the chair next to it. Tan, upholstered, resting next to a short glass table. No depression or wrinkles in the fabric, indicating little, if any, use.

The clock on the wall was round and analog. Old-style and reading 8:23. And next to that, a wall-mounted oscillating fan.

"John?"

His attention returned to Dr. Williams.

"Any more visions?"

"Some."

"Like what?"

Reiff looked back to the blank wall in front of him. "Usually things that aren't there."

"And when was the last time?"

"Just before you walked in."

"So, it's happening even when you're awake now."

Reiff shrugged and returned his focus to the room around him. He could finally see clearly and noted the large chrome handle on the door.

"We can give you something to help."

"More drugs?"

"John, your body has been through some extraordinary trauma. If these visions are becoming more frequent—"

"No more pills."

Williams looked at Rachel with a grimace. "Fine," he said, and returned to his clipboard and paper. "Can you remember your address?"

"Just a PO box." When Dr. Souza raised an eyebrow, he added, "I move around a lot."

"I see." Dr. Williams continued scribbling. "Our records indicate you were in the army."

"That's right."

"And what did you do?"

"Staff sergeant."

Finally, Dr. Williams lowered his clipboard. "Do you remember anything from the accident yet?"

"A little."

"Do you remember where you were going?"

"Sioux Falls, I think."

"And why was that?"

"I don't remember."

"Do you have a job?"

Reiff's attention returned to the foot of the bed and then to himself. "I'm between jobs." He raised his right hand and examined it. Stretching it open, then closing it. Followed by an examination of his fingers. One at a time.

"Where was your previous job?"

"Are you worried about me paying the bill?"

Dr. Williams smiled. "We're just trying to gather some information."

"Why?"

The older doctor shrugged. "For example, if you have any previous health issues we should know about. Maybe allergic to any medication. That sort of thing."

As he spoke, Reiff's attention moved to the wristwatch on the man's left hand. It looked well-worn, with a metal gold and silver band.

He studied more of the man's appearance. White lab coat over blue collared shirt and dark slacks extending below the coat to a pair of leather shoes.

He then looked at Dr. Souza. The clothing beneath her coat was more casual. A simple blue blouse and comfortable cotton pants. And white sneakers.

"Is everything okay?"

"It would be nice to get some fresh air."

"We can do that once you're more mobile. In the meantime, let's talk a little more about your medical history."

Reiff's attention returned to his hand. Opening and closing. Faster this time. And smoother.

"Have you had any surgeries? Any unusual results or issues from previous checkups?"

"No."

"Do you remember the last time you had a medical exam?"

"In the army."

"And how long ago was that?"

"Seven or eight years."

Dr. Williams jotted it down.

"Any injuries or broken bones that needed medical attention?"

"How much attention?"

"Surgery?"

"No."

"What about jobs in the army? Anything resulting in medical attention? Exposure to dangerous chemicals or anything else unusual?"

He shook his head. "Nothing everyone else wasn't exposed to."

Once again, Williams lowered the clipboard. "Do you know your blood type?"

Reiff's eyes turned to him. "Don't you?"

"I do." The doctor grinned. "Do *you*?"

"A-positive."

"Correct. Is there anything else we should know?"

"Not that I can think of."

Williams sighed quietly and turned to Rachel, who was observing. She noticed Reiff examining the pen in Williams's hand, and she reached out to take it. Then motioned for his clipboard, where she pulled the top few pages free, returning them to Williams.

She handed the clipboard and remaining pages to Reiff, along with the pen. "How about a little fine-motor testing? Can you try to write your name for us?"

He took the items, carefully positioning the pen between two fingers.

Without speaking, she stepped in beside Reiff to watch as he wrote. When finished, he turned it toward her. The letters of his last name.

"A little rough but not bad," she said. "How does that feel?"

"Like I'm in the first grade again."

She laughed. "Why don't you go ahead and practice while Dr. Williams and I check on some things."

29

"Dear Lord!" said Williams. "The man's a damn enigma!"

Standing inside her lab, Rachel folded both arms. "Maybe he just doesn't like talking about himself. A lot of people don't."

"Well, that doesn't help us much, does it?"

She returned a bleak look. "It may just take time, Perry."

"No kidding."

She strolled forward, peering at the animals in the adjoining room. "I don't like lying to him," she said. "It feels—"

They were abruptly interrupted by a loud screech from Otis, the chimpanzee, hanging from a swinging perch in his giant cage and staring at them through the open doorway.

"It's the least of our concerns at the moment," said Williams.

Absently, Rachel noted the small capuchin monkey in the cage beside Otis, calmly watching them. "Did you see the way he was looking around the room? It's like he knows."

"How would he know?"

"I don't know, but I think he *knows* we're lying, which makes it even worse. I feel guilty just looking him in the eyes."

"It's for his own good, Rachel. You know that. Even what we're doing now, it has to be—"

The door behind them suddenly burst open, and a winded Henry Yamada rushed in, nearly shouting. "Someone's in our system!"

Rachel stared at him in surprise. "What?"

Yamada checked over his shoulder before letting the door close behind him. "Someone is in the system," he repeated, "right now."

"What, like being hacked?"

"Maybe? And that's not all; they're using Nora's account."

"How is that possible? Our system uses our faces for security."

"I don't know, but somehow, they got past it. And the connection is originating from someplace I don't recognize." Yamada looked back and forth at them. "What the hell is going on?!"

"We've been wondering the same thing," answered Williams. "A lot of things are not adding up."

"So then, something *is* going on?"

"Keep your voice down," Williams hissed, stepping forward and pulling Yamada away from the door. "Something's not right. That much is clear. But we don't know what yet."

"Then what do we do?"

Williams remained calm, thinking. After a long pause, he said, "Nothing."

"Uh, pardon?"

"Nothing," he repeated. "Clearly, we're not being told everything. But none of us are exactly in danger. My guess is someone else is involved in our project that we haven't been told about."

"Like who?"

"How the hell would I know?"

Yamada looked back at the door. "If Nora is in on something, we have to tell Masten."

Williams rolled his eyes. "Please. If Nora's involved, do you seriously believe *he* isn't?"

"Henry," interrupted Rachel, "where is the connection coming from?"

"I don't know."

"You can't locate it?"

"I tried. But it doesn't trace. I've never seen that before. But I'm not exactly a hacking expert either."

"Let's all just take a deep breath," said Williams. "We're not in the loop about something, but like I said, it's not life and death either. We have time to figure this out. So, the best thing to do . . . is nothing."

"Seriously?"

"Yes." Williams nodded. "At least for the moment."

"And what if this is some kind of secret conspiracy?"

"Then so what. It's not *our* conspiracy. We just keep doing our jobs while we try to unravel things."

Rachel and Henry both looked at him uncomfortably.

He went on. "Let's not forget: We don't *own* any part of this project. Or this lab, for that matter. We're just employees. Pawns."

"Pawns?"

Williams glared at Yamada. "On a chessboard. Jesus, how old are you?"

"Thirty-two."

"I was being facetious."

He turned to Rachel. "The best thing we can do is stay the course—but stay alert. Sooner or later, Masten or Lagner will have to reveal *something*. Especially," he said, turning to Yamada, "when you tell her about the hacking."

Yamada nodded, then said, "What if it's not a hack?"

"What do you mean?"

"What if it's *her* logging in?"

Williams raised an eyebrow. "Do you know where she is right now?"

"In her office. It seems crazy, but it's possible she gave someone her login credentials."

"Wait," said Rachel. "There's still a chance we could be misinterpreting things. I mean, it's still possible there's a normal explanation to all this. Something we're just not aware of."

"It's possible," agreed Williams. "But what we're talking about is 'likelihood.'"

"Okay, so worst case is that others are involved. But we're still working toward the same goal, right?"

Williams tried not to roll his eyes again. She was, without a doubt, one of the brightest young minds he'd come across in medicine in a long time, but this was where her lack of experience became notably less helpful. Rarely had Williams seen silent partners actually help a project. Which was why they were kept silent. But even this felt different. Something he couldn't put a finger on yet.

"Henry," he finally said. "Tell Nora about the hack, or 'possible' hack, and see what she says. Rachel, you stay with Reiff and see if you can get any more out of him. Maybe he knows something, and maybe he doesn't."

"What are you going to do?"

"I'm going to have a talk, with *Robert*."

30

Robert Masten's office was ornate, matching the man's persona and self-image. It was a giant space paneled in dark *bocote* wood with an oversized desk in the center of a windowless room. The lighting overhead provided a soft glow off several pieces of matching white furniture, along with a wooden ebony bar sporting two glass shelves of brandies and cognacs, where Masten was standing when he called Williams to enter.

Upon seeing the man, Masten, in a dark blue suit, raised and tilted his glass in his direction. "Why hello, Perry. Care for a drink?"

"No, thank you," replied Williams, easing the heavy door closed behind him.

Masten smiled and poured himself another shot. Recapping the crystal bottle, he gave his full attention to his lead physician. "What do I owe the pleasure?"

The older man approached and stopped several feet away, both hands in his pockets. "I need some answers."

Masten laughed. "You always have more answers than I do."

"We'll see."

Noting the seriousness on Williams's face, Masten pursed his lips and nodded, then gave a welcoming swipe with his free hand. "By all means."

"Who else?"

"Excuse me?"

"Who else," repeated Williams flatly. "Who else is involved?"

Masten paused for a moment before tilting his head. "What are you talking about?"

"I think you know exactly what I'm talking about."

What was left of Masten's smile fell into a frown. "I'm not sure that I do."

The doctor continued, closing the distance. "It feels like you're hiding things, Robert."

"Hiding things? From who?"

"From us."

"What makes you think I'm hiding something?"

"For starters, you keep breaking protocol."

"Perry," he sighed, "I already explained that. Communication can be a very delicate matter—"

"It's not just that. I know when things aren't right."

"So, it's instinct then." When the doctor didn't respond, Masten's face grew more earnest. Emptying his glass, he put it down and turned away, drifting toward his desk. "You know, Perry, I hired you not just for your medical expertise but for your experience. Both in medicine *and* business. Believe me, that kind of balance is rarer than you think. The ability to understand *and appreciate* not just the mechanics of medicine, but the practicality of it."

"I'm aware of that."

"Are you?" Masten asked rhetorically. He took a deep breath and continued to his desk, turning and sitting against the edge. "Exactly how easy do you think all of this has been?"

"Not very."

"Not very," smirked Masten. "Just getting this building renovated without anyone knowing was a Herculean task—if I do say so myself. As was finding just the right people, like you, without attracting unwanted attention to our project. Considering everything else going on outside of these walls, it was a damn miracle."

"I get it."

"Ninety percent of this project had nothing to do with medicine." After a moment of reflection, he shrugged. "Okay, maybe eighty-five. My point is that the world is a different place. I admit I did take a few liberties." He glanced around the room. "Care to guess how expensive *bocote* wood is today?"

Masten continued. "In the beginning, I thought we had it made. Naively. A rough road, yes, but I made it all happen. Either through blood, sweat, or tears. At the time, I thought this office was a reasonable splurge—back when we had the money."

"What are you talking about? Did something happen?"

"Life happened," answered Masten, looking back up. "Life. The world. What should have taken me one year took almost ten. Ten long, unrelenting years, fighting obstacle after obstacle. Every imaginable problem. Every roadblock. One after another. Until . . ." His eyes stared forward. "It's a miracle," he said again. "A miracle that we're even standing here."

"What happened?" pressed Williams.

Masten stared back, sighing. "We lost a lot of it."

"A lot of what?"

"Our funding. In one fell swoop. One of our largest backers just . . . walked away."

Williams's instinct was to ask which one. But it didn't matter. Most of their backers were anonymous.

"When?"

"About six months ago. After our string of spectacular failures."

"We knew it was a possibility."

Masten shrugged. "Knowing something is a possibility and then watching it happen over and over are two different things, my friend."

"Reiff is alive and healthy. That alone is worth a hell of a lot."

Masten stared at him, bemused. "He's *alive*. That's all we know at this point. And you and I always knew that everything, the project itself, would come down to him and him alone. Our diamond in the rough," he said with a grin. "Our one in a million."

Williams stepped forward again, pulling his hands from his pockets. "That's another piece that doesn't make sense."

"What's that?"

"With Reiff being so unique. So valuable to us. How is it we know so little about him?"

Masten leaned back on the desk. "A lot of that data has been lost, Perry. You know that."

"Then tell me," countered Williams. "Where did we find Reiff?"

"I already told you."

"Then tell me again. *Where exactly did the man come from?*"

31

"Not bad."

John Reiff looked up from his bed to find Rachel observing from the doorway before moving forward and picking up one of the papers.

"I see we've moved on to drawing."

"You can only write your name so many times."

She chuckled and examined the page. "Looks like you've had some experience at this."

"I did some sketching in school."

Rachel gave an approving nod and studied the image. A building or a farmhouse. Surrounded by what looks like a patchwork of trees or an orchard. "Your dexterity is recovering nicely. That's a good sign."

"Better than the alternative, I guess."

"It certainly is."

Reiff lowered the pad of paper and pen and stretched his fingers. "How long have you been a doctor?"

"Almost fourteen years."

"What kind?"

"I'm a vascular surgeon."

Reiff gave her a curious look. "The circulatory system?"

"Very good."

"And you were assigned to me because?"

"The accident you were in was in the snow. In icy conditions. Your vascular system had to be rewarmed very carefully."

"I see. So, I was a Popsicle?"

This time she laughed and gestured with her thumb and finger, leaving a small space between them. "Just a little."

She picked up another of the pages and looked over the sketch. The lines still revealed a light shaking in Reiff's hand, but nothing alarming and not enough to prevent her from recognizing a crowded city block with dozens of lightly shaded figures. People, and behind them several more buildings.

"Where is this?" she asked.

"No idea."

She stared at it thoughtfully. "If you can do this well now, I would have liked to see what you did in school."

"I didn't win any contests, if that's what you're asking." He inhaled and moved the paper and pen to the rolling table next to him. He then looked at her expectantly. "So, when can I eat?"

It was a question she was prepared for. At least, she had been ready for it before her last conversation, which had now called into question any number of things, leaving her lingering momentarily before answering.

"We still need to ensure your GI tract is ready for food," she replied. "But the rest of your system seems pretty stable, so I'll talk to Dr. Williams. Of course," she continued, "if we can start giving you food, we'll have to start slow." She picked up another of his sketches and said with a wink, "The good news is you clearly have the motor skills to feed yourself."

Reiff grinned at that.

Rachel then moved backward, sitting in the chair against the wall. "Is it just me or do you not like talking about yourself?"

His response was neither immediate nor evasive. "Not much to tell."

"I find that hard to believe."

Reiff turned and glanced absently at his IV line. "I'm not that interesting. Just a normal guy."

"Normal how?"

"I put my pants on one leg at a time, just like everyone else. At least when I have them."

"Are you saying you'd like some clothes?"

"That'd be nice."

"You didn't come in with much, but I'll see what I can do. On one condition."

"What's that?"

"You talk to me."

Reiff smirked playfully. "What would you call this?"

"Not what I mean. I mean a real honest-to-goodness conversation. About your background. Things that might help us."

"Like what?"

"You mentioned you travel around a lot. Where are your medical records?"

"Where?"

"Yes," she said. "As in, who has them? A hospital? A doctor? They must be somewhere. Maybe the army?"

Reiff thought for a moment. "I saw a doctor a few years ago in Butte. Can't remember his name, though. It was just a clinic."

"What did you see him for?"

"Fractured wrist."

"Did he have your records?"

"No. It was a walk-in clinic. Records would probably still be with the army."

"Okay," replied Rachel, folding her arms. "Where were you stationed?"

"All over."

"What did you do in the army?"

"I worked in communications," he replied.

"And when were you discharged?"

"July 2015."

She stared at him with a look of curiosity. "So, from there you just moved around?"

"I thought I would take some time to see more of the country I'd been defending."

Rachel nodded. "I see. And?"

"And what?"

"And where did you go?"

Reiff gave a thoughtful tilt of his head. "Everywhere really."

"Did you always travel by bus?" she asked.

"I prefer trains, but they don't go everywhere. The rest of the time, it was either bus, hitching, or good old-fashioned walking."

Rachel couldn't hide her cheeky expression. "So, you just traveled aimlessly around the country for several years?"

"More or less," he replied.

"What about money?"

"When I need money, I work. Otherwise . . ."

"Otherwise?"

"Otherwise, I just pick a direction."

Rachel leaned back in the chair. "And what kind of work would you do?"

"Construction, cook, day laborer. Whatever people were looking for."

"So, you can cook?" she teased.

"You know there's an old maxim about judging a book by its cover."

She raised her hands. "No, no. Not judging. Just . . . surprised."

"Why is that?"

"I don't know. You just don't look the role. Construction, yes. A cook, meh."

"And what about you?"

Rachel raised an eyebrow. "Pardon?"

"What's your story?"

"My story?" For some reason she hadn't expected that question. "There's not much to tell."

"I thought we were *talking*."

Caught off guard, she could feel herself stammer. Her instructions were to keep personal details out of all conversations. Which was easier said than done. Without at least some level of detail, a discussion quickly began to feel forced. Still, they couldn't afford to let something slip.

"Um, pretty straightforward, I guess," she finally said. "I went to medical school and, after graduating, cut my teeth working ER for several years. I burned out, as everyone eventually does, and decided I wanted to do something more interesting."

"Like defrosting people."

She laughed. "Kind of."

"Interesting," he said. "But can you make a perfect pancake?"

"Uh . . . no."

"That makes two of us."

The room fell silent, prompting Rachel to slap the tops of her knees and stand up. "Okay, why don't you get a little more rest, and I'll go see when you can eat."

"Bring a wheelchair, too."

She stepped forward and briefly patted his arm. "We'll see."

32

"We're running out of time," Rachel said when Williams returned to her lab. "Figuratively *and* literally."

"What do you mean?"

"He wants to eat."

"Okay. That was inevitable."

"Yes, it was."

"Let's begin with a liquid diet, as planned. Did you get any more out of him?"

"A little. Sounds like the army is where we should be looking for more information. And look at this," she added, moving to her desk.

She picked up the pages Reiff had drawn on and handed them to Williams.

"What's this?"

"Fine motor skills."

"He did these?"

Rachel nodded.

"Nice."

She moved beside him and pointed. "Look at the lines."

"A little shakiness but not bad."

"His NCV tests are mostly normal, suggesting minimal damage."

"All areas?"

"Yep. So, unless there is something seriously wrong in his GI that we can't detect . . ."

Williams nodded in agreement. "Then it's time for food." He lowered the papers onto one of the lab's nearby counters, glancing up when their chimpanzee Otis screeched again, this time repeatedly, from his cage. Grasping the top of his perch and swinging wildly. Next to him was the capuchin, once again watching them, and the small dog Rachel had warmed up to, standing on her hind legs against the front of her cage, with her tail wagging excitedly.

When he turned to Rachel, he saw her silently watching him.

"What?" he asked.

"The patient also wants a wheelchair."

Henry Yamada pushed back through the door to find both doctors talking on the far side of the lab. Upon his entering, they both stopped and turned, crossing the room.

"Well?" they asked in unison.

"Well, *that* was weird," Yamada said. "Something is definitely going on."

"We already know that, Henry."

"No, I mean *with Nora.*"

"What did she say?"

"First off, let me clarify that I am not an expert on this cybersecurity stuff. At all."

Rachel rolled her eyes. "We *know.*"

"However," he went on, "I *do* know enough that I'm not a complete idiot either." He spotted the impending joke on Rachel's face and stopped her. "Don't!"

"I didn't say anything."

"Anyway, that was one strange conversation."

"How so?"

"For starters, it almost felt like she was waiting for me. And she didn't deny it at all. She said someone else was using her ID because theirs wasn't working."

"Did she say who?"

"One of the engineers. In India."

"Do you think that's true?" asked Williams.

"No."

"Why not?"

"Because most of India is sleeping."

"A lot of Indian teams work our hours."

"That's true," agreed Yamada. "A lot of consulting companies work at night to match the working hours of their clients. But not ours."

"Not ours?"

"Our team is purely R and D. Which doesn't have to happen

simultaneously. And when they do reach out, they reach out to me. Not Nora."

"And did you say that?"

"I began to, but she insinuated they couldn't get ahold of me, so they called her."

"Would that be unusual?"

"Not really. What's unusual is that in the past, she would call me herself. And I would reset their password for them. Pretty standard stuff."

"Maybe she couldn't get ahold of you."

"Yeah, no."

"Not possible?"

He shook his head. "Even if I didn't answer, I would have seen that she'd called."

"Maybe she *thought* she called?" As she spoke, Rachel glanced at Perry, who was listening stoically.

"Nora doesn't forget," Henry pointed out. "And, believe me, she knows better than to give her level of access out to someone else." He turned and looked at Otis, who once again began whooping loudly. "She also said they were just verifying some things with 'the Machine.'"

"Okay?"

"The engineering team already has all the information from the Machine. All the specs, all the test results, and *all* of the data logs. I sent them myself. There is nothing else for them to get from the system."

"So, whoever was accessing the system is not one of us."

"I don't think so."

"Does she still want it dismantled?"

"Yes. Don't even get me started on that."

The three grew quiet for several long seconds, and were all contemplating when Yamada glanced at the counter and noticed the papers and drawings. He stepped forward and picked one up.

"What's this?"

"Some sketches."

He beamed at her in admiration. "I didn't know you could draw, Rach."

"Neither did I."

Yamada peered closer at one of the pages and looked up with curiosity. Then down again.

"This one is your lab?'

She frowned. "What?"

Yamada raised the paper to eye level. "Your lab."

"What are you talking about?" Rachel stepped in and took the piece of paper, turning it over. On the face were several rectangular boxes of varying sizes. Lightly sketched with faint crosshatching. "He didn't finish this one. They're just blocks or something."

Yamada took the paper back and held it up so they could both see it. Then lowered it so they could see the far side of the room over the top of the paper. "Um."

It took Rachel several seconds before her eyes widened.

The animal cages were on the far side of the room through the doorway. All against the wall a few feet from each other. In ascending size and height, beginning with the rabbits' cages and ending with Otis's, which was the widest and tallest, reaching just a few feet from the ceiling.

Side by side, the cages stood, each with its own rectangular shape. And dimensions that matched the shapes in the patient's sketch.

33

John Reiff looked up when the door unlocked and Rachel rushed in.

"You forgot the wheelchair."

She crossed the room and stopped in front of him, looking Reiff up and down as he stood on both feet with only one hand on the bed.

"What are you doing?"

"Practicing."

Momentarily piqued, she let the thought go and held up the picture in front of him. "What is this?"

He stared at the page and its square images. "I don't know."

"You don't know?"

"Well, I know what it is. But not where."

"What—" started Rachel before suddenly stopping herself. Searching for the pen, she found and picked it up, handing it to him. "Finish."

"Excuse me?"

"Finish the picture."

Reiff stared at her. "Are you okay?"

Rachel took a slow breath and composed herself. "I'm fine. Please finish the picture."

Reiff's eyes didn't leave hers but instead gazed at her, perplexed. "Why do you want me to finish?"

"I want to know what this is. I want to know what you were drawing."

"Or I can just tell you what it is."

Rachel blinked. That hadn't occurred to her. "Fine. What is it?"

"They're cages."

"What kind of cages?" she asked coolly.

Reiff continued studying her. "Are you asking what they're made of, or what's in them?"

"What's inside?"

He glanced again at the unfinished picture. "Animals."

From his oversized office, Masten stared at his monitor, awash in the ambient glow, while wearing a look of disbelief. As though he hadn't heard correctly. But the expression on Rachel Souza's face, even through the live video feed, looked exactly like Masten's. Incredulous and stunned.

34

It was less than a minute before Dr. Williams entered the room and stood beside Dr. Souza, this time without his white coat. Instead, he wore a yellow, short-sleeved shirt and dark slacks.

"Hi, John."

Reiff turned his gaze. "Hey, Perry."

Williams noted Reiff in his standing position. "Going somewhere?"

Their patient grinned. "My ride didn't show."

"I see." The older doctor caught his breath and brought both hands to his hips, motioning at the picture still in Rachel's hand.

"What can you tell us about his picture?"

Reiff raised an eyebrow. "Why do you ask?"

"Was this one of your visions?"

"Yes."

"And are these"—Williams nodded at the paper—"cages?"

"Yes."

"Where are they?"

When Reiff didn't answer, Rachel did. "He said he doesn't know."

"I see. And what are in the cages, John?"

"Animals," mused Rachel.

Reiff studied the two. The picture had gotten them both excited. If he didn't know where the cages were, something told him they did.

"John, do you know which animals you saw?"

Reiff's eyes remained on Williams. "I think it's your turn, Doctor."

"Pardon?"

"It's your turn. For answers."

Williams slowly lowered his hands. "Okay."

Reiff looked back and forth at them. "Let's start with . . . where am I?"

Both doctors feigned surprise at the question.

"We already told you. In a hospital."

"I don't think so. If that were true, you two wouldn't be the only two rotating in and out of my room. There's no television or phone line. Or window." He then peered past them at the door. "There's no noise outside when either of you come and go, telling me there's probably no one else on the other side of this wall. And most hospital room doors don't have locks." He folded his arms across his chest. "I think it's time you tell me where I really am."

Rachel began to speak, but Williams cut her off with a raised hand. After thinking for a moment, he nodded. "You're right. You're not in a hospital. You're in a special facility. The only one with the equipment to save you. You're also correct that there are no other patients in the building. Just you."

"Why?"

"Because of the severity of your condition," answered Williams. "You suffered an extreme case of hypothermia. Most acute victims are treated within minutes or hours. It took longer with you, requiring extra precautions to resuscitate you. Just like Dr. Souza said."

Reiff looked at Rachel.

"As for the lock on the door, it's a precautionary measure. Patients subjected to severe trauma, like you, often experience illusions or hallucinations that cause them to panic and even flee. That would be bad."

"Is that right?"

Williams nodded, noting Reiff's dubious expression. "You don't believe me."

"I'm a cautious fellow," replied Reiff, looking back at the door. "Maybe we should take a look."

Williams became solemn. "After you finish answering our questions."

"A dog, couple of monkeys, and a pig."

Williams felt his heart race. "Is that all?"

"Some rabbits," added Reiff, "and a few rodents."

The older man remained still, facing Reiff but saying nothing. Wavering slightly. Processing. Until he finally spoke to Dr. Souza.

"Get the wheelchair."

35

Henry Yamada stopped typing and picked up the ringing phone from his desk.

"Hi, Nora."

"Hello, Henry. Busy?"

"Uh . . ." He glanced up at his screen while switching the phone to his other hand. "Not too much. What's up?"

"I need you to do something for me. Something urgent. I need you to pull up our security feeds and look back over the last few days."

Henry tilted his head to secure the phone and lowered both hands back to the keyboard. "Okay. What are we looking for?"

"I need you to go through the video footage, frame by frame if you have to, and tell me if John Reiff ever left his room."

"Uh, isn't the room locked?"

"It should be. But it's possible it was left open. Regardless, we need to know if he left the room. And if so, when and where he went."

"Okay," Yamada said, and resumed typing. "Anything else?"

"That's all for now. Call me as soon as you know. Thanks."

With that, Nora Lagner ended the call, leaving her computer engineer staring at his monitor with both hands outstretched over the keyboard.

It wouldn't take long. Both the camera in Reiff's room and the door alarm were connected and controlled by the same security system. All Yamada had to do was have the video feed skip forward to each time the door was opened or closed. Which, unbeknownst to his boss, Yamada was already in the process of checking.

36

A few minutes later, Reiff was wheeled into the hall outside his room, pushed by Dr. Williams and followed by Dr. Souza, who calmly pulled the door closed behind them.

From the chair, Reiff looked left, then right. In both directions was an empty hallway; they looked exactly alike, other than one being slightly shorter than the other.

Reiff turned his head and spoke over his shoulder. "You're the tour guide."

Without a word, Dr. Williams turned to the right, pushing Reiff forward. The man said nothing while they traveled toward the end of the hallway and turned right.

Another long stretch appeared before them, brightly lit and just as empty. The doctors' steps echoed as they walked. The three continued another fifty feet or so forward, past a set of double doors. Both were painted and perfectly matching the walls except for the chrome door handles and two darkened rectangular windows.

"What's this?" asked Reiff.

Dr. Williams slowed and nodded to Dr. Souza, who moved past to grasp one of the handles, and waited for Williams's signal before opening the right side to reveal a dark interior. She stepped inside and flipped multiple switches on, causing the room to explode into bright light.

"This," said Williams, pushing him through the open doorway, "is where you were saved."

Reiff scanned the room while his chair rolled forward. It looked like a combination of a research lab and a hospital emergency room. On the far side, below an overhead wall made entirely of glass, was a long console that appeared to be some kind of control system for the room.

Several monitors lined the console, some of which were powered on and displaying various data windows. It all reminded Reiff of a NASA control room.

On the right side were two long counters connected in an L shape, crammed with dozens of machines and unfamiliar—but probably medical—devices. Perhaps for diagnostics. And above them, shelves of carefully labeled containers and bottles, as well as several smaller computer monitors, all positioned at eye level.

Reiff looked up to see a long overhead rail system snaking across the ceiling and over their heads, ending near the strangest device he had ever seen. He could only describe it as an *electric sarcophagus*. A giant, casket-shaped metal container with roughly the shape and dimensions of a human body. Something one might expect a high-tech mummy to be extracted from. It had hundreds of small wires attached to virtually every square inch of its exterior, all neatly bound and organized, running up and around the thing in all directions.

"What the hell is that?"

Dr. Souza stepped next to him with both arms behind her back. "We call it 'the Machine.'"

Dr. Williams leaned in from behind. "*That* is what saved your life."

Reiff marveled at the precision of it all, and how it managed to look both modern and retro at the same time.

"What does it do?"

"It thaws Popsicles," joked Dr. Souza.

Reiff's eyes continued to roam over the rest of the room. Next to the Machine and along the wall were several more devices. Larger, square, and painted in a muted beige. Apparently, the standard for hospital systems. All in various dimensions and sporting their own computer displays, and next to them, a device Reiff recognized immediately. A hospital-sized defibrillator.

"Did you have to use that?"

Williams sighed. "Don't ask."

After leaving, they turned left and resumed their walk down the remainder of the hallway, passing several more closed doors on the way.

"And these?"

"Nothing important. Just supply rooms or wiring closets."

They continued on toward a set of elevator doors in the distance. Also painted to match the walls. Finally, they stopped at the end, where Souza leaned forward to push the silver call button.

When the elevator arrived, both doors opened, and the three proceeded inside, where Souza selected the floor directly above them.

It was the floor that housed her lab, and upon entering, Reiff immediately understood their interest in his sketch. Several cages lined the wall through the open door in the adjoining room.

The doctors stood quietly behind Reiff, seemingly waiting for his reaction, which was only to raise his hands and calmly roll the wheelchair forward.

He reached the smallest cage through the door first, before continuing past the next. Then the next. One at a time until he reached the capuchin monkey, which was standing up and grasping the thin metal bars in front of him, and looking up at him. Then to the last one, where he paused curiously in front of the giant cage housing the chimpanzee. Swinging quietly and contently on his low-hanging perch.

From the doorway, Williams spoke. "Is this what you were drawing?"

37

Traversing the bright halls of a large corporate building in Bethesda, Maryland, the man Masten and Lagner knew only as their "handler" slowed his pace when his phone began to ring.

Noting several people approaching, Liam Duchik spotted a small open conference room and stepped inside. He closed the door and answered the call.

"Yes?"

"It's Masten. We have a development."

"What is it?"

"It's John Reiff."

Duchik turned and peered back out through the long narrow window next to the door. "Who else would it be?"

"The visions he's having may not be hallucinatory."

Duchik's dour expression did not change. "Explain."

"He's been drawing things. Things that he's seeing."

"We already know that."

Masten's voice hesitated. "One of them appeared to depict Dr. Souza's lab."

Duchik blinked and slowly turned away from the glass. "Go on."

"He drew the cages."

The handler lowered his voice. "Of the test subjects?"

"That's right."

"Are you sure?"

"Not a hundred percent, but it seems pretty obvious."

"What do you mean 'it seems'?"

"The sketch wasn't finished, but the images appear to match. And then there was his reaction when he finally saw the room."

"They took him to the lab?"

"Yes."

Duchik became thoughtful. "The patient must have left his room."

"Maybe, but we can't find any proof from the security cameras."

"Then someone told him about the lab. Perhaps the woman."

"We're going through all the audio now. So far, nothing about Souza's lab was mentioned. And nothing about the animals."

"Well, it had to come from somewhere," said Duchik harshly. "Even if he wasn't conscious at the time. Go all the way back, to the time he was revived. One of them must have referenced the animals."

"But if he was unconscious—"

"His subconscious was active long before he woke up, which absorbs far more information. Find out when and where Souza, or Williams, discussed the test subjects."

"Okay."

Duchik paused thoughtfully. "Does this mean Reiff is ambulatory?"

"Not quite, but close."

"What else has he seen besides the lab?"

"Just the top floors. Souza's lab and the main lab."

"He saw the Machine?"

"Yes."

"And he's still experiencing the hallucinations?"

"Some."

Duchik was no fool. He was acutely aware that Masten would downplay any significant problems and even lie if need be. Leaving him the task of reading between the lines of their reports. It was something Duchik had become exceedingly good at. With all types of individuals.

Masten was smart, but not smarter than him.

"Keep him to those floors," he said. "Tell him there are security issues with the other levels."

"What about Reiff himself?"

"I will give you seventy-two hours."

A compromised mental state was useless for his purposes. But Reiff might still hold some value physically, particularly around Williams's autophagy and cellular therapy regimen.

"What are we supposed to do in three days?"

His response was sharp and emotionless. "Prepare to dispose of him. And make sure your people keep their mouths shut."

Duchik ended the call and looked out through the glass pane with a detached gaze.

His parents had barely escaped the crumbling Eastern Bloc in the seventies and learned firsthand the value of survivability. The kind some might even label as "ruthless."

And their now sixty-two-year-old son, Liam, had taken every bit of that discipline to heart. The importance of focus and conviction in a world that had so little of either. A world filled with human beings without the slightest sense of purpose or meaning. Instead, they were brainwashed by the same herd to which they all strived to belong.

None of it had been a surprise to him. None of what had happened or how the masses had reacted. It had all been programmed by a world the sheep had created, and acting precisely as his parents had said they would. It had culminated in a devastating event that had taken far longer to play out than was expected. With consequences far worse than even *the herd*'s experts had feared.

As his parents had always said: Surprise was a symptom of the naive.

Several hours later, Perry Williams sat anxiously within a darkened room in his home, silently staring at the older computer monitor atop his wooden desk. The office was sparsely decorated, with a bookcase behind him supporting an extensive set of medical textbooks, and beside it a broad-paned window, darkened by the night sky.

The desk itself was decades old, faded and crowded with framed pictures of a smiling wife along with several more of their children. Many were of their children's youth, but others were when they were grown, in portraits with their own families. All smiling happily. Frozen in time.

He had been sitting there for nearly an hour. Waiting and nervously watching a small window on his computer screen.

And then it happened.

In a secured chat box, a string of letters suddenly appeared.

Hello?

Williams abruptly leaned forward and typed a response. *I'm here.*

    Identify yourself.

He swallowed, apprehensive. His hands trembled ever so slightly as he typed. He was going entirely on faith now. And on Henry Yamada's word. *Dr. Perry Williams.*

    Where are you?

They already knew where he was. Why were they asking again? *At home.*

    Are you alone?
    Yes.
    What is your social security number?

Williams hesitated again. Yamada had said they would want all his personal information. To verify Williams was who he claimed to be. Uneasy, he typed the nine-digit number.

    What is your FRN?

He picked up a small plastic card from his desk, angled it under the light, then began typing again. When finished, he lowered it and pressed the Enter key then waited for their response.

    Stand by.

It took several minutes for the next message to appear.

    Verified. Did you leave the connection open?
    Yes.
    Give us the 13-digit alphanumerical code provided to you.

Now Williams held up a piece of paper. This one with his own hand-writing. Typing out the thirteen-character security code.

Another long wait as the chat window remained idle. Until:

Connection verified. Give us 24 hours. We will provide the
requested information along with the remaining payment
instructions.

Williams barely had time to type *OK* before the chat session disconnected. He eased back in a combination of relief and lingering nervousness. Relieved that they accepted but nervous in the vulnerability he
was feeling.

He had no idea who he was dealing with. Only a referral from Yamada. Williams wallowed in a fleeting moment of regret, suddenly
wondering just how well he even knew the engineer. Asking him for
this kind of help could land Williams in jail if someone found out. Or
worse, if whoever was on the other end of that secured text window was
not who they said they were.

Williams had just put everything in the hands of a thirty-two-year-
old kid he'd known for barely over a year. He'd given these people
access by creating a connection from his office computer and purposefully leaving it open, which the hackers would use to tunnel back into
the lab's private network.

38

The following day, Rachel was unsurprised to open Reiff's door and find him standing again. Having already disconnected himself from his IV, he was walking back and forth around the foot of the hospital bed with minimal support.

"Well, aren't we looking spry?" she said with a grin.

Reiff looked up and then at the tray in her hands, and the large bowl of fresh fruit. "What do we have here?"

"Breakfast," she replied. "Like I said, we have to start slow to make sure your stomach is ready for it."

He rounded the bed and lowered himself onto the edge while Rachel moved the wheeled table closer and set the tray in front of him.

He immediately picked up the fork and raised it over the bowl before pausing.

"Something wrong?"

He stared at the fruit. "I'm not as hungry as I thought I'd be."

"That's normal. It's a result of the nutrients in your IV and a process called autophagy."

"What's that?"

"A deep-cleansing cycle that occurs when your system doesn't digest food for an extended period. Like during fasting."

"Hmm."

Rachel laughed. "Believe it or not, it can become very powerful over time."

Reiff let it go and speared a large strawberry, put the whole thing in his mouth, and chewed slowly. He then ate another just as quickly and turned to her in awe. "These may be the best strawberries I've ever had."

She laughed again. "Hunger can have quite an effect on the taste buds."

"Then I can't wait for some steak."

"It'll take time to get to the steak," she cautioned. "Fruit is the best food for reintroduction. It has lots of nutrients and is mostly water, so very easy to digest."

She glanced at the stand next to his bed, noting more drawings. "May I?"

Reiff nodded and continued to eat.

Two more drawings, both depicting crowds of people. One was around a large building that looked to be in flames. She stared closely at the picture for several seconds, until they were interrupted by a knock at the door.

Williams stuck his head in and looked over at Reiff making quick work of the fruit.

"Just wait for the steak," he said with a laugh.

"That's what I said," Reiff mumbled with his mouth full.

Williams looked at Rachel. "Can I talk to you for a moment?"

"What's up?"

Williams waited for the door to close. "Masten wants to see us."

"Now?"

"Apparently."

She took a breath and acquiesced, pushing the door back open to let Reiff know they would be back.

In the conference room, the two lowered themselves into their usual seats, facing Masten and Lagner. "Where's Henry?"

"He's busy," said Lagner. "And not necessary for this."

The doctors looked at Masten, waiting, while he calmly lowered both hands onto the table and began.

"We have some concerns," he started. "Over Reiff's hallucinations. We believe they're symptomatic of a larger biological issue that may require a change in his treatment. I know outwardly it may not appear—"

"Wait a minute," interrupted Rachel. "A biological issue? Where exactly is this diagnosis coming from?"

"From Doctors Soliz and Bennett."

Rachel looked at Williams. "That's not what they told us."

Robert Masten raised his hands in an innocent gesture. "I don't know what to tell you; maybe that was before—"

"Before what?"

"Rachel, listen. I know this is a delicate situation—"

"Why is it a delicate situation? He's getting better."

Langer shook her head. "He's not."

"Just because he's communicating normally," Masten added, "doesn't mean his brain is—"

"What?"

"Rachel."

"His brain is *what*?"

"Let's not get upset."

"I'm not upset. I would just like to know why you're trying to convince us of something we're not seeing. The only two people actually *treating* him."

"We've watched everything, too, Rachel. All the video. We can see things just as well as you."

"I see. And, of course, you have the medical training to go with your keen eyesight."

"Soliz and Bennett do. Even more than you do."

"Bullshit!" she snapped.

Masten's gaze hardened. "You're a vascular specialist. Not a neurologist or a psychiatrist. It's out of your area of expertise."

"You don't have to be a neurologist to see he's getting better. Or a psychiatrist! You just have to be honest."

Irritated, Masten turned to Williams for support but found none.

"I agree with Rachel," he said.

Masten exhaled. "Okay, let's just take a step back here."

"Back to what?" asked Rachel. "What exactly are you trying to do?"

"We're not trying to *do* anything."

"Are you sure?" Her tone began to rise, and Williams quietly put a hand on her arm.

"What's going on here, Robert?" he asked calmly.

"What do you mean?"

"None of this is what we agreed on. None of this was part of the plan. Something has clearly changed, and we want to know what it is."

"I don't know what you're talking about," said Masten.

The doctor's response was matter-of-fact. "Who else is involved?"

"Jesus, Perry. We already talked about this."

Williams calmly removed his glasses and placed them on the table. "We talked. But I don't recall an answer."

Masten's face reddened. "Now, you listen to me. You're not in charge here. I am. Not you. Not you," he said, looking at Rachel, "and not you," he finally said to Lagner. "*I* am. And I decide what we do with this project and how we do it! Is that understood?"

Both doctors stared back at him stoically, until Rachel folded her arms.

"I'm not doing it anymore."

"Doing what?"

"I'm not lying to him," she said. "I'm done. The man's a human being, for Christ's sake. *And* a patient. And patients have rights."

Masten's voice hardened. "Watch yourself, Doctor."

"Watch myself? Or what? Are you going to have Dr. Bennett give me a psych eval?"

Williams squeezed her arm again, this time more firmly.

"The patient signed away his rights," said Lagner.

"Really?" replied Rachel. "Something tells me he never got a chance to *sign* anything."

It was then that Williams suddenly stood up. "Okay, let's take a break. I think everyone needs to cool off. Dr. Souza?" he said, pulling Rachel to her feet.

He pushed her forward, rounding the table. Around Masten and to the door, opening it and pushing Rachel through. Turning, he raised both hands apologetically. "Let's all reconvene later."

39

In the hallway, Rachel whirled around, trying to turn back.

"No!" growled Williams, taking her by the shoulders and continuing forward while she attempted to wrest herself free.

"What the hell is going on, Perry?"

"Quiet!" he cautioned.

"Then let's—"

"No! Arguing will get us nowhere. We have to calm down. *You* have to calm down!"

He twisted her around and marched her toward the elevator. Upon reaching the familiar double doors, he slammed his palm against the call button.

The doors opened almost immediately, and Williams pushed her inside, hitting the button labeled L.

Masten and Lagner remained at the table.

"It seems we have a new problem," she said.

Masten nodded in agreement. Still fuming.

His phone rang, and he retrieved it. Almost slamming it down onto the oval table in front of him. He put it on speaker.

It was Duchik.

"Someone is in your system."

"Excuse me?"

"Someone," he repeated, "is *in your system*. Someone else."

"Are you sure?"

"My team just notified me."

Masten turned to Lagner, who immediately reached for her satchel on the chair beside her and yanked her laptop out. Flipping it open, she began to log in.

"What are they doing?"

"Going through things," said Duchik's voice. "Everything. Including the grant and financial records."

"Those are encrypted."

"And yet somehow they're *unencrypting* them."

Lagner was now in, looking for signs of activity. "I don't see anything."

There was a pause on Duchik's side before he spoke again. "They're tunneling through one of your internal systems. I have the MAC address."

Lagner pulled up a digital map of their network, displaying hundreds of different connected devices or nodes. "Give me the last four digits of the MAC."

"4DR2."

She typed them in and hit the Enter key. An icon was immediately presented with both the identified device and its name.

She turned her laptop, showing the screen to Masten.

It was the computer in Williams's office.

40

Williams ushered Rachel out of the elevator and through the building's lobby, pushing through one of the outer doors and into the bright sunshine.

Together, they descended the short set of steps and continued before stopping over a hundred feet from the entrance, where Williams spun her back around. "We can't talk about this anymore. Not in there. They'll hear us."

She peered over his shoulder. "What do we do? Go to the police?"

"With what?" he scoffed. "That people aren't following the rules in our secret project?"

Her eyes returned to his. "So, we do nothing?"

"We *have* nothing, Rachel. Not right now."

"We could still 'talk' to the police."

"Things aren't like they used to be. You know that. Besides, who's to say Masten doesn't have connections in the police department? We need more before we talk to anyone, and when we do, it shouldn't be someone local."

"But what if we don't have time? What if they're planning something?"

"I'm sure they are, but we need to understand what it is first."

"And what if we're too late? What if . . . they're about to do something to John?"

Williams hesitated, glancing back over his shoulder. "Okay, listen. I'm working on something."

"What does that mean?"

"It means exactly what it sounds like."

She gave him a dubious stare. "What are you working on?"

"I can't tell you. Not yet. But I should have more information soon."

"Information about what?"

"About what's going on here," answered Williams.

"*Then* we go to the authorities?"

"It depends on what I find."

"And what if you don't find anything?"

"Then we keep looking."

"For what?!"

"*Anything.* Anything pointing to who else is involved in this. Like who was given access to our systems." After hesitating, he added, "Or how John Reiff came to be our patient."

With Williams's words hanging in the air, Rachel looked past him again, making sure no one else had followed them out. Then she pulled a piece of paper from her pocket. "You mean like this?"

Williams took the page and unfolded it. "What's this?"

"Another picture. He drew it this morning."

After examining the sketch, Williams shrugged. "Okay, so . . ."

"Look again," she said. "Closer."

The older doctor inspected the paper, unsure what he was looking for. Then he finally saw it, prompting an immediate change in expression.

With widened eyes, he said, "Is this what I think it is?"

Otis screeched when Rachel burst into her lab. Rushing to her desk, she nearly fell into her seat.

Two cages down from the chimpanzee, Bella, the tiny Chihuahua-terrier, was already on her hind legs, eagerly wagging her tail and whining.

Rachel brought up a browser and typed in a short sentence. Then waited. A moment later, she began scanning through the results, and selected one of the links at the bottom of the page, which brought up an extensive news article along with several pictures.

As she read, something caught her eye, and she glanced away from the screen, noting the flashing red light on her desk phone.

She tried to focus on her monitor, but, unable to ignore the light, she returned to the phone. With a sigh, she reached forward and pressed the voicemail button next to the receiver to play the message.

"Hello, Dr. Souza. Samantha Reed here from the AZA, calling about the transfer to Phoenix Zoo next week. I just have a few details to go over regarding transportation, so if you could call me back, we can get everything sorted. You can reach me on—"

Rachel pressed the button again and ended the playback, then glanced at the date on the phone's digital display.

Damn it. The transfers were next week. She still had to do fresh blood workups for each of the animals.

The zoo was taking the primates, but Bella, the rabbits, and pig Lester were bound for the Humane Society. Her heart sank at the thought. She'd been distracted and hadn't thought much about it. The rabbits were not all that social, and Lester only marginally so. But Bella. Bella was different. After several weeks Rachel wasn't ready to lose the little dog.

She closed her eyes and forced herself back to the task at hand: the computer screen in front of her and the article. Scanning again. Through several paragraphs and skimming down to the photos.

She knew it as soon as she saw it. Three of the images had what she was looking for, but it was the last that presented the best angle. She enlarged the picture and then held Reiff's sketch up next to the screen.

Dear Lord.

41

With her heart beginning to race, Rachel swiveled and rose from her chair, walking quickly to the printer. She grabbed the paper as soon as it spit out onto the output tray and turned it over.

It was beyond coincidence. Unmistakable. And even more than that . . . frightening. There was no explanation at all for what she was looking at.

Unless Perry had an explanation. No. That was just desperate thinking.

She continued staring, mesmerized, knowing in her gut Williams would have little more to offer than theoretical platitudes. They had agreed to meet at his house in two hours to figure things out. But that was before *this*.

She was roused from her trance by another ear-piercing screech from Otis, excitedly grasping the bars of his cage and shaking his body. And through the racket, she could see Bella's soft gray nose pressed through the small bars of her own cage, whimpering and calling for Rachel by wagging her entire body.

Rachel watched the screaming chimpanzee through the doorway as she crossed the room. Then, once inside, noted the always quiet capuchin monkey, Bella, then Lester, and finally, the rabbits.

If she hurried, she could get their blood work done before meeting Williams. Maybe even a few minutes with Bella. A welcome distraction from what was happening.

She continued past the cages, prompting Otis to stop and pause as he watched her. Then on past the others, where she lightly touched the tip of Bella's nose, finally stopping at the opposite end. Only two of the smallest cages were being used after the death of one of the mice. But when Rachel peered down at the two remaining, she noticed something in the sleeping rodents.

They weren't breathing.

Rachel stiffened and immediately reached for the clasp of one of the cages. Opening it and reaching inside, she retrieved the mouse and splayed it out in her open palm.

After a careful examination, she lowered it onto the counter and reached for the second.

Both were dead.

Rachel stumbled back, trying to rationalize and calculate.

Was it possible that all three were within the same life-expectancy windows?

Yes. It was possible, she told herself. But was it likely? No two animals lived to the exact same age. Every creature had its own unique DNA, determining each and every facet of the animal's life. Its makeup. Its size, its health, and, in the end, its mortality. But could they all be part of the same "chronological" litter? Born around the same time. In the same conditions. The same—

Together, she raised them up, one in each hand, and gently rolled them over with her thumbs. Sensing the coolness of each tiny cadaver. Cool, soft, and stiff.

The dread was returning. Like a mass of unease swelling behind her breastbone as she tried to fight against it. With her mind. With logic that told her, while it *was* possible, the odds were against it. Heavily.

Logic that was growing ever more desperate in her mental search for more explanations. Before even that came to a screeching halt. Truncated in midthought by her two eyes as they came upon the next cage.

One of the rabbits did not appear to be moving either.

42

Perry Williams lived in an old two-story home with a wooden wrap-around porch traversing the entire house's left side, connecting the back of the house with a large and lightly painted front porch.

The front lawn was a patchwork of tufts of uncut grass.

Rachel climbed the seven wooden steps and ducked beneath a long row of rusted but still singing wind chimes.

She knocked loudly and waited for the door to open. When it did, his stoic outline appeared behind the darkened screen.

"Sorry I'm late," Rachel said over the ringing of the chimes that hung above her.

Williams opened the screen door and welcomed her inside.

"We have a lot to talk about," she said as she made her way to a faded fabric couch and lowered her purse, then herself.

"What did you find out?"

She shook her head and relaxed against the soft backing. "You go first."

He nodded, sitting in a wooden rocking chair directly across from her. "I've been doing some digging."

"What kind of digging?"

"Electronic," he replied, then paused, considering his answer. "'Hacking' would be a better word."

"Computer hacking?"

"Yes."

"Do you know how to do that?"

He shook his head. "No. I had to ask Henry."

"Henry said he didn't know hacking either."

"He doesn't. But he knows someone who does."

"Ah, okay. And?"

"And I called them. In a manner of speaking. I sent an encrypted message."

Rachel grew more curious. "And?"

"They replied," he said. "Then they proceeded to investigate me. To make sure I was who I claimed to be."

"When was this?"

"Tuesday."

"Wow. How long—" began Rachel.

Williams cut her off. "They've already sent me what they found." He glanced at the clock on his wall. "About forty-five minutes ago."

Her eyes widened with interest. "And what did they send?"

"Some of the financials," said Williams. "For the project. Masten's files."

"What, like a ledger?"

"Among other things. But it wasn't how he spends the money that I was interested in. It was how he *got* the money in the first place."

"He said it was all grant funding."

"It *is*," confirmed Williams, who began rocking gently in his chair. "Care to take a guess what they found?"

"Am I guessing how much or who it came from?"

"Either."

Rachel pondered. "Masten said hundreds of millions, so I presumed that was accurate."

Williams nodded. "It is, for the most part. But we were told it was all in the form of grants from private donors. Lots of them."

"And you found otherwise?"

"There are definitely hundreds of grants. But only a few from private donors."

Rachel sat forward. "So what then, they're all from the same donor?"

Williams nodded again.

"And . . . they're not private?"

"Nope."

"Then who?" she asked.

"The NIH."

Her eyes widened. "NIH? As in the National Institutes of Health?"

"Yep."

"*They're* the donor?"

Williams continued rocking. "Over ninety percent of them."

"Ninety percent of the money is coming from the NIH?"

"Mm-hmm."

Rachel's expression changed from bewilderment to confusion. "The NIH is the primary funder? But their mandate is public health. Not—"

"Not what?"

She stammered, staring at him. Then past him. "But this isn't what they do."

Williams shook his head. "This is *exactly* what they do."

"Their reach is supposed to be for the public benefit. What we're doing is . . ."

Williams watched as Rachel's thoughts gradually steered her toward the same conclusion.

"I'm mean, sure," she continued, "you can *call* it a public benefit, I guess. Eventually. But they're part of Health and Human Services. That's a pretty broad definition. Why would they be involved . . ."

"It's the government, Rachel. They don't need a reason to be involved. Especially these days."

She was still working through it. "So, all the grants said 'NIH'?"

"It wasn't that obvious. But most trace back to them. Through other entities. Hundreds of them."

Rachel's puzzlement deepened again. "But why? Why would they issue hundreds instead of just one large grant? I mean, if they have the power to include this in their mandate."

Williams gave her another knowing smile.

"Oooh," she finally breathed. "Unless they couldn't."

"Small grants are less likely to trigger scrutiny than large ones. That's how a lot of government funding works. Hiding money in plain sight."

". . . And the NIH is huge. It issues grants all the time. If the project is approved, then the project is approved . . ." Her words slowed as she spoke them. "Unless . . . it wasn't approved."

"Hard to say. But it's one or the other. Either approved or not, our money was hidden among thousands of tiny sub-awards."

"If it was approved, they wouldn't have to do that."

"Probably not."

Rachel began nodding. "Well, that would explain Masten's paranoia this whole time."

"It sure would. And why they still haven't done a press release."

The press release! It was one of the things Masten changed. Or more like canceled. Part of the plan throughout the project was to eventually hold a press release if and when they were successful. When their patient was deemed to be out of immediate danger.

And after what they'd accomplished, why else would Masten not want to do a press release?

"They never intended to announce this," she whispered.

"That's my guess," replied Williams.

"But that doesn't make sense."

"It does if you go far enough down the rabbit hole."

"What does that mean?"

"What it means," said Williams, "is that other people are involved. That much is obvious. All the deviations from our original plan are making more sense."

"So, you think someone else is changing the protocol?"

He shrugged. "Or it was never intended to be followed in the first place. Which would explain a lot."

Rachel continued thinking. "It would. But why would the government want to be part of our project?"

The older Williams smiled beneath his white mustache. "You're looking at this wrong, Rachel. The government doesn't want *in* on our project. They are the project."

"What?"

Williams leaned forward in his chair. "*We* are working for *them*."

Her mouth dropped in surprise. "Oh my God. So, what then, it's all been a lie?"

"Who knows what is true anymore," said Williams with a shrug.

Rachel fell silent, thinking of everything this changed. Not just with what they'd accomplished but going forward.

"We're not in charge anymore?"

"Assuming we ever were."

"Do you still think Masten is in charge?"

"I have no idea."

She had begun to speak again when something occurred to her. "Wait a minute. How do you know these hackers were legit?"

"I don't. Henry assured me they were, which is all I had to go by."

"And how did they get the information?"

"I created a secret channel for them using my computer at work, allowing them to access our systems." He immediately read the concern on her face. "But you don't have to worry about that."

Rachel was not comforted. "Do you know that for sure?"

"Trust me. These guys were legit. And thorough. And frankly, more than a little paranoid."

"But were they invisible?"

"Yes."

"Are you sure? As in, *completely* sure?"

Williams glared back at her. "What are you getting at?"

"What I'm getting at," she said, "is that Henry once told me everything digital leaves a trace. *Everything.* He said even looking at a file changes its properties. Something about every file maintaining the date and time it was last opened."

"Rachel, we're fine."

"How do you know?"

"Because no one knew we were looking. And therefore, no one would have a reason to be checking the time and dates of the files. Especially files that are years old."

She thought about it before finally nodding. "That's true."

"Trust me. These guys are sharp. They knew what they were doing."

"And how would you know that?"

"Because they were damn expensive."

The room remained quiet for several uncomfortable minutes as they both thought through the ramifications.

Who isn't getting government funding these days, thought Rachel. But then again, if the NIH was so interested in what they were doing, why didn't they just do it aboveboard, or even do it themselves? They had more than enough resources at their disposal. They did their own research all the time.

Williams finally spoke up. "Your turn?"

"Huh?

He motioned to her purse sitting beside her on the couch. "What did you find?"

"Oh, right," she said, pulling her purse onto her lap and withdrawing the printed photo. She held it momentarily in her hand before extending it over the wooden coffee table.

"It's probably good you're sitting down."

Williams took the paper and unfolded it, staring at the picture. After scrutinizing, he asked, "Do you have Reiff's sketch?"

"Yes." She dipped back into her purse and retrieved a second sheet.

Taking it, he held both up, side by side, examining them. Looking back and forth until finally exhaling in a single audible word.

"Jeeesus."

43

"How is this possible?"

"I have no idea," said Rachel. "I was hoping you might."

Williams eased forward in his rocking chair, placed both papers on the table, and studied them side by side.

When Rachel had shown him the sketch earlier, he'd said it looked too general, but looking at them together it was unmistakable. No amount of chance could explain this.

"Even if we mentioned the animals in Reiff's presence and somehow forgot," offered Rachel, "do you *ever* remember us talking about this?"

All Williams could do was shake his head.

"What about Henry?"

"I only remember Henry being in the room twice," he answered. "Both times before Reiff was conscious."

"But even when unconscious—"

"I know all about the subconscious, Rachel. Could a few words have slipped out without us remembering? Sure. But not with enough context or detail for the man to draw *this*."

"Context can be very subtle. Cues that a lot of us don't think about."

Williams peered up in a look of sarcasm. "Seriously?"

"Then you tell me. I'm out of ideas!"

"I don't know," said Williams absently. "I just don't know. I've got nothing."

"There has to be an explanation."

He leaned back in his rocking chair. Pondering. "We've both been in medicine long enough to have seen things," he finally said in resignation. "Things that don't make sense."

She slid forward on the couch and rotated the pages toward her. Viewing them again. "Yes. I've seen things before. Witnessed things.

But nothing like this. The picture of my lab? Okay fine. Somehow, some way, the man knew something. Heard something. Maybe even guessed. The sketch wasn't even finished. So yes, there was room for some level of coincidence, or chance, or whatever you want to call it. But this? This is *not* the same."

"Nope."

"There's no television or radio in his room. No phone, no means of communication, except through us. We all agreed. Frankly, if any of those things *were* in the room, maybe I wouldn't be all that shocked. Perplexed maybe, but not shocked."

Williams listened from his chair, studying her before replying. "It is weird; I'll give you that. More than weird. But we've both seen lots of things that couldn't be explained, so why not this?"

"You're asking why I'm so bothered over it?"

"Yes."

"I'll tell you why," she said. "Because we're still lying to him." She rose from the couch in agitation. "It's a miracle the man is alive, and we're *still* lying right to his face. Doesn't that bother you? After what he's gone through, is still going through, haunted by these hallucinations or whatever they are. And we're *still* playing games?"

"Rachel—"

"You know what I keep thinking about, Perry?" she said, crossing her arms. "Through all of this. Day in and day out."

"What?"

"That, as hard as all this has been for us over the course of this entire project. All of the struggles. All of the testing, the failures, all the deaths! I keep wondering what the hell that man must be *thinking*! I mean, just step back and consider that. The guy only vaguely knows what happened to him. But he has no idea how he got here or who we are. Who we really are. Or why he can't leave his room without supervision. Whether he's going to be all right. While no one, except us, even knows he's alive! And we just keep lying. Giving just enough information to keep him from asking more questions. Like he's just some kind of test subject." She turned away angrily. "I'm sick of it. I'm absolutely sick of feeling like I'm this horrible, heartless person!"

She closed her eyes in aggravation, then slowly opened them again. "And now we have a much bigger problem."

"Like what?"

"Our test animals are dying."

Williams's eyes widened in shock. "What did you say?"

"They're dying, Perry. One at a time. First the mice, and now one of the rabbits."

"There . . . there could be several reasons—"

"Oh really?"

It took him a moment. "Animals don't live as long. Especially mice. They may be from the same—"

"Same what? Litter? You think I haven't thought of that?"

Williams stammered. "Maybe . . . there's something in the lab. A contamination we don't know about. Maybe some contagion."

"Or *maybe*," said Rachel, "it's something else. And far more obvious."

Williams fell quiet.

"They're dying, Perry. And I don't think it's a virus, or some contamination, or their immune system, or anything else like that. I just did fresh blood workups on them, and everything looks normal. Everything looks *completely* normal.

"The only significant difference," she said, "is what you and I both know is the most obvious, which is what we've done to them."

44

Things were coming apart. Quickly.

Robert Masten sat solemnly in his office, watching the exchange between Rachel and Perry outside the building—caught in the distance by one of the building's exterior cameras.

He couldn't hear what they were saying, but judging by their body language, both were clearly excited over something. And in a conversation not meant to be overheard. But even without the benefit of sound, the subject of the discussion was easy to guess.

Repeating the video multiple times, he watched over and over as Perry glanced cautiously over his shoulder while he spoke, back at the building's entrance. Seemingly missing the camera positioned in the shadow beneath the southwest overhang. After several more seconds, Rachel could be seen producing a sheet of paper and presenting it to Williams.

Too distant for Masten to make out, but the presumption was easy. Another drawing by their seemingly prescient patient. Much to Masten and Lagner's chagrin.

He continued watching until the video reached the end of the segment, ending with the two turning and reapproaching the building.

Things were more than unraveling.

Their handler was now fully involved in the lab's affairs, whose team had uncovered the traitorous actions of Dr. Perry Williams. The doctor would have to know the truth behind the funding grants by now.

But how much more did the old man know? How much more could he know? The NIH connection but probably little else. In other words, the "when" and the "who," but not the "why."

And yet, while Masten remained confident of that, he also knew the greatest vulnerability in any conflict or discord was not knowing what your adversary knew, which left plenty of room for paranoia and suspicion. Shortcomings Masten was not accustomed to.

But this time was different. He was losing control, and he could feel it. Not just over his staff but control of the entire project, creating a sickening feeling inside his gut.

Masten was suddenly interrupted by something on an adjacent monitor directly to his left, when on it, another video feed suddenly went black.

Only minutes later, a tired Rachel Souza reached out for the door handle of the recovery room and noticed something odd upon touching it. The resistance in the handle's motion was different. Something absent from what she normally felt.

A dead bolt that had, on every other occasion, automatically unlocked in the same motion as turning the handle. This time, rotating it down felt almost limp. As though there was no engagement from the dead bolt at all.

Her moment of confusion was short-lived.

Instinctively, she continued forward and pushed the door open, whereupon she was met by instant surprise.

The room was pitch black.

Halting in midstep, she looked around with what little help she had from the ambient light behind her.

John Reiff's bed appeared empty, as did the rest of the room.

Still grasping the door handle, she glanced down and wiggled it, working it up and down in the usual fashion until seeing the dead bolt beneath suddenly resume its normal in-and-out motion.

She reached to her left and found the wall switch, bathing the room in blinding light, before peering around the opposite side of the door.

The dead bolt, located precisely below the shiny chrome handle, had something protruding from its keyhole.

It took her only a few minutes to find Reiff, after running down the long illuminated hallway, checking every door until traveling up one floor and reaching the most logical place he would go: her lab. Where she pushed the heavy door open to find him inside.

He had his back to her, sitting at her desk.

"John?" There was no answer, prompting her to approach and call again.

Reiff slowly swiveled in her chair until he faced her. His face was somber, and his body leaned slightly forward.

"How did you get out of your roo—" she started, but quickly changed in midsentence. "Are you all right?"

He watched her without comment. Without any reaction at all. Sending a tingle of apprehension down her spine.

She stopped moving. The expression on his face looked angry.

His body was still, with his eyes focused intensely upon her.

"John?" she said again, just above a whisper.

Still, he did not speak.

Inching closer, she peered over his left shoulder at the data displayed on her computer monitor. "Were you . . . reading my emails?"

"Tell me," he finally said.

"Excuse me?"

"Tell me . . . *now*."

Another chill ran through her, and she could feel her heart pounding faster in her chest. She didn't know what to say. Or even where to start.

"Listen . . ."

"Tell me *now*!" shouted Reiff.

She jumped, startled by the sudden rise in his voice. "I will," she stammered. "I promise. Anything you want to know."

He leaned forward in the chair and stood up with some difficulty, reaching for the nearby counter for support. He stumbled toward her, stopping within just a few feet.

"Where am I?!"

Rachel swallowed. "In a research facility."

"No shit," he growled. "Where?"

"You mean—"

"I'm not in Minneapolis."

She shook her head slowly. "No. You're not."

"Then where?!"

"Arizona," she answered. "Near Flagstaff."

He took another step forward. "Why?"

"It's complicated."

"What's the date?"

"The date?"

"The *date*!" yelled Reiff.

"It's, uh, Thursday, the twenty-first."

His eyes hardened, and he shook his head. "That's not what I mean."

She knew what he was asking. With her heart pounding like it was about to explode, she took a deep and fearful breath. "You were frozen for twenty-two years."

45

They stood motionless, facing one another. His eyes looked as though they could catch fire. Or bore a hole directly through her. Until they blinked.

"What else?"

"W-what do you mean?"

"What *else*? What else have you lied to me about?"

Rachel was suddenly awash in a wave of guilt. "A lot," she confessed. "But it wasn't for the reasons you think. We weren't trying to hurt you."

"What the hell does that mean?"

Her hands were trembling. She wanted to step back. But she didn't. "It was to help you. Believe it or not."

"Help me?" he scoffed. "How?"

"To adjust."

"You lied to me to *help me*."

"Yes!" Rachel nodded. "To survive."

"Bullshit."

"It's true! I swear. It was all to help you." She caught herself. "*Almost* all of it."

"Almost?"

"Okay, okay. Some of it was to protect us, too."

"From what?"

She sighed. "Like I said, it's complicated."

"Then start uncomplicating it," seethed Reiff.

Rachel felt herself deflate inside. This was not what she had hoped for. And not at all how she wanted to tell him.

"You . . . were in an accident," she said, almost pleading. "That much is true."

"Where?"

"We don't know. Not precisely. In Minneapolis, we think, or somewhere nearby. Believe it or not, there's a lot we don't know either."

A short distance away, in the Reiff's room, the bright overhead lights switched back on, followed by the open door being eased closed from the inside.

Robert Masten examined the door and the tiny piece of metal still jutting from the lock below the handle. It resembled a thick, straight wire, still and unbending when Masten touched it. He turned and continued searching the rest of the room.

Finding nothing of note, he moved across the tiled floor to the end of the bed. Touched the metal frame and continued to its opposite side, closest to the wall.

Checking the mattress, he spotted something and bent down. A short fraying appeared along the side of the seam, and upon fingering the small hole, Masten could feel another end of broken wire within.

He rose to his feet and continued his search until he noticed several pieces of paper on the bedside table.

Masten moved back around the bed to the table and examined more of Reiff's drawings. Lightly sketched in blue ink, they depicted different settings and objects—none that he recognized until reaching the last.

He tossed the rest away and studied the final image. First casually, then more closely. It appeared to show a series of columns. Ten of them, side by side. Fading into an undrawn background. But it was some of the other details that caused Masten to instinctively reach for his phone.

"What do you mean there's a lot you don't know?"

Rachel frowned. "I mean about *you*. It's what Perry and I were trying to figure out. Why we were asking you so many questions."

Reiff's expression suddenly became blank—dazed. He wasn't hearing anything she was saying as he slumped against the metal counter.

Twenty-two years. Jesus!

"How . . ." he said, "could you not know who I was?"

Rachel tried to explain. "Your accident was a long time ago. We knew your name and a little about your background, but that's all. Until last week, when we brought you back."

Reiff became listless. "I was dead for twenty-two years?!"

She sighed. "Kind of. You were preserved. For a long time. Frozen, but not exactly dead. Not clinically." She stopped. "Well, maybe. It's hard to explain."

"Try!"

"Please believe me; this isn't the way I wanted to do this."

"I don't care what you wanted."

She hesitated, noting the video camera overhead. The man had a right to know. "Do you know what cryonics is?"

"Basically, but please, enlighten me."

"Cryonics is the science of preserving a person after death. With the hope of being revived later. It's been around for decades. The preservation part, that is. Legally, a person cannot be preserved until they are deceased. At which point, preparations commence. Immediately. But after all biologic activity in a body has stopped."

"That's what happened to me?"

"Yes," she said. "Kind of."

He glowered.

"Your circumstance was different. You were in an accident in the dead of winter, when you drowned in a partially frozen river. Which we *think* caused you to freeze very close to, or even slightly before, the point of biologic cessation."

Reiff pushed himself up into a straightened position. "So, was I dead or not?"

"I don't know. It's a gray area."

"You don't *know* if I was dead or not?!"

"I wasn't there. None of us were. We don't know exactly what happened. But we had to assume your condition at the time was deemed to be nonrecoverable."

"Nonrecoverable."

"Unlikely for successful resuscitation."

He rolled his eyes.

"It's just medical jargon. And our best guess. Again, we don't know for sure."

"How could you not know? You had me frozen for twenty-two years!"

"John, listen to me—" She turned and again looked at the camera overhead. This time Reiff noticed and followed her gaze toward the ceiling.

"Who is that? Who's watching us?"

They didn't have much time. "That's what I've been trying to tell you. Things are complicated."

Reiff pushed past her. Stumbling to keep his balance. "*Who* is watching?" he asked again, louder.

Rachel pleaded in a hushed tone. "John, listen, please. There's a lot of tell you; it's just—"

"Just what?"

She opened her mouth to speak but wavered. Allowing Reiff to study her.

He then turned, looked at the camera again, and returned to her. "Something tells me things aren't going well."

She pursed her lips. Anything she revealed to him now was in the danger zone. For her and for him.

Suddenly, the animals began shrieking.

46

A blanket of darkness masked everything like a thick veil beneath a moon-filled sky. Crickets chirped in a cacophony from every direction, their incessant stridulations filling the cool air of night. A time when most predators were still inactive.

One sizable human predator was present and very much awake. Sitting quietly among the dense foliage, he watched from the large grouping of bushes just beyond the perimeter of a broad unmanaged lawn.

So far, there appeared to be only one person inside the house. On the second floor. In one of the bedrooms, or perhaps a converted office. A patch of white hair could be seen in the window over the top of a computer monitor.

The man in the bushes scanned the yard again, ensuring that his eyes were fully adjusted. Oversized and unkempt, the lawn presented over a hundred feet of open, unobstructed space he would have to traverse.

Option two was circling around the perimeter of the property, among the foliage, until reaching a line of trees on the opposite side, but that would put him within view of a neighboring house. It wasn't worth the chance of accidental detection.

Instead, he chose to remain still. Waiting in a crouched position for an opportunity. He had plenty of time.

It was less than twenty minutes before the target rose from his seat upstairs and turned away from the window. Heading through the doorway and into what looked to be an upstairs hallway.

A bathroom break.

The figure in the shrubs waited several seconds before rising smoothly from the darkness, ensuring that there was no sudden return by the man upstairs. Then he darted forward over the tall grass in light, quick steps, settling into another shadowed spot less than ten feet from the large wraparound porch.

A few moments later, he could hear the abrupt flow of water through pipes inside, followed by a return to silence. The flushing of an upstairs toilet.

He turned and peered back over the grass, now searching from the opposite direction for anything he'd missed.

The move to the porch would have to be done slowly. Even in darkness, people could detect movement from a distance if it was sudden enough. But move slowly, and a neighbor would have to be looking almost directly at him to notice.

The biggest problem was the porch.

He was a good twenty feet from the door leading into a dimly lit kitchen, and that would take time.

Because old wood always creaked.

He'd have to move at a snail's pace. Carefully distributing the weight of each boot step as he rolled from heel to toe.

It took several minutes to reach the exterior door. One agonizing step at a time. Discovering, several times, the onset of a squeak before immediately raising and lowering his boot to a sturdier plank. When he finally did reach the door, a gentle turn of the handle told him which lock was engaged. To his surprise, it was the knob, not the dead bolt.

Slow and smooth, and with both hands together, he increased the torque until the old locking rod within the wood strained and cracked. Then, with more gradual pressure, the old knob failed and broke at the neck with a loud clunk—somewhat muted beneath the intruder's thick gloves.

Keeping the knob fully turned, he pushed inward on the door, gently testing for resistance along the aged doorframe.

Upstairs, Perry Williams stopped reading at a sudden noise.

He remained still, while trying to remember if he'd left something out. Something that could have tipped over.

He pushed up from his chair, head cocked and listening; he heard nothing else. He took a few steps to the door and stopped again.

Silence.

Cautiously, he continued through the doorway and into the hall, stopping again at the top of the stairs to peer down over the railing.

The intruder hadn't moved since opening the door except for one step inside and backward, around a corner, to conceal himself.

The kitchen design was a modern rustic, with a large island in the center, surfaced by a giant polished slab of dark wood. Elegant. But not ideal.

When the man came downstairs, and he *would* come, there were two options for entering the kitchen. That was a problem.

He waited, listening to the subtle movement upstairs.

Williams lingered at the top of the staircase but heard no other sounds. After a few moments, he turned and walked carefully toward the master bedroom. With ears still tuned, he moved gingerly over the carpet to his oversized closet, reaching high above the doorframe and coming down with a set of keys.

One more pause before inserting the key and unlocking his gun safe.

He would come down.

They always did. Given enough time.

Investigating a noise that was never quite loud enough for them to guess what it was.

The easiest, of course, was to simply turn on the faucet.

The faint trickling sound of water was enough for most victims to conclude they'd accidentally left it running.

It was always the easiest.

Contrary to popular belief, trying to locate a target within the house was never a good idea. Every house made noise, especially when stairs were involved. Much too noisy. And the absolute last place he wanted to be was trapped in a stairwell by an armed homeowner.

Coercing them downstairs was always better. Because it rarely took more than five minutes for the victim to eventually lower their guard and come down to investigate. So, his position had to be near their entry point: in this case, the bottom of the stairs. Somewhere to conceal himself while still close enough to reach the target quickly. Ideally, when they were examining the faucet and had lowered any potential weapons.

And then, of course, was the cleanup.

47

Rachel Souza was in front of the cages, trying to calm the animals, who were still crying and screaming from behind their metal bars. All except the capuchin, Dallas, who was up on both legs like the others, watching intently.

"Easy," called Rachel. "Easy!" Simultaneously with either hand, she reached into separate cages and stroked both Bella and Lester's heads. But her eyes were on Otis, the larger chimpanzee, who remained against the cage door, excitedly pressing his flaring nostrils through the gap in the bars and yanking as though trying to break them.

"What's wrong?" Reiff asked.

"I don't know." She shook her head, shushing the animals.

He stepped closer and leaned toward the chimpanzee. Then toward the capuchin in the cage next to him, whose hazel-brown eyes were following him.

Reiff tilted his head, then, without a word, turned and walked back to Rachel's desk. Studying the screen for a moment before beginning to type.

"What are you doing?"

"Nothing."

"It looks like something to me."

Now seated, Reiff finished with a final click of the mouse and twisted back around in the chair. "We need to get out of here."

"Why?"

He rose and began moving toward the outer door.

"Wait!" She rushed across the room and stopped in front of him. "Wait! Just wait." She rotated her back to the camera and whispered, "We can't just leave. Not like this."

"Actually, I can."

She held up her hands in a pleading gesture. "I need time."

"For what?"

"To arrange things," she said in a low voice.

At that, Reiff shook his head. "I've been here long enough."

"Wait, wait," she cried before reaching into the back pocket of her jeans. She quickly unfolded two pieces of paper, handing him the top page.

"First, tell me what you know. About this."

He took the page and examined his drawing. "What about it?"

"What you drew on this paper," she said, "happened a long time ago. *Before* we revived you."

"So?"

Rachel tried again. "These letters," she said, touching the page, "'A' and 'U.' What are they?"

"Letters," he repeated sarcastically.

"No. What I mean is . . . where did you see them?"

He returned the paper to her. "On a wall. Just like I drew."

"And what is this, around the rest of the building?"

"Flames."

"That's right. Flames. Around the entire building. And surrounding it is what?"

"People."

"Exactly!" she said excitedly. "And how was the 'AU' painted?"

"What do you mean?"

"I said, *how* was it painted?"

Reiff stared back at her. "It was spray-painted."

"In what color?"

"Red."

Suddenly, as if unable to believe the confirmation, Rachel raised a hand over her mouth.

"What?"

She shook her head from side to side. "How did you know that?"

"I don't know. I saw it. Multiple times."

She was speechless, holding out the second piece of paper. The photograph she had printed from the news site.

"Is that what you see in your vision?"

"You keep calling them visions."

"What would you call them?"

Reiff shrugged. "I don't know. They feel like memories." He took the second page. His sketch and Rachel's picture both showed the same four-story building, modern and stylish, with a giant glass awning extending over the entrance, and behind it two enormous glass towers rising up and out of the picture.

And on both pages, the entire lower structure was consumed in flame, with the two giant towers behind it engulfed in thick black clouds of smoke. In both images, on an open area of yet unconsumed building, were two enormous letters, A and U, painted within a red circle.

"Do you know what the event was?" Rachel asked.

"A riot."

"That's right. An enormous riot. In Frankfurt, Germany." She took a deep breath. "What I want to know is how. *How* did you envision something that happened fifteen years ago?"

Reiff raised both brows. "What?"

"You heard me," she said. "How did you know about something that took place *while* you were frozen?"

48

Before Reiff could answer, the door to the lab was thrown open, re-vealing Robert Masten in the doorway. Nora Lagner followed behind him, and behind her, two larger men Rachel didn't recognize—both wearing suits.

Reiff squinted over Rachel's head as the director stepped into the room, trailed by the others. "Who are you?"

"Mr. Reiff," he said with a warm smile. "It's a pleasure to finally meet you. My name is Robert Masten, the director of this facility." He gave a pointed look to Rachel as he stopped in front of her. "And of this project."

"What project is that?"

"The one that brought you back," he said, broadening his smile. "And you're welcome, by the way."

"Great. What do I owe you?"

Masten suddenly laughed, then spread his arms in a broad gesture. "Welcome," he said, "to Project Recrudesce."

"Pardon?"

"Recrudesce," Masten repeated. "It means to return. To recur."

Reiff looked at Rachel. "That's a terrible name."

Again, Masten laughed. "I'm afraid Dr. Souza never liked the name, either. A strong, intelligent woman who has never hesitated to speak her mind. Just one of the many reasons she is one of the best in her field." He turned to his left. "Allow me to introduce Nora Lagner, our proj-ect's CTO and the brains behind much of the technology that made this possible. That made *you* possible."

Reiff nodded politely to the woman, before his eyes moved silently to the men standing behind her. Both young and chiseled, in their late twenties or early thirties, with hair cut short and neat. Between 200 and 220 pounds and looking slightly uncomfortable in their dark blue, single-breasted suits. Almost as well dressed as Masten.

The director turned back to Rachel. "How is our number-one patient today?"

"Good. A little weak but no longer in need of a wheelchair."

"So I see. That's wonderful. And I see you brought him to see our other patients," he said, motioning to the animals.

Rachel took a moment to collect herself. She hadn't brought Reiff to her lab—this time. Masten probably already knew that. And he probably also knew about the picked lock. Her only safe response was to avoid the question. "I was just explaining," she said, turning to the animals, "that they're due to be transferred this week."

Masten nodded. "Unfortunately so. But it's time to find them a good home."

"No one likes to be caged," replied Reiff.

"Indeed."

Rachel cleared her throat nervously. "Well, we should get you back to your room to rest."

Reiff politely shook his head. "I'm not tired."

An uncomfortably long silence ensued before Nora Lagner finally spoke up. "If you're feeling up to it, Mr. Reiff, we'd like to ask you some questions. I'm sure Dr. Souza has explained that we still have several tests to run. Nothing too strenuous, though. I promise."

"What kind of tests?"

"Simple cognitive tests. Things like concentration, comprehension, and recall. To measure acuity and look for any lingering effects from the procedure. Would that be all right?"

"Only if you're feeling up to it," added Masten.

Once again, Rachel intervened. "I think we should give him a little more rest—"

"That's fine," said Reiff, looking around the lab again. "But first, I have a few questions of my own."

The director raised his eyebrows expectantly.

"For example, how the hell did I get here?"

"I'm sorry?"

"How did I get here?" he repeated. "Physically."

Masten and Lagner looked at each other. "I don't . . ."

"And where exactly have I been for the last twenty-two years?"

A forced smile returned to Masten's face. "We're happy to answer any questions. Following the assessments, of course. We don't want to overwhelm you." His expression managed to turn cheerful again. "Believe me. There's a lot to explain."

49

Rachel was left standing alone, idly, in her lab. Staring at the metal door after it shut with a loud click.

What the hell had just happened?

In less than five minutes, Reiff was now in the hands of Masten and Lagner. Willingly. She was left in stunned silence, feeling as though the rug had just been pulled out from under her. Not just the rug. The entire floor.

How was she supposed to get him out if he was with "them"? And even more importantly, what was Masten up to?

Her stomach began to churn in a growing sense of helplessness.

What in the world was the man thinking?

Eventually, her attention returned to the animals, who strangely had calmed down, and watched her in silence. No doubt able to detect the distress in her as she tried to think what to do.

In the hallway, Reiff appeared relaxed as he followed Masten and Lagner—almost cheerful. Strolling behind them with difficulty but still managing to keep up as they headed for the familiar elevator at the end of the hall.

Once inside, he remained quiet among the four, wordlessly examining each of them.

The larger men hadn't spoken at all. Grunts. While Masten and Lagner continually glanced back at him. Politely, but with a strange air of apprehension. As though they couldn't believe he had agreed to go with them so easily.

Otherwise, why the grunts?

Reiff knew he was in no condition to resist. Even if he wanted to.

The weight of what Dr. Souza had revealed still had him reeling in a somewhat surreal state. She'd said it so matter-of-factly, but now the significance was beginning to take hold. To sink in. Along with the repercussions.

Twenty-two years. Jesus, twenty-two years! All while the world simply moved on. If true, it meant the entire planet was now twenty-two years older. In the blink of an eye. At least in the blink of his eye.

He suddenly had a strange thought—of prisoners being locked away and released twenty years later. How different would the world look to them? Probably not much if they had access to a television. But what about someone who didn't? What about someone detached from each and every day? Not just from the world but from life itself.

Which led to another question. *Did I actually die?* Even Rachel wasn't sure. He did remember the accident. Pieces of it. Enough to know it happened. He remembered being trapped in the bus, with water rapidly filling the interior. Death would have been the most likely outcome. But had he died first or frozen first?

They reached a lower floor, and the elevator made a loud ding before its doors parted with a low rumble. The five exited one at a time and continued forward down another hallway just like the others. Off-white and featureless—with gray tiling extending perhaps fifty feet to where, at the opposite end, the hall split both left and right.

Together, they passed several more locked and painted doors before reaching one that led into a decent-sized conference room with a table ringed by several leather chairs.

"Can I get you something?" asked Lagner. "Maybe to drink?"

Reiff picked a seat and lowered himself into the soft leather. "A beer would be great."

"I meant some water."

"Then why didn't you say that? Fine. Just add a little fermented barley and hops."

"Very funny."

She motioned to one of the grunts, who grumbled and disappeared as she closed the door, selecting a chair next to Masten. The second grunt remained outside, expressionless and unmoving.

"Now then, Mr. Reiff," she started. "How are you feeling?"

"How am I *feeling*?"

"Are you in any discomfort? Any pain?" she asked.

"Nothing out of the ordinary."

"We can get you something if need be."

"Don't bother."

Lagner lowered a pad of paper and a pen onto the table in front of her. "I'd like to start by testing your recall. Beginning with some recent things, then progressively moving backward. For example, can you tell me what you ate for lunch yesterday?"

Reiff didn't answer.

After jotting the time and date, she looked up again. "Mr. Reiff?"

Still no answer, or movement, from Reiff.

Lagner studied him carefully before turning to Masten.

"John?"

He didn't respond to Masten either. Not at first. Allowing the lull to linger before he finally replied, "I'm still waiting."

"For what?"

"For my answers."

"Listen, John. I told you we need to go through our assessments first. It won't take long."

Silence.

"I promise."

Still nothing.

Masten huffed with a look of annoyance. "Fine. What were your questions again?"

"How did I get here?"

Masten gave a half shrug. "The truth is . . . we're not exactly sure." He quickly held up a hand when Reiff's expression began to change. "Let me explain." After a moment of contemplation, he continued. "This is probably going to seem hard to believe. Like everything else, I'm sure. But your participation in our program is a little fuzzy."

"Fuzzy?"

"What I mean . . . is that some records were lost."

Reiff's eyes narrowed.

"We *did* save you. Let's not forget that, okay?"

"How would I know?"

"Are you suggesting we didn't?"

"All I know is what I've been told. And yet, I'm not in a hospital. But rather an experimental lab somewhere and seemingly unable to leave. While you claim I've been brought back years later. All without anyone telling me how I supposedly became part of your experiment."

"That's not what I said."

"You lost my paperwork."

"We didn't lose your paperwork!" said Masten, pounding the table with a fist. He stopped and seemed to regain his demeanor. "There is a great deal you don't understand, Mr. Reiff. John. A lot has happened. A lot more than you know."

"No kidding."

Masten shot a wary eye at Lagner, continuing in a tempered voice, "The vast majority of what we've told you is true. Given some tweaks here and there. But that was for your own good." He lowered his hands flat onto the table. "We knew it wouldn't just be about reviving you. *If* we were successful. We knew there would also be some cognitive challenges. Assuming your faculties were even still intact. If they were, there would have to be a period of adjustment. Psychologically. To the realization that your accident didn't happen last week. Or even last month."

"So you decided to let me find out myself."

"That was not our intention," sighed Masten. "We just weren't ready yet. Regardless of what you may believe, we *are* still trying to keep you alive. No one has ever done anything like this before. No one. Which means you're it. You're the first one. And the procedure, while so far successful, is far from perfect. Your system, unfortunately, has experienced a lot of damage."

"You should have told me that in the beginning," said Reiff.

"Told you what exactly?"

"What year it is, for starters."

"Right," scoffed Masten. "'Hello there, Mr. Reiff. Rise and shine. It's a miracle you're alive, and we might lose you at any moment, but we wanted you to know that you've been dead for a long time.' Yes, that would not have caused any trauma to your system at all."

"Nonrecoverable."

"What?"

Reiff smirked. "Dr. Souza said I was nonrecoverable. Apparently, being dead is a gray area."

"Call it whatever you like. But there was a lot we had to take into consideration. A hell of a lot more than you know."

Reiff tried to relax. Turning away and glancing around the room. "Okay. So why did it take so long?"

"Like I said, it's never been done before."

Nora Lagner spoke up. "Bringing a person back wasn't just difficult,

Mr. Reiff; it was an impossibility. Until a few weeks ago. It required years of development and testing, and there were many failures."

Reiff turned away from the room and back to her. "How many failures?"

"Many," she repeated.

"So, that's why you have the animals."

"Correct."

"Which means the animals in the lab . . . would have to be the survivors."

"That's right."

"It's taken us a long time to get here, Mr. Reiff," said Masten. "A very long time. A little appreciation would be nice."

Reiff continued thinking. "So, you started the whole thing?"

"No. I was brought on six years ago to take over the project. Recrudesce was started years before by a man named Munn. He was a molecular biologist and talented scientist but a terrible businessman. When he died, I came in to overhaul the project. Tapping Nora here to help me. By then, all the theoretical work had been done, but making it actually work was a different story."

"They needed someone to build it?"

"Design *and* build it." Masten nodded. "And get it funded."

Pensively, Reiff lowered his gaze. "And you said I'm the first."

"The very first."

He peered at Masten. "Why?"

The other man raised both eyebrows. "Why what?"

"Why me? Haven't hundreds of people been frozen over the years? For this very reason?"

"Thousands," corrected Lagner.

"Fine. Thousands. So again . . . *why me?*"

Masten leaned back in his chair. "Because cryonics is complicated." With a sigh, he said, "In 1952, the first sperm cells were successfully frozen and used to inseminate three different women. It was a breakthrough. Then years later, a professor named Ettinger proposed the idea of freezing actual humans. From there, the idea snowballed, and five years later, the very first human was cryonically frozen. Since then, thousands have followed suit. Tens of thousands, actually."

"So, why didn't you resurrect one of *them*?"

"Because we can't. And we'll likely never be able to. The early patients will never benefit from the advancements cryonics has made since then and from what we've learned. Specifically, that being frozen causes severe and permanent crystallization in each and every cell of the human body. In other words, irreparable damage to all cell nuclei. Way beyond anyone's ability to fix it. Probably ever. This eventually led researchers to develop something called cryoprotectants, substances that helped prevent this severe crystallization. Reducing cellular damage to levels experts hoped one day would be either repairable or survivable."

"Like antifreeze."

"In a way, yes. But created specifically for human cells."

"So, how many frozen patients have this protectant?"

"It varies. Cryoprotectants, like all things, have also evolved. And improved. Gradually becoming more and more effective. Today we use a cocktail of them. Three different protectants that can often reduce a body's cellular damage to below ten percent. Close to what some experts believe could be survivable. The next problem was thawing them." He turned to Lagner.

"There are three problems in the thawing and resuscitation puzzle," she said. "Speed, temperature, and tissue density. Heat a body too slowly or unevenly, and it dies from extreme hypothermia before it can be reanimated in time. This time forever. Heat a body too quickly, and you cause more tissue damage than the crystallization, pushing the subject back out the window of survivability.

"What we had to do was find a way to thread multiple needles at once. Not too fast and not too slow. Warming different parts of the body without overcooking others. Liquids like blood warm faster than denser tissue—say, an organ. Our early attempts reliquefied the blood but left the organs too cold to achieve refunction. Other attempts warmed the organs but simultaneously boiled pockets of the body's blood and plasma. So, we had to develop a system that could heat throughout, but in accordance with cellular density."

Across the table, Reiff remained listening. "That's all very interesting, but it doesn't answer my question."

"It took years and tens of thousands of man-hours to perfect the technology. Or should I say, 'achieve the ability'? It's still not perfect, but we've finally reached survivability. Obviously."

"In the end," said Masten, "it proved to be a much bigger dilemma than the crystallization. But it still wasn't the biggest."

"And what was that?"

"Death," Masten replied simply.

"Death?"

"Understand that, to date, everyone who has been cryonically 'prepared' has been so *after* they were pronounced dead. This is because it's still illegal to freeze oneself before death. Before taking that final breath, when the brain's synapses are still firing and the heart still pumping. All of which must officially end, clinically and legally, before a person can be cryonically frozen."

Masten swiveled his chair, looking directly at Reiff. "Which brings us to you."

50

Back in front of her desk, Rachel stared absently at her phone screen, listening as it dialed. Once again, it rang five times before forwarding to voicemail.

Perry wasn't answering.

She swiveled back and forth in her chair. She needed his help if they had any chance of getting John out. And probably Henry's, too.

She gave up and tried Henry Yamada. Again, waiting as the phone dialed and rang repeatedly.

Come on!

After five rings, Yamada's voice recording began playing.

Damn it!

Rachel rose and shook her head. She busied herself with checking and refilling the food and water for the animals. But when she finished, she gathered her things and walked briskly to the other side of the lab, pulled the main door open, and flipped the overhead lights off.

It wasn't until the door had closed and the room was plunged back into darkness that the small capuchin monkey softly leaned its head against the cage's slim metal bars to continue probing the lock's keyhole with his tiny finger on the other side of the cage door.

The drive took a little over twenty minutes. It was nearing midnight as Rachel eased her dark gray Camry over a long, tree-lined gravel driveway and into the open clearing in front of Dr. Williams's house. Its two stories with light yellow siding gave it a soft, welcoming glow beneath the arid autumn moonlight.

She slowed her car to a roll as she wound around the sizable over-grown lawn to the far side of the house, stopping in front of the matching two-car detached garage.

The entire house was dark. All lights were off, both upstairs and downstairs. He usually heard her coming up the drive by the distinctive crunching of a hundred yards of graveled stone.

With the engine idling, she remained still and peered up, waiting for a light to come on. When none did, she frowned. Was he already asleep? It would explain why he wasn't answering his phone.

Rachel exhaled, then leaned forward, laying both arms over the top of the steering wheel. Should she wake him up? After a few minutes of silent thought, she began to feel an inkling of foolishness.

It wasn't as though Reiff was in imminent danger. Danger? Possibly. Imminent? Hardly. Masten seemed surprisingly polite when introducing himself in the lab. But it was more than that. He seemed casual. Even conversational. Slightly irritated, perhaps, but still welcoming.

Had she and Perry overreacted in their fear of what Masten and Lagner were up to? Now, sitting quietly in her car, it certainly seemed possible. After all, if it wasn't enough to keep Perry up, then maybe . . .

In her head, Rachel's questioning was quickly turning to self-doubt. She had to admit, she wasn't sleeping much lately. And she *was* tired. Exhausted, really. Which, over time, could make anyone overreactive.

She spread her arms and rested her forehead on the steering wheel. She was really tired.

Her mind began rewinding. Fighting its way back through the last several days. Reexamining the conversations with Masten. If she was this tired and on edge, surely Masten was, too.

One by one, she went over several of their exchanges. Her words, Masten's words, Perry's, even Lagner's. Was it overreaction? Or just misunderstanding? Among several people, all of whom were worn to the bone?

Yes. It was possible.

Except—

She could envision some misunderstandings. Several of them, if she changed her viewpoint enough. It was possible. But through all the replaying in her mind, through all the logic and forced objectivity, there was one thing that still wasn't changing. No matter how objective she tried to be.

The feeling.

The feeling in her gut never changed. It was the same through every word, or gesture, or tone. It never wavered.

Her gut simply never came around.

It was still there, now. Radiating the same sickening sensation in her stomach. That something *was* wrong. Something fundamental. Something instinctive. And whether it was paranoia or some faint hint of a woman's intuition, the end result was always the same, prompting Rachel to finally raise her head and look again at the house.

No. She had to talk to Perry. Maybe he'd think she was overreacting. Or just irritated at being woken up. But she had to talk it through.

Turning off and exiting her car, she closed the driver's door hard, hoping it might be loud enough for Perry to hear, but no lights came on.

She approached the wooden-handrailed steps to the front door, where she glanced through the window into the darkness, before taking a deep breath and knocking. Praying that he wouldn't be mad.

After a full minute and no answer, she knocked again—louder.

Nothing.

Did he wear earplugs? Or use an apnea machine?

She knocked once more, this time on the glass pane next to the door.

Nothing.

She tried the door handle. Locked. Then peered more intently through the glass. Possibly detecting a movement inside. Or was it a reflection from the trees behind her, swaying from the breeze?

Stepping back, she turned to her left and followed the wooden porch as it wrapped around the side of the house. One by one, she paused at each window, repeatedly raising her hands and trying to see inside.

Near the end of the porch, she reached the side door and went to turn the knob, but immediately looked down. She wiggled it loosely from side to side.

Rachel studied the knob only briefly before pushing it forward, causing the door to squeak as it opened.

She leaned in and called out, "Perry?"

Still hearing nothing, she stepped gingerly into the kitchen and glanced about through the streaks of light traveling across the kitchen and the island's natural brown wood. The rest of the house remained dark. Ensconced in blackness, she felt her way forward, around the island to the doorway leading into the dining room. It was then that she finally found a light switch and flipped it on.

And screamed.

51

John Reiff looked up when the second grunt returned and opened the door, stepping past Masten and Lagner to place the glass of water on the table. Then, without a word, the man retreated, closing the door behind him and taking his place beside the other.

John's attention then returned to Masten. "What do you mean 'it comes back to' me?"

There was a strange feeling in the room. Not between Masten and Reiff, but—oddly—between Masten and Lagner. Something that felt like tension or an unspoken strain. Adding to a slight hesitancy in Masten's reply.

"You," he said, "are an anomaly."

"What a nice thing to say."

"What I mean is that you are an aberration. Put more positively: You're an exception. One in a million." Masten shrugged. "Well, we don't have a million others to count, but the exception still proves the rule, as they say. For what is still possible."

"I think you're losing me."

"I'm talking about the crystallization. The destruction of cells during the freezing process that has plagued thousands of patients since the advent of cryonics. You are the exception.

"What I'm trying to tell you—" Masten glanced hastily at Lagner. "—what *we* are trying to tell you . . . is that you had no crystallization."

"I'm sorry?"

"You had no crystallization," repeated Masten. "Well, almost none. Well below one percent, which in medical terms may as well have been zero."

"And why is that?"

Masten blinked. "Why zero or why you?"

"Both."

"We don't know. We've run every possible test on you, before and after, and we still don't know. Perhaps there's something different about your biological makeup. Maybe it was due to how the hypothermia set in following your accident. There are five distinct hypothermic stages your body would have traversed and quickly. Was there a unique pattern or process in how you passed through those stages? Was the temperature or series of temperatures involved? Were there chemicals or compounds in the water at play that we don't understand? We have no idea. We weren't there. All we know now is that you, for whatever reason, did not experience the same level of cellular damage that every other frozen patient has. Which, in the end, made you the ideal candidate to attempt resuscitation."

Reiff stared back across the table. "Why?"

Again, Masten appeared confused.

"For what purpose?"

At this, both Masten and Lagner let out a smile as though answering a childish question. "To see if we could," he said simply. "To prove our technology worked."

"And what if it hadn't worked?"

"It *did* work," said Lagner.

Reiff examined the woman. "But if it hadn't . . . you would have lost your best candidate."

Neither replied. Not immediately. But Lagner eventually grinned. "We were confident."

It wasn't confidence, thought Reiff. *Try hubris.*

"So I'm a guinea pig."

"Not at all," replied Masten coolly. "There was an important reason to bring you back."

"I can't wait to hear it."

"You're the key. You're the key to helping us figure out how you did it. How you managed to avoid what has doomed so many others." Masten leaned forward with an air of excitement. "Don't you see? You may be the one person able to help us finally figure it out. The breakthrough. The one piece that could allow us to break the bonds forever."

"Bonds?"

Masten's eyes widened. "Of mortality. An actual and bona fide end run around death. Not just for a select few but everyone. An end run around disease. Around age. Around every major scourge the human race has been afflicted with. In time, of course. But the ability is here."

A dubious Reiff slowly shook his head. "Death is not a scourge. It's a fact of life. It's a *part* of life."

Masten grinned. "Spoken like a philosopher. But no. Claiming death as being a *part* of life is hogwash. Nothing but emotional and metaphysical nonsense. Something to give meaning to a culture incapable of dealing with a bitter and inescapable truth. If we can't avoid it," he said sarcastically, "let's make ourselves feel better about it. Let's convince ourselves that death provides some perverse sense of virtue. That it makes us *better* for it. More alive. More consequential."

"Sounds like you've given this some thought."

"I have, Mr. Reiff. I have. And do you know what I've deduced? I have deduced that this is it. All of this," he said, spreading his arms, "is *it*! There is nothing else but this. Our one and only chance."

"One and only chance for what?"

"*For everything!* Existence. We have one singular chance. One life. One brief window to exist and to experience this extraordinary world around us. Before we're gone. Forever. Every single one of us."

Reiff's moved to Lagner, who remained quiet with no visible reaction. Then to the two men standing outside. Both still and unflinching. Oblivious to Masten's outburst of excitement.

"And you . . . want to extend this *window*," said Reiff.

"No," gleamed Masten. "I want to destroy it!"

"The window?"

He nodded. "Shatter it. Destroy it completely. To extend our agonizingly brief existence here on earth into something longer. Much longer. And more significant. More consequential."

"And you don't think life now is consequential?"

"Of course I do. Our existence here is profoundly consequential. But *far* too limiting. Too brief to reach our full abilities. Our full significance."

"Maybe you should try being more productive with the time you have," quipped Reiff.

Sarcasm at which Masten laughed. "Touché. If only we didn't need to sleep, eh? Imagine what else we could get done."

"Something tells me you already don't sleep much."

Masten laughed again, genuinely. "Believe me, it's not for lack of trying. And I daresay you've made that much more difficult recently."

"Not my fault."

"No, it's not. But it doesn't change the fact that you're here now. Nor the role you must play."

"By helping you."

"Correct." Masten motioned to himself and Lagner. "By helping *us* figure out exactly what it was that allowed you to avoid what no one else could. Mother Nature's curse: the crystallization."

Masten finally began to calm and relaxed in his seat. "So, have we now answered your questions?"

"Sadly, yes. At least most of them."

"Good. I trust we can now dispense with the Q and A and get on with our testing? It may seem trivial to you, but we must be sure your brain has come through this experience in one piece if you are to help us. After all," Masten joked, tapping his temple, "if you're not all here, what's the point?"

Beside him, Nora Lagner finally returned to her paper and her notes, continuing with the questioning. While Masten settled in to observe.

One by one, Reiff began answering the questions. Quietly studying the two across from him. Momentarily satisfied but certain, based on their physical and verbal demeanor, that they were still hiding something.

In truth, Robert Masten and Nora Lagner already knew why Reiff's cells had never crystallized. Despite Masten's clever explanations, there was no magic involved. What they really wanted from Reiff was something entirely different.

52

Rachel Souza sat within the surreal glow of flashing red and blue lights. Hunched and facing outward from the police car's open rear seat.

Her face was despondent. Morose. She gazed absently down upon the inert gravel beneath her feet.

"You okay?"

There was no reaction.

"Ma'am?"

Rachel's eyes refocused and traveled upward to the partially silhouetted face of a woman.

"I'm Detective Weinberg. Can you answer some questions?"

Rachel nodded.

"The officers told me you know Mr. Williams?"

Her eyes fell, staring forward, and she nodded again. "Dr. Williams."

"I'm sorry, Dr. Williams." The detective glanced back at the house. "Do you know anyone who would have wanted to hurt Dr. Williams, Ms. Souza?"

She felt like she was in a trance. "Dr. Souza."

"*Doctor* Souza."

Rachel's eyes suddenly blinked, and she peered up again. "Wait? Hurt him?"

"That's what I said."

Rachel whirled around inside the patrol car's back seat. "B-but no one hurt him. He was just . . ."

"At the table."

"Yes."

Weinberg sighed, then lowered her head closer while resting one arm over the open door. "I'm afraid we've found some indications of a struggle."

Rachel stammered. "But . . . I just saw him, there at the table. He didn't seem—It just looked . . . natural."

"Apparently, someone wanted it to appear that way. There's no bruising on his neck, so something was probably used to avoid that."

"You're saying he was strangled?"

"Looks that way."

Rachel wore a look of incredulity. "What did they use?"

"Probably some kind of cloth. It helps distribute the tension to avoid pressure points." Seeing the look on the younger woman's face, Detective Weinberg changed the subject. "Do you know of anyone he was having problems with? Maybe a neighbor? Maybe someone else?"

Rachel shook her head. "Not that I know of."

"Anyone else living with him?"

"He lived here by himself."

"Divorced?"

"Widowed."

"I see. Any children around?"

She tried to think. "He has two daughters. In Florida. And some grandchildren. Three, I think."

The detective scribbled notes on a small notepad. "Where in Florida?"

"I'm not sure. Miami, maybe."

"Different last names?"

"Yes. But I can't remember what they are at the moment."

The woman standing over her continued writing. "And how did you know Dr. Williams?"

"From work."

"And where is that?"

"At a research lab. In Flagstaff."

The detective nodded. "And what do you do at this lab?"

It was then that Rachel paused. Their project was secret. And Williams warned her about going to the police. Her eyes shifted. *My God, the lab. Masten!*

"Something wrong?"

She shook her head. "No. I, uh, just remembered something. Something I forgot at work."

"Something important?"

"Something I forgot to turn off," lied Rachel.

It was impossible. Masten would never have done anything like this.

Or Lagner. Not over a project. Not over—Rachel gazed absently at the back of the passenger's seat.

"Dr. Souza?"

But Perry had just discovered those things about Masten. And the project. And the money.

"Dr. Souza?"

She turned when she felt the detective's hand on her shoulder.

"Are you okay?"

"Yes. I—I just can't believe it. We were just talking a few hours ago."

"About what?"

"Just work stuff."

"And how did the conversation end?"

Rachel looked up at the detective. The face was still shadowed, preventing Rachel from making out the woman's expression. "What?"

"I said, how did your conversation end?"

"What do you mean? Are you asking if I had an argument with him?"

The detective shrugged. "Did you?"

"No! No, we weren't arguing. We were colleagues."

"Sometimes colleagues argue."

"What are you saying? That *I* did this? That I," she sputtered, "*strangled* Perry? What is wrong with you?"

"Easy, Doctor. I'm just asking. It's my job."

"Yeah? Well, guess what? I didn't do it! I came here to talk to him about something. And I found him there, sitting at the kitchen table. Just . . . slumped forward."

"What did you come to talk about?"

Rachel began to answer but stopped. Incensed at the implication in the woman's voice. Was she a suspect? Were they trying to tie her to this? Perry was right. The police couldn't be trusted. Not these days.

"I came," she finally said, "to talk to him about work. About part of our project. About something we were working on together. I've been here many times *for work*."

"What did you say this project was again?"

Rachel glared at the woman. "I didn't."

"What kind of doctor are you?"

"A vascular surgeon."

The detective continued writing. "And what is that exactly?"

"The circulatory system."

"I see. Was Dr. Williams a vascular surgeon, too?"

"No. He's an internist."

"Which is what?"

Rachel sighed. "And organ specialist. The heart, lungs, kidneys . . ."

"I see. And what time did you get here?"

"I already told the officer."

"Tell me again please."

"A little before midnight," said Rachel.

"Isn't that kind of late to be collaborating?"

"Doctors have erratic schedules."

"I guess so."

Rachel then stood up, out of the car. Facing the detective.

Under the glowing lights, Weinberg studied Souza, noting the look on the woman's face. And smirked. "Something on your mind?"

"Am I under arrest?"

"Pardon?"

"You heard me."

Weinberg tilted her head, examining. "You seem a little anxious, Doctor."

"Of course I'm anxious. I just found my friend and colleague dead at his home. Wouldn't you be?"

"I don't know. Would I?"

"I know how this works," said Rachel. "If I'm not being arrested for a crime, then I'm free to go. At least I know *that's* still the law."

"I'm just trying to get information."

She shook her head defiantly.

"Dr. Souza, I'm not implying anything. Now, if you're inferring something based on my questions, then perhaps—"

"Hey, Detective!"

They both turned to one of the officers, perhaps a hundred feet away, studying part of Williams's unkempt lawn, beneath the bright beam of a flashlight.

"We have footsteps over here." The man's silhouette knelt down and appeared to touch the grass. "Looks like someone running through this grass. Maybe a possible print."

Weinberg's eyes returned to Rachel and remained on her as she called back, "How big?"

The officer's light flashed forward and then back to the ground in front of him. "Looks pretty large. And heavy. Probably male."

Weinberg lowered her eyes. Down Rachel's body to her feet. And her white size-six tennis shoes.

Her eyes returned to Rachel's. "Stay in town."

With that, the detective turned and walked away, wading out into the tall grass, leaving Rachel alone and fuming.

She tried to focus and grabbed her phone, redialing Henry. If it was true that Henry Yamada put Williams in touch with someone to dig up that information, then Henry could put *her* in touch with them, too.

She listened as the ringing repeated and once again rolled over to Yamada's voicemail.

"Henry, it's Rachel. Call me right away. Something terrible has happened."

She paused, wondering if she should say more, but instead ended the call. She didn't want him to find out over a voicemail.

How could it come to this? she thought. How could Masten do this to Perry? It just seemed so impossible. So . . .

Still grasping her phone, she had a thought. What if the police were wrong? If the detective jumped to conclusions about her, maybe they jumped to conclusions with Perry, too?

She returned to the image in her mind. Turning on the light and finding Perry. Motionless. Leaning forward, with both hands on the table in front of him.

What if he wasn't murdered? What if there was another reason they didn't find marks on his neck? And what if the impressions in the grass they were now studying were Perry's? After all, it *was* his house. And his lawn.

Before talking to Henry, she asked herself, what did she actually know for a fact?

If the police were wrong, if they had jumped to conclusions, what would that mean? That there wasn't any foul play inside Perry's house? And if that was true, then her assumptions about Masten were wrong, too. Was she about to accuse an innocent man of murder?

It was possible. Believable if one just removed the element of suspicion. And paranoia.

Was there still something underhanded about who was funding the project? Most likely. But how unusual was that really in the grand scheme of things? How many businesses, or governments, had never engaged in some level of grift? Rachel didn't know, but if she had to guess, she'd put the number close to zero.

She remained standing on the gravel of Perry's drive for a long time, thinking carefully, before raising the phone to dial a different number. *Innocent until proven guilty.* And if Masten was indeed innocent, he, of all people, should be told about Perry. That their friend and top medical expert was gone.

53

Several miles away, below the conference room's bright recessed lighting, Masten remained somber as he listened as Nora Lagner continued their assessment. Testing Reiff's short-term memory, then long-term, and now on to simple questioning to test deductive reasoning.

"If you found a wallet on the ground," asked Lagner with a tilt of her head, "what would you do?"

"Is it my wallet?"

"Not the point."

"Context is important."

Lagner shook her head and moved on. "If you see the lights of a police car behind your car, what do you do?"

"What state am I in?"

Unamused, Lagner looked at Masten, who suddenly glanced down when his phone rang inside his pocket, interrupting them. He silenced it.

Masten waved his CTO off and once again leaned forward. "I think that's enough for now. What I'd like to do now, Mr. Reiff, is switch gears and ask you about something else." He reached into his shirt pocket and retrieved a piece of paper. Unfolding it, he flattened the large sheet against the table with his hand and slid it across to Reiff.

John Reiff studied the image without touching it, then looked back at Masten.

"Can you tell me what that is?"

"One of my sketches."

"When did you draw it?"

"Yesterday."

Masten nodded approvingly. "What time?"

"In the morning."

"And what is it a picture of?"

"I don't know," answered Reiff.

"Please describe it for me."

Reiff studied the paper. "A large room. With several large objects inside."

"What kind of objects?"

"Cylinders of some kind."

"How many?"

"Ten."

"Can you describe them?"

"Metal. Painted white. With openings near the bottom. Rectangular pieces of glass like small windows."

"Anything else?" asked Masten.

"The rest of the room was plain. Mostly empty. Tall ceilings, though, and some mechanical equipment on the far wall. Nothing much else."

"There was glass in the cylinders?"

"Yes," answered Reiff. "To see inside."

"What did they show?"

"Some kind of liquid." Reiff thought for a moment. "With a green tint."

"Green tint?"

"Yes."

Masten grew more curious. "Were there any markings on these cylinders?"

"Not that I remember."

"Do you think this was a hallucination or something else?"

"No idea."

"You have no idea at all?"

Reiff shook his head.

Masten then frowned. "So, you have no idea whether what you're drawing is real or not."

"No."

"One of your pictures looked a lot like Dr. Souza's lab."

"I guess." Reiff reached forward and slid the paper back to Masten. "Or I drew some scene out of an old movie. A lot of labs look the same."

Masten nodded. Taking the picture and studying it again. "Well, the good news is you appear to be in relatively good health, physically and mentally. Which means with any luck, you can help us figure out why your system is so unique. If we can find a way to avoid cryogenic crystallization, just like you, it could be one of the greatest scientific breakthroughs in human history."

"And people could live forever."

"Not forever," said Masten. "But long enough."

"Long enough for what?"

"Like I said. Long enough to mean something. To be truly satisfied with one's time here. Our one chance."

John Reiff leveled his gaze across the table thoughtfully, all expression fading from his face. "People are never satisfied."

54

Rachel had barely made it off the property when her phone rang, causing her to slow just as she reached solid asphalt again.

The small screen illuminated the inside of her car, displaying an unknown number with what appeared to be an international code beginning with 44.

She contemplated while still rolling, before pressing the button to ignore. Then dropped the phone on the passenger seat and accelerated.

Less than a minute later, it rang a second time. This one from a different number but still beginning with the digits 44.

Rachel slowed again, this time coming to a complete stop on the edge of the road before checking behind her to see if the police cars were still visible. They weren't. Only the afterglow of their pulsating blue and red lights on the far side of a cluster of ponderosa pines.

She moved the phone to her left hand and put the car into park. Apprehensively, Rachel answered the call.

"Hello?"

"Rachel. It's Henry."

"Henry?" She was both surprised and confused. "What number are you calling from?"

"It doesn't matter. Where are you?"

Another look over her shoulder. "I'm just leaving—" She stopped speaking and gulped, fighting the trembling in her voice. "Perry just died, Henry! He's gone."

The other end of the call fell silent. The silence lingered until Yamada finally replied, "Oh, God."

"I'm just leaving now. The police are there. They're still—"

"Rachel, stop talking."

"What?"

"Stop talking," repeated Yamada. "Listen to me carefully. Hang up and download an app onto your phone called AllinCrypt."

"What, right now?"

"Yes. Right now." He spelled out the app name. "Download it and call me back on the number you see me calling from. Do you understand?"

"Yes. But why?"

"Just do it," he said, and ended the call. Leaving Rachel in complete silence. Alone in her car.

She did not move at first. She merely stared forward, blinking uncomprehendingly, until her fingers began to move by themselves.

Her signal was weak, and it took several minutes to find and download the app. When finished, she copied over the last number he called from and pressed the call button within the application.

Yamada answered on the first ring.

"Can you hear me?"

"Yes."

"Good. Where are you, Rach, exactly?"

"On the road leading to Perry's." She checked one more time. "The police are still there."

"Okay. We need to meet and talk."

"Are you even in the country?"

"Yes," he replied. "I'm in Flagstaff. I'm just rerouting my calls."

"What for?"

"I'll explain when I see you. How much gas do you have?"

"Gas?" Surprised, she leaned forward to check. "A little less than half a tank."

"Okay. That's plenty."

"Henry, what the hell is going on?"

"Rachel, just listen. Do you know where the Rogers Lake hiking area is?"

"Uh, I think so."

"It's about ten miles southeast from where you are. West on Highway 40 and then south on 231. I think it's called Wooden Mountain Road or something like that."

"Okay."

"It's a rough road, so go slow. I'll meet you at the entrance."

"When?"

"As soon as you can get there. Are you awake enough to drive?"

"Are you kidding?"

When Yamada said rough, he meant it. The road turned to gravel a few miles from the main interstate and then to dirt, where it narrowed and became even harsher. Constant and unmanaged weather-strewn ruts made it feel like she was driving over a giant mile-long washboard. Buffeted by sporadic gusts of wind beneath a star-studded night sky, she could make out the distant reflection of what appeared to be a small lake in the distance and, stretching out before it, a long rolling prairie. By day, the expanse was covered in a thick carpet of brown and green scrub brush.

The constant jarring of the road slowed Rachel to less than ten miles an hour, and took forever before the reserve's large, white-painted sign finally appeared in her headlights. Slowly and steadily, she edged closer until she could make out the largest of the printed letters.

WELCOME
ROGERS LAKE COUNTY NATURAL AREA

When she was within a few hundred feet, a bright flashlight beam appeared next to the sign and motioned to an open space to pull off to.

Turning and applying some gas, she powered up and over a modest hump before bringing her Camry to a stop, immediately ensconced by a cloud of dust billowing forward past the car and into the bright beams of its headlights.

Turning off the engine, she remained inside until the person approached the passenger-side window and shined the flashlight at his face.

She quickly opened and pushed her driver's door open, stepping out onto the hard, arid ground.

"Henry, what the hell is going on?" she called over the wind.

He put a finger over his lips and turned off the light. "Turn off your headlights."

She reached back inside and complied before Yamada circled the front of the vehicle and took her hand. Guiding her away and toward a row of trees.

"We're in trouble, Rach," he said, turning around. "Serious trouble."

"Why? What do you mean?"

"First, tell me about Perry."

She gazed through the darkness, still distraught. "It was horrible, just horrible. I went to his house. Late. And when I got there, none of the lights were on. I should have known something was wrong. But for some reason . . ." She let it go with a shake of her head. "I got in through the side door and found him. Sitting at the table. Slumped forward. I almost jumped out of my skin."

She inhaled and continued more slowly. "I called the police as fast as I could. And tried to search for a pulse . . ."

Yamada's voice was low and patient. "What happened?"

"I-I don't know. It looked like he had a heart attack. Just sitting there at his table. Waiting for me. But the police . . ."

"The police what?"

"They don't think so."

"Meaning what?"

Her voice trembled. "They think someone killed him!"

"Why do they think that?"

"They said they found signs of a struggle. I don't know what it was. I didn't notice anything. But they think it might have been strangulation."

"Did you see any signs of that?"

"Like what?"

"Like marks."

"I'm not an expert. And I wasn't *looking* for anything at the time. The police said there wasn't any bruising on his neck, but there were ways around that. Like with a cloth or something."

"So, they think he was murdered."

"Yes," she exclaimed, "and the detective was asking questions like she thought it was me."

"But they let you go."

"Only after they found some large footprints in the grass."

Yamada looked down at her sneakers. "Lucky for you."

"Henry, what is all of this? What is going on? And where the hell have you been? I haven't seen you for two days."

"I was at home," he answered. "Working. Looking into some things. Things that didn't feel right."

"Nothing feels right anymore!"

"It was the stuff Nora was having me do. With all the code and all the data. Asking for things that didn't make sense. And then Perry. Asking me to put him in touch with some hackers."

Rachel pulled strands of whipping hair from her face. "He told me this morning. He said they found a bunch of stuff about the project's funding. Through the NIH."

"It's true. A lot of shit, Rach. A lot of grants that look like they might be fake. Or fraudulent. Along with a bunch of secret payments."

"Payments? Perry didn't say anything about that."

"Maybe he hadn't read that far. They found a lot of stuff."

She peered at him, crossing her arms in the darkness. "Why are you telling me this?"

"Because I think the police are right. About Perry."

"That he was murdered?"

Yamada raised his hands, covering his face momentarily before letting them fall. "I put Perry in touch with my cousin, who works at a security firm. And he put him in touch with the guys who broke in and did the digging. The hackers."

"And?"

"My cousin is dead, Rachel. I just found out. And maybe those hackers are, too."

55

"Oh my God." Rachel spun around in a panic, staring into the darkness in the direction of her car. "What do we do?"

"I don't know." Yamada's face became grim. "I don't know."

"I was ready to give Masten the benefit of the doubt . . . ."

"Why?"

"Because I thought the police might have been wrong. That Perry *could* have died of a heart attack. But now, with him. And your cousin. And the hackers."

"I don't know that part for sure."

"Does it matter? The timing can't be coincidental."

"No, it can't."

Rachel then gasped. "Wait. Do they know that you know?"

"Who?"

"Robert and Nora. Do they know that you know? About what the hackers found?"

"I don't think so." Yamada's eyes switched from reflective to worried. "Do they know about *you*?"

Rachel stopped to think. "I don't know. Perry told me outside. So, I can't see how they—"

"Wait," interrupted Henry. "Outside where? Our building?"

"Yes."

"Oh Jesus, Rachel! That building has cameras all over the place! Inside *and* outside! Where were you when Perry talked to you about it?"

"You mean—"

"Where were you standing?"

"Uh, about a hundred feet from the entrance. Maybe farther. Near the street."

"Right in front of the building? Are you two stupid? That whole area is covered!"

"I didn't know!" she shot back. "How were we supposed to know?"

Yamada closed his eyes. "Okay, okay. I'm sorry. You didn't know. But, we have to assume those cameras picked up everything you said."

"Not that far away!"

"It's possible," said Yamada. "Even if they didn't, Masten and Lagner would probably suspect you two were up to something by leaving the building. Either way, we have to assume they know that *you* know."

"This can't be happening," Rachel said, shaking. "This *cannot* be happening!"

Yamada sighed. "We need to go to the police."

"What?"

"I said—"

"I heard what you said. But Perry said we shouldn't. He was adamant."

"That was before he was dead! *And* my cousin."

She stared apprehensively at Yamada in the night air. Lingering, saying nothing, until finally acquiescing in a nod.

"We have to talk to the cops and give them everything."

Still in thought and nodding, Rachel suddenly froze. "Wait, what?"

"We have to tell them everything."

She slowly shook. "You said *give* them everything." When Yamada didn't reply, she inched closer, squinting. "Give them what, Henry?"

He didn't answer.

"*Give them what, Henry?*" she repeated, louder. Then, while she stared at his darkened face, it hit her. "You have a copy."

Yamada swallowed.

"*You* have a copy?"

"Yes."

"You're worried about them knowing about me while *you* have a copy of what the hackers found?"

"My cousin sent it to me. Before."

"And you don't think that if they knew about your cousin and the hackers, that somehow they wouldn't know about you, too?"

Yamada mumbled, "Maybe."

"Maybe?"

"Okay, fine. They might find out. Probably. Eventually."

Rachel raised her hands to her face. "My God," she said. "Then, whoever did this to Perry and your cousin also knows about you and me." She shook again, almost crying as she spoke. "This just cannot be happening."

"Time to go to the police," he said.

With her eyes closed, she dropped her hands. "How bad is it?"

"How bad?"

"The information they found." She opened her eyes again. "How bad is it?"

"It's pretty damning. Not just for Robert and Nora, but some of our consulting doctors are in on this, too. And it may go even deeper than that. Or should I say higher."

"Then don't tell me any more. Let's just take it to the police."

Resigned, both took a deep breath and turned back the way they came. Stepping carefully along the winding footpath as it descended back out from the trees toward the park's giant sign.

They made it twenty feet before Rachel slowed and grasped Yamada's arm. "Wait! What happens when we turn them in?"

"What do you mean?"

"I mean, what happens, specifically?"

"To them or us?"

Rachel blinked and gazed past him over the distant lake. "Not to them, *by them*."

"I don't follow."

She looked at Yamada. "What are they going to do?"

"You mean like deny it?"

"No, like covering it up."

He thought a moment. "I guess that's possible."

Rachel, still staring, then asked, "How hard would it be to cover it up, Henry? Everything."

"The whole project?"

"The whole project. It's not that big. How long would it take them to get rid of it all? Like emptying out the labs?"

"That's a good question."

"They wouldn't even have to get rid of it all," she said. "Just the main systems. The Machine. Most of the testing units. The DNA sequencers. A few other things."

"But the rest would still be there. If someone came to investigate . . ."

"The easiest thing to do, and the most expedient, would be to divert, not deny."

"What does that mean?"

"Think about it. Cleaning *everything* up would take time. But just a little cleanup would be faster. A lot faster."

"But the lab would still be there," he repeated.

"That's what I'm saying. They don't have to get rid of it all. A diversion rather than a denial could make things much easier. And more believable."

"What *diversion*?"

"All labs look the same," said Rachel. "At least most of them, to an untrained eye. All Robert and Nora would have to do is get rid of the cryo-related systems and claim Recrudesce was something completely different."

Now Yamada got it. "Wow. I didn't think of that."

"It would be the easiest thing, right?"

"That's evil genius."

She nodded and gripped his arm again. "And we both know how methodical Robert is."

"And Nora."

"*And* Nora," agreed Rachel. "So, what do you think the odds are that they already have a backup project in mind as a contingency?"

"Jesus," breathed Yamada. "I wouldn't put it past them."

"Neither would—" Rachel gasped. "Oh my God, Henry!"

"What?"

She stared up at his darkened face. "If they have to get rid of everything relating to the project, that would also have to include John Reiff."

56

Upon returning to his office with Lagner, Robert Masten was startled to find someone waiting for him inside. The person stood waiting in darkness, standing behind Masten's large glowing computer monitor.

The man's face was immediately recognizable, even before Masten flipped on the lights—squinting briefly at the sudden brightness.

His features were strong and chiseled. Eastern European had been Masten and Lagner's original guess, but it was obvious now, seeing him in person. With short, peppered hair and deep eyes.

Liam Duchik spoke as they approached. "It's time."

Masten tried to appear relaxed, adjusting the sleeves of his suit jacket. "Time for what?"

"For our patient to exit."

"What? Why?"

"Things have gone too far."

Surprised, the director looked at Lagner, then back over the top of his desk. "Reiff is stable now. Finally. This is not the time to just—"

"The patient has become a liability. Or perhaps you can't see that."

"He's a larger asset. We just—"

Duchik interrupted again. "Save your breath. I watched your interview. Your assessment. Whichever you'd like to call it, the man is a threat."

Masten stepped forward, almost pleading. "Listen to me: There's something going on here. Something big. *Huge.* The man is not just stable; he's an anomaly."

"An anomaly?"

"It's inexplicable," admitted Nora.

Duchik's eyes moved to her. "Is that right?"

"Whatever it is that's happening to Reiff," she said, "it's real."

Duchik let the statement hang in the air before changing tack. "Is he mentally stable?"

"We think so."

"You think so."

Masten clarified. "By every measurement, his cognitive abilities appear to be completely intact. Which was the goal."

The man nodded. "A goal that has been achieved."

"It has. But there's something else. Something we never expected. Something we can't even explain! That might just be *miraculous*."

With no reaction from Duchik, Masten continued. "You saw what he did. The drawings. You *have* to see the possibilities. The potential staring us right in the face!" He grew almost desperate. Incredulous. "Jesus, don't tell me you're going to ignore it. Tell me you're at least a *little* fascinated. Just like we are."

Duchik's face remained like stone. A faint look of curiousness in his two dark eyes, but not in response to what Masten was saying. In response to how he was acting.

"Have you never been duped, Mr. Masten?"

"What?"

"Have you never been swindled?" The handler's face grew sardonic as Masten could only gawk. "Have you never met a Thrillist?"

The director could only stare back in frustration.

"This man is deceiving you," said Duchik. "He is reading you. And you cannot see it."

He couldn't believe his ears. Without a word, Masten reached into his jacket pocket, retrieved the drawing, and tossed it onto his desk. "You're telling me this is made up?"

The other man glanced at the paper, wearing a bemused look.

"How?" inquired Masten. "How would he know about that?"

"It's a tad vague, is it not?"

"Vague?"

"I see what could resemble columns in what *could* resemble a large room. The rest is the mind seeing what it wants to see."

"What it wants to see? You've got to be kidding!"

"The mind seeks order, Mr. Masten. It seeks structure and explanation. Familiarity. It is a well-known technique. A tactic of the brain for dealing with an infinitely complex world around it. Something I'm sure Dr. Bennett can explain in great detail."

Masten was speechless. Utterly speechless. He turned to Lagner for confirmation of the idiocy before them, but she was reactionless.

"The truth, Mr. Masten, is that I don't care. I don't care whether our patient is a charlatan or some sort of medical miracle; it doesn't change anything. The man is still a liability. Not just to me, but to others."

"I-I can't believe this."

"Believe it," replied Duchik. "You've done your job. You've completed your mission. Revel in that. Now exit our patient, or I will."

57

The long familiar hallway was once again bright and empty when he exited the elevator. It lacked a single adornment upon the featureless beige-painted walls, periodically interrupted by assumedly locked doors, and painted in the same monotonous tone—almost like camouflage.

The only discernible sight in the hall length was the twin narrow glass panes in the double doors at the end. The main lab where he had supposedly been brought back to life. That was still assuming he had been dead in the first place.

He moved slowly in the loose-fitting pants and a shirt given to him by his doctors. Similar in look and feel to a doctor's scrubs, along with a pair of plain, light gray tennis shoes. His rubber soles squeaked with each step over the spotless tiled floor.

He paused at the door to Dr. Souza's lab. It was closed and he couldn't hear anything on the other side, leaving him wondering if she was okay as he continued forward.

When he reached the double doors, he then stopped to peer through one of the narrow windows. The room was dark. Revealing little more than Reiff's reflection in the tempered glass. All he saw were the reflections of Masten's goons, who stood directly behind him. Escorting him.

Leaving the double doors, Reiff followed the hall's left-hand turn, which led to another. Passing more locked doors until he spotted the door to his own room. The fragments of the bedspring he'd used in the lock had been removed, and the door itself no longer locked at all.

When he turned on the lights, nothing else appeared to be different. Drawings on his table, the bed neatly made, and the two familiar medical devices: a Dinamap and an infusion pump, still affixed to the wall and powered off.

On the opposite side of the room were the familiar plant and chair, next to the sink, and a bright blue plastic bio garbage bag. Higher on the wall, a clock read a few minutes past four fifteen, which he assumed was A.M.

Reiff turned and watched both men assume guard positions outside. After a long, tired silence, he closed the door and glanced wearily at the camera just below the ceiling. Then he leaned forward to flip the lights off.

One floor above, the long hairy arm of the tiny capuchin remained quietly extended, reaching through and softly petting the short dog's white head.

While she wagged her tail cheerfully, the monkey's second hand emerged to stroke Bella's neck and chest, then moved to the slim collar around her neck, where both sets of tiny fingers came together and continued fiddling. Searching for a way to get it off.

58

Flagstaff was located at the southwestern edge of the Colorado Plateau within a scattering of dormant volcanoes known as the San Francisco field. It was over seven thousand feet above sea level, and where American astronauts trained before landing on the moon seventy-five years before, many of the city's historic buildings and houses still remained. Some, over a hundred and fifty years old, constructed from original red sandstone quarries upon which Flagstaff was founded. It gave the relatively small metropolitan expanse a much more substantial feel than its population of two hundred thousand.

The first rays of sunlight were beginning to lighten the sky south of nearby Mount Elden. They were both in Henry Yamada's car, having left Rachel's Camry in a nearby parking lot.

Exhausted, Henry slowed the vehicle and turned right onto an empty East Butler Avenue before steadily accelerating again. Ignoring the majestic scene unfolding upon the distant horizon, he glanced at Rachel, sitting in the passenger seat and staring intently at her phone.

"What are you doing?"

"Trying to find the names of Perry's daughters."

"Where?"

"Perry emailed them to me once," she said. "Before taking a trip. I think I still have it somewhere."

"To give to the police?"

"Yes. They deserve to know what happened to their father."

Yamada nodded without replying. The streetlights were still on, with only a single set of headlights approaching on the opposite side of the median until passing them.

"We are doing the right thing . . . right?"

Rachel turned and glared. "This was *your* idea."

"I know, I know. It's just easy to start second-guessing yourself."

"Oh, that's great to hear. Less than a mile from the police station."

"Sorry." He gripped the steering wheel tighter and forced his weary eyes open. After a few blocks of silence, he looked at her again. She was no longer scrolling through her emails but instead fixed on something.

"Find it?"

She didn't answer.

"Rach?"

Yamada slowed, preparing for a right-hand turn onto Sawmill Road. "Rach?"

She appeared still and unmoving, prompting him to lean forward and check her face.

Her eyes were open but blinking oddly at the tiny screen.

"Rachel, are you okay?"

Her head of long dark hair finally twisted toward him. "I'm not sure."

Yamada slowed the car and pulled over. "What's up?"

She handed him the phone and looked away, thinking. Replaying a scene in her mind.

"What is this, an email?"

She nodded.

He still didn't understand what he was looking at. "Who is Waterman?"

"I don't know."

Henry examined the email details. "I don't get it. You sent an email to yourself about someone you don't know?"

"I didn't," she whispered.

He reexamined the screen. "Well, if you didn't, then it must be some kind of spam."

"Or something else."

Yamada handed the phone back and shook his head, exasperated. "Rachel, I'm tired. I don't have the energy for twenty questions. Just tell me what's bothering you."

She turned and stared at him. "I didn't send this email. And it's not spam."

"Then what is it? The email has your address as both the sender and recipient."

"Yesterday evening, before I went to Perry's, John Reiff was in my lab. He'd picked the lock on his door. And I found him in my lab. Looking at my computer."

"You already told me that. You said that's how he discovered what year it is."

"That's right. We were there for several minutes together before Masten showed up. With the others."

"Okay."

"Several minutes," she repeated. "Talking. Except when I had to attend to the animals for a minute."

A tired Yamada rolled his eyes. "Get to the point!"

"When I turned back around, John was on my computer. Again. Typing."

"Typing what?"

Still staring at him, Rachel raised an eyebrow.

The inference took only a moment. "Wait. You think *this* is what he was typing? An email. To you?"

"Yes."

"Why would he do that? Why wouldn't he just tell you to your face?" Yamada took the phone from her again, rereading the email. The natural question was to ask why. Why would Reiff do that? But rereading the message now made the answer obvious. In four short words.

Find Waterman in Pahrump

59

"Who's Waterman? And where is Pahrump?"

"I have no idea."

Yamada frowned. "He didn't mention that name to you before?"

"No. Never."

"Are you sure?"

"I'm positive." Rachel switched applications on her phone and began typing. Then waited a few moments for the search results. Looking back at him, she said, "It's in Nevada."

"Nevada?"

"Just outside of Las Vegas."

"What's in Pahrump?"

Rachel shrugged. "Someone named Waterman, I guess."

Yamada turned and scanned the empty street. "Or someone who *used* to be there. Twenty-two years ago."

"Right."

"And what made Reiff send this to you? Just out of the blue?"

Again, she thought back to the previous evening. Finding him in her lab, their conversation, and finally, Reiff leaving with Masten and Lagner. "All I can think of," she said, "is that he knew something was about to happen."

60

Robert Masten stood on a redwood deck, raised and perfectly positioned to view the southern hills of Arizona's famed San Francisco Peaks over an endless green ocean of swaying pine trees.

The man's face was contorted in a mixture of frustration and anger as he leaned on a waist-high railing with one hand and held his phone in the other. "He's insane!" he barked. Veins were bulging from his neck. "Can the man not see what's right in front of his face?"

"Apparently not."

"I'm not doing it, Nora. I'm telling you, I'm not doing it! It's a miracle Reiff is alive at all. Let alone healthy. More than that, he's a goddamn telepath, or something! *You* tell me how he knows what he does."

"I can't explain it either." Her voice sighed on the other end. "I don't know what it is. I honestly don't. But—"

"But what?"

"I'm not going to lie, Robert. It worries me. A lot. Do I think we should kill him? No. But what *else* does he know?"

"Does it matter?" Masten exclaimed. "This isn't some trick. It's a phenomenon. A bona fide medical phenomenon."

"So, what are you saying?"

"Nora, think about it. Whatever it is going on with Reiff, it's, it's . . . *metamorphic.* Whatever changed, it happened *after* we revived him. And that means that it had to result from the cryonics." Masten turned around and stared absently at the luxurious mountain home behind him. With giant overhead beams, floor-to-ceiling windows, and a living area that would shame some hotel lobbies. Ornately decorated with porcelain tiles and rich Italian leather furniture.

"*We* did it, Nora. Somehow, we caused this change in Reiff. Which means it belongs to us."

Lagner pondered. "I suppose that's true."

"It *is* true. Not only is it a miracle Reiff survived, but it came with a giant bow on top. Think about what it could mean. Not only can we extend human life, but we also hit the proverbial jackpot! We just need to figure it out. And we will. In time, we'll figure out what happened inside the guy's brain and eventually replicate it."

"That could take a long time. A very long time."

"Sure, but who knows if this will ever happen again."

"But at what cost, Robert? And for how long? What if we never figure it out? Even in our lifetimes."

To her surprise, Masten laughed. "But that's the beauty of it. We just got a new lease on life. Extended for who knows how long. Imagine what we can figure out now. Not just about Reiff, but everything. Imagine the problems humankind will be able to solve now that we have more time. A *lot* more time. It's what we've been dreaming about for decades. Imagine, Nora, if all the greatest minds in human history, inventors, creators, innovators, imagine if they hadn't died. Imagine if we were able to keep them from dying and eventually *heal* them. Imagine if their knowledge, their understanding, their unique view of the universe was never lost. If their ideas kept going. And their unique abilities kept contributing to society. Well, guess what? We're here! We can't go back for those in the past, but all the brilliance in the world right now, in all its forms—we can keep it!"

There was a long pause for Lagner. "That really is a huge step."

"It's beyond huge! And now, imagine if Reiff's ability came along *with* it. Good God, Nora!"

"I see it," she said. "I really do. But Reiff still scares me. I'm sorry, but he does. Whatever this ability is, it still scares the hell out of me. Especially the thought that we may only be seeing a glimpse of it."

"Even better!" cried Masten. "So, we study him longer. Forever if we have to!"

"You know we have his DNA."

"Yes, I know that."

"Before and after revival," she added. "All we have to do is compare them. Find out what changed and where."

From his deck, Masten shook his head. "You know as well as I do it's not that easy, especially without the ability to study and test things firsthand. In person."

"It would take longer, but we could still—"

"Nora, it would take forever. This isn't just about tracking down nucleotides. We're talking groups of them. There could be hundreds. Thousands!"

"And what if it truly is an Occam's Razor?"

"What do you mean?"

"If it's not a trick," offered Lagner, "then it would have to be something else. What if he picked these images up another way? Some other kind of stimuli, perhaps, maybe even while frozen. We don't know."

"What are you talking about?"

"I'm talking about something we haven't considered, Robert. Something simpler. Something unknown but ultimately explainable."

"Another form of stimuli," Masten repeated.

"Not another form. Another source. Through the glass or some other means. Electrical impulses. Photons from a television screen somewhere. There's a lot we haven't considered."

His voice grew quiet.

"Then," she added, "it wouldn't matter how it happened. Would it still be an anomaly? Yes. But not a miracle."

"Then we wouldn't need him," said Masten dryly.

Lagner sighed. "We already have the data. Every byte, from the very beginning. Including the DNA sequences. All of them. We can literally examine every byte and every molecule. So, why risk the project?"

"You mean Reiff."

"Yes, I mean Reiff! Why take the risk of him exposing something? You said it yourself, 'we're here.' So, let's not take chances."

"Sometimes you're *too* logical, Nora."

"There's no such thing."

"There is. When it comes to human biology, there is." There was another long pause. "I'm not doing it," he finally said. "And I'll tell you another thing: I know who our friend is."

"Our friend?"

"Our visitor. The handler we've been using. His name is Duchik. He's part of the NIH."

"How do you know that?"

"It doesn't matter. But he's not just a go-between like we thought. He's one of them."

"One of who?"

"Them. The higher-ups. Which explains all the funding. Something tells me there wasn't much approval needed beyond him."

"How do you know?"

"I told you. It doesn't matter. What matters is that we resist."

"Resist how? He said he would kill Reiff if we don't."

"Then we find a way to change his mind. Help him understand exactly how big this opportunity is with Reiff. That it's worth some risk. And then some." He shook his head. "We have to control this, Nora. Us! You and me. Just like we knew we would. Someone has to be in charge of this technology. Someone who understands its true possibilities. The power of what it can really be used for! Duchik is hell bent on taking it, but we can't let him. We have to maintain control!"

"I'm not sure if that's possible," said Lagner.

"Trust me, it is. Anyone can be swayed. Eventually. We just need to figure out what his agenda is. And then leverage it."

"Then we'd better do it quickly."

"I agree. So let's do some digging."

Masten ended the call. He remained standing—the phone in hand—before raising his head and looking out over the trees. As if only just noticing them again, with their wall of needles glittering in the cool breeze.

They had a new mission.

On the other end, Nora Lagner listened for the disconnection before tilting the phone up off the short glass table and verifying the call was over. Then laid it back down.

After a fleeting thought, she refocused her attention, then put both hands on each arm of the chair and pushed herself up onto her feet.

Walking gingerly across the carpet, she reached behind and removed the pins to let her hair down. Shoulder-length, brown, highlighted by wisps of light gray. She was in her mid-fifties, and her eyes and face were aged, perhaps a bit plain, but still attractive.

Her eyes dropped to the opposing chair, and she grinned at the man seated before her. "He's not going to comply."

Liam Duchik's dark eyes stared up at her. Never changing expression. "I know."

Lagner took another step forward and stopped. Reaching both hands behind her back, she unzipped her dress and lowered each side down over a shoulder before allowing the garment to drop to the floor. She was wearing nothing else.

61

Rachel Souza woke to a sudden vibrating of the car and shot up from her seat. With a pattern of upholstered fabric imprinted neatly into her cheek. Next to her, Henry sat idly behind the wheel, staring ahead. They were pulled over on the side of the freeway.

"What's wrong?"

He continued staring forward, absently, with eyes drooping. "I'm falling asleep at the wheel."

She followed his gaze through the insect-covered windshield. "Huh?"

Yamada widened his eyes and stared again. "I'm too tired."

The engine remained idling with desert in all directions and wavering heat rising from the sunbaked ground.

"Where are we?"

It took him a moment. "Highway 93. North of Kingman." He turned to her with heavy eyes. "I need you to drive."

"Sure." She raised the seat and unfastened her seat belt. Then pushed her door open with a squeak and stepped out onto the broad shoulder of sand and gravel.

She was instantly hit by the heat. Dry and hot, like an oven. She circled the aged Nissan as quickly as possible and waited while Yamada groggily climbed out.

A large SUV passed in the far lane with a whoosh, followed by a blast of hot air and a light shaking of their vehicle. But once inside, she pulled the door closed behind her and said a small prayer for the working air conditioner.

She adjusted the seat and rearview mirror, while Yamada climbed into the passenger side and leaned his seat back without hesitation.

"Get some sleep," she offered, and merged back onto the vacant freeway.

The only Waterman they could locate in Pahrump was named Devin. Devin Waterman. With an address on Pioche Street and nothing else. No description. No phone number. Nothing of any use for contacting or even identifying the man. Assuming he was still there. A lot had changed in the last two decades, making the odds of Waterman still being there reasonably low. But at this point, it was all they had.

Even if Waterman was gone, hopefully they could find out where he went. And pray that he wasn't too far away, and was still alive. The mortality rate had skyrocketed over the last several years, and she and Henry both worried those fatalities had taken Reiff's friend, too.

At least, she hoped they were friends.

She checked herself in the mirror and stretched open her jaw to wake up.

A few trucks appeared like dots on the opposite side of the freeway, slowly approaching and passing. Reminders of the long struggle to recover. The Great Struggle, as it was called. Devastating for everyone and terminal for many. Making the project with Robert Masten all the more miraculous. At a time when landing any job would have been an achievement. But something that could actually help people at the same time was beyond exciting. It had been almost beyond belief—too good to be true.

But it had been true. Just as Masten had promised at the time, he found funding when funding was nearly impossible to come by. And resources and equipment. Just attaining the materials necessary to build the Machine had seemed miraculous. But he'd done it.

How, she had no idea. And frankly, at the time, she hadn't cared. The Struggle had been so hard for so long; the last thing she wanted was to jinx it. Of course, now, in retrospect, she realized she'd been a fool. A stupid, naive fool. Williams was dead, and everything they'd worked for had been a sham. She didn't know what they wanted, but she knew it couldn't be good. People don't get murdered to keep good things secret.

62

Pahrump had seen better days. At least, Rachel hoped it had. Run-down and only a step away from seedy, the town still supported what a quick online search claimed to be a population of about ten thousand. Far lower than its peak decades before, but in many ways, not all that much worse than some of the other towns in Arizona.

The Great Struggle had been tough for everyone. Everywhere. And not just in the United States. So, the timeworn appearance of Pahrump was not entirely surprising.

After almost two hours of sleep, Henry Yamada's tired eyes were focused on the map on his phone, navigating as they made their way through town. Pioche Street was on the south side past an abandoned golf course, whose large open stretches of yellow grass looked out over the distant Nopah mountain range just beyond the California border.

A few cars passed as they made their way through multiple blocks of neighboring streets. The cars were old and dusty but functioning.

They found the address and pulled over out front of the small, well-kept prefab with a long concrete driveway, skirted by a waist-high chain-link fence, with a small rock garden for a front yard. Nothing fancy, but it was clear that whoever lived there took care of it.

They climbed out, squinting beneath the glaring late-morning sun. The temperature indicator on Yamada's dash was broken, but it had to be somewhere in the mid-nineties. Together, they headed for the chain-link gate, but no sooner had they reached it than a large German shepherd erupted from behind the house, charging at full speed and barking ferociously.

The dog came to a sliding stop less than ten feet from the fence causing his chain to go taut, clearly aware of where his range ended. But his barking remained relentless, powerful, and frightening. Rachel was pretty sure he could have chewed through the restraint had the thought occurred to him.

"Geez!" said Yamada, putting a hand on his chest. "Thank God for the chain."

Shaken, they remained standing by the front of the car, keeping some distance between themselves and the dog on the other side of the fence.

"What do we do?"

Rachel shrugged and placed one hand above her brow, trying to see inside the house's front window. "I can't tell if anyone's home."

"Well, I'm sure as hell not going up to ring the doorbell. Then again, something tells me they don't need the doorbell to know we're here."

"Probably not." Rachel continued watching the front window, looking for any movement.

"What do you want?"

Rachel and Henry whirled at the sudden voice behind them. On the opposite side of the street, a woman stood behind her own fence and watched them. Her entire length of fence was lined by tall weeds, and in the yard was a decrepit, rusted swing set, which looked like it was struggling to remain standing. Not far from that were remnants of an old garden bed.

The woman—probably in her seventies—wore baggy, wrinkled clothes. Her face looked like leather from years in the hot, dry climate.

Rachel cleared her throat and cautiously approached across the hot pavement. "Hello."

"What do you want?" the woman repeated.

"We're, uh, looking for someone. Someone who used to live here."

"Like who?"

"Waterman," said Yamada, following behind Rachel.

"Waterman?"

"Yes. Devin Waterman."

"Why?"

They glanced at each other. "Why?"

"Why are you looking for him?" The woman leaned onto her fence, squinting at both of them as they drew near.

"Uh, we're here about a mutual friend."

"What friend?"

Now Rachel furrowed her brow and motioned to the house behind her. "Does Devin Waterman still live here?"

The old woman continued scrutinizing as though looking for something. Until she finally nodded. "Yeah, he lives there. Been in this hellhole for thirty years. Hell, he was here before me."

"Do you know if he's home?" asked Rachel.

The woman shook her head. "Not during the day. Which is why he has Fluffy over there."

They both looked at the dog and then back to the woman. "His dog's name is Fluffy?"

She laughed at them, then raised a fist up to her mouth and ended with a short cough. "I'm just yanking your chain. Its name ain't Fluffy. It's Sparkles."

There was another brief look of surprise, quickly replaced by doubt.

"All right, I'm just joshing. His name is Max. And it's a good thing you didn't go any closer. That damn dog is mean. Like the thing's on steroids or somethin'."

"Do you know where we can find Mr. Waterman?"

"He's always at the same place."

"And where would that be?"

"At the range."

Rachel looked at Yamada. "The range?"

"There's where you find most range masters, ain't it? *On* the range."

"Range master? Of what?"

The woman grimaced. "You don't know nothin' about him, do you?"

"Not really."

"Then why you looking for him?"

"We're trying to help someone. An old friend of Mr. Waterman's."

She laughed with a small cackle. "I didn't know good old Devin *had* any friends." Watching the two youngsters, she finally waved her hand. "He's a range master up the road. At Prairie Fire. Where they do all the training. That's where he always is when he's not outside tending to his rocks."

Rachel feigned a smile and looked in the direction the woman had pointed. "Thank you. Where is it exactly?"

"Back the way you came. About fifteen minutes. When you see the sign, turn right. You can't miss it. It's the only thing out there."

"Thank you," she said again. Followed by Yamada. Halfway to the car, Rachel abruptly turned back around. "Uh, what does—How old is he?"

The old woman gave a haughty cackle. "Older than you!"

63

Prairie Fire had also seen better days, but the compound, comprising about a dozen buildings, was in much better condition than the town in which it resided. The buildings still being used were clean and in good shape, and the expansive gravel parking lot was more than half full.

It was a training university for military and law enforcement that also taught safe, effective weapons tactics to members of the public. Anyone interested in learning proper use of their weapon for self-defense purposes.

Which appeared to be a lot of people.

The popping could be heard from a half mile away, even before they reached the entrance, on an aged but still very usable two-lane road. As they skirted the parking lot, the popping became louder and constant—from approximately a dozen different shooting ranges, judging from a nearby sign. All seemingly spread out over several hundred yards.

From the lot, they spotted four of the ranges and part of the fifth before looping back to the buildings that were nearest the entrance and that made up most of the university's operations. There was a large hall surrounded by several smaller buildings, all with well-maintained signs that said things like STORE, AMMO, and GUNSMITH. At which point, Rachel spotted and parked in front of the building labeled ADMINISTRATION.

Inside, she and Yamada were met by air-conditioning and a long, waist-high counter, and behind it sat two people at their desks. One of whom immediately stood up to greet them.

"Good morning," the middle-aged woman said with a smile. She appeared to be in her late forties, and was dressed in a desert-colored uniform.

Rachel returned a friendly but nervous greeting. "Hello. We're looking for Devin Waterman."

The woman reached down behind the counter and brought up a binder, examining the day's printed schedule.

"He's teaching on range seven today. It's close enough to walk, or you can just drive down to the far end of the parking lot."

"Wonderful. Thank you." They were both turning to leave when the woman stopped them.

Looking them up and down, she said, "Do you have your eye and ear protection?"

Rachel and Henry looked at each other. "Uh . . . we forgot."

"You can't go down to the range without them. You can either buy some in the store or just wait." She checked her watch. "Everyone should be breaking for lunch in about thirty-five minutes."

"Thank you," said Rachel, with a look of gratitude. "We'll wait."

Outside, they climbed back into the dusty Nissan and turned the engine back on. Then they slowly idled down the length of the lot, try- ing to avoid creating more dust, until signs for ranges 7, 8, and 9 came into view.

They continued forward, pulling in beside a group of cars in front of 7, and parked, but left the engine and air conditioner running.

"This is quite the operation," mused Yamada.

She nodded. "Not exactly my cup of tea, but I can see why it's popular."

"On the way here, I read that it used to be called Front Sight. They went through a bankruptcy some years back, but it doesn't seem to have hurt them much."

"Yeah. Makes me wonder how big it was before."

Thirty minutes later, and still in the car, they spotted students leav- ing the other ranges and heading toward the main buildings. On range 7, the students were still on the range but had ceased shooting. It looked like they were now standing in the bright sun, listening to their two instructors.

Turing off the engine, Rachel and Henry both climbed out and ap- proached, noting the large pergola with metal roofing providing shade to a couple of dozen metal chairs, empty and littered with various per- sonal items from the students.

They stopped in the pergola's shade and waited. The two instructors were sharply dressed and outfitted in the same desert-style fatigues as the woman in the office. One instructor appeared to be the junior instructor, but both men wore boonie hats and polarized sunglasses.

The class broke when the senior range master ended his instruction, and everyone headed back toward the chairs, each carrying holstered handguns.

Rachel and Henry stepped back and watched as the students approached, chatting with one another as they retrieved their belongings. After a few minutes of private discussion, the two range masters followed.

Rachel could feel her heartbeat quickening.

"What are you going to say?" asked Yamada.

She shook her head. "I have no idea."

When the instructors reached the shade, they moved to a side table, and each picked up a water bottle to drink from. As they did so, Rachel approached and looked for name tags and saw DEVIN stitched into the shirt of the instructor who close up looked a little older than the other.

She swallowed nervously. "Mr. Waterman?"

The man lowered the bottle and gazed at her from behind his reflective sunglasses. "In the flesh."

"Uh, my name is Rachel Souza," she said, stammering, "and this is, uh, Henry Yamada. Could we . . . have a word with you?"

Unable to see his eyes, she watched the man's lips move within a trim white beard and mustache. "Shoot."

"Uh, I mean, privately?"

Waterman looked up, and he scanned the area behind them. "About what?"

She was fidgeting. "To talk about something. It's important."

"Who are you with?"

"Uh, no one. No one. Just . . ." She paused. "It's a little hard to explain."

Waterman turned and nodded to his junior instructor, who gave them a quick once-over before heading out behind the last of the students. Waterman then lowered his bottle back to the table. "Okay. Go ahead."

She eyed Yamada, who looked even more nervous than she was, then opened her mouth to speak. "Do you know a John Reiff?"

Waterman became still.

"Who?" he asked.

"A man named John Reiff. He was in the army."

Waterman continued staring, unflinching. "Yes. I knew John Reiff. Why?"

Rachel's mouth suddenly became dry. "I'm not really sure how to say this . . ."

64

If Waterman seemed unflinching before, he now appeared like stone. Completely motionless, standing partially in the sun with the hot desert breeze whistling around him.

"What did you just say?"

Rachel felt herself wanting to take a step back but forced herself to remain where she was. She twisted her head to the side to find Henry in her peripheral vision, over her left shoulder.

At a few inches over six feet, Waterman's intimidating figure gazed down upon them. His expression was utterly unreadable behind the sunglasses.

"I said," answered Rachel nervously, "John Reiff is alive." She swallowed and added, "In Flagstaff."

The two watched him anxiously before Yamada's eyes dropped down to the .45-caliber handgun on the man's right hip.

"That's impossible."

"It's true," said Rachel. "He's a patient. In our . . . lab." She couldn't think of a better word at the moment.

"Your *lab*?"

"It's . . . kind of complicated—"

Waterman cut her off before she could continue. "John Reiff is dead!" he suddenly shouted. "And has been for a long time!" He looked past them again through the bright sunbaked parking lot. "I don't know who you're with or what game you're playing, but I suggest you turn around and leave. Now."

"Wait," Rachel pleaded. "Just listen—"

"No!" growled Waterman. "You listen to me. If you think I or anyone else is going to let you desecrate John Reiff's memory for some godforsaken reason, you better think again. In fact, why don't you turn around—"

Yamada suddenly stepped out from behind Rachel and thrust his phone up in front of the man, holding it less than a foot from his face.

Waterman glanced at the screen, taking a moment to focus, before hesitantly removing his sunglasses. He stared closer at Yamada's phone with a pair of intense blue eyes, taking note of the picture displayed on it.

It was a still image captured from one of Yamada's video feeds in the lab. It showed John Reiff in his room, looking up at the camera from his bed.

"This is from a video taken four days ago," said Yamada. "From his recovery room."

Waterman's eyes remained fixed on the tiny screen as he reached forward and plucked the phone from Yamada's hand. Using two fingers, Waterman touched the surface and enlarged the image.

It was slightly pixelated. Common for a still image taken from a video. And the colors were washed out. But the face in the image, and the eyes, were unmistakable.

"How do I know this is real?" he asked.

"Are you kidding?"

Waterman glared at Yamada. "I mean, how do I know it's recent?"

Rachel then stepped in front of Henry. "Why else would we be here?"

65

Waterman's large frame settled into a nearby chair with a resounding metal thump, followed by a brief sound of moving gravel beneath it. He was still staring at the phone's screen. He stayed closemouthed for a long time until finally glancing up at Rachel. "I think you better show me some ID."

Surprised, she scrambled for her back pocket and retrieved a slim wallet and, from it, her driver's license. Followed by her security badge from the lab.

Waterman studied them and turned to Yamada, who, without a word, provided the same.

"How?" he finally asked.

Rachel inhaled and then replied in a single word. "Cryonics."

"What's that?"

"The practice of freezing people—after they die—in hopes of bringing them back later."

Waterman's eyes widened briefly in surprise before quickly narrowing again. "That can't be right. John was in an accident. His body was never recovered from the river."

Rachel and Henry looked at one another. "We don't know the details of what happened. We know about the accident, but we don't know exactly how Mr. Reiff ended up in our program. I know that might be hard to believe, but it's true."

"Your program," said Waterman.

"We don't blame you for being skeptical."

"Skeptical?"

"Suspicious?" offered Rachel.

The older man pushed himself up from the chair and walked to the edge of the pergola's shade, staring outward again.

"I know this is a shock," said Rachel. "But we're here because we're trying to help John. And time is of the essence. We'll answer any questions you have, but we need to hurry."

He turned around to face them. "And why is that?"

"Because we think he's in danger."

Waterman had to keep himself from scoffing. How did he know this wasn't some weird, twisted joke? His mind was already searching for reasons to dismiss the story as nonsense.

He mulled it over for a long time, before his eyes eventually grew hard again, and he turned to scan the surrounding area once more. This time more carefully. Still finding nothing, he gradually returned his attention to the two at the table.

"So, what kind of trouble is John in?"

"We can explain it on the way," offered Rachel.

"You can explain it now."

She slowly nodded her head while staring up at Waterman. "Fine. But please believe that what we're about to tell you is the truth."

With no response from him, she continued. "Henry and I are part of a project that began a little over seven years ago. Code-named Recrudesce. A privately funded project, or so we thought."

"Meaning?"

"Meaning that while we thought it was private, it wasn't. We think now it was a secret government project."

Waterman's expression dimmed. "And you're just now finding this out?"

"Correct."

"What took you so long?"

They looked at each other. "Naivete mostly. The last seven years were comprised primarily of research and development. And testing. Mine being medical and Henry's mechanical. Starting small and gradually building on our successes, and nothing ever seemed out of the ordinary."

Waterman approached the table as she spoke. "Or maybe you didn't want it to."

"It's entirely possible. Our eventual goal was to successfully resuscitate, or reanimate, the first cryonic patient. Something that had never been done before. The project was run by an expert in the technology sector named Robert Masten, and required new technology designed from the ground up. It took us over seven years, but we finally did it. We succeeded. With John Reiff."

"And what happened to the failures?"

"John was the first human subject. After animals."

The older man grew contemplative. "So, what, you've had John this whole time? Frozen?"

Rachel nodded. "*We* have had him for about three years. But we didn't know where he came from. We still don't. He was—" She stopped, trying to find the right word. "—*sourced* by the head of the project."

"Sourced," repeated Waterman.

"I'm sorry. I'm tired. It's not the right word, but you get the idea. Where John was before that, we don't know. And the information we got on him was limited."

"So, he was your guinea pig."

She sighed. "You have to understand; we weren't just trying to re-animate him; we were also in the process of saving his life. From a condition that, for all practical purposes, left him in a state of death."

Waterman smirked. "I see, so you *saved* the guinea pig."

"We'd really rather not use that phrase," said Yamada.

"We prefer to refer to him as the first one. The first of many, or so we thought."

"And what does that mean?"

"Honestly, we don't know what to think now. Whoever is really behind this project, we think has already killed two people. Or more. One was my boss, a doctor named Perry Williams."

"And the other was my cousin," added Yamada.

If Waterman was surprised at the mention of the murders, he didn't show it. Instead, he merely continued listening.

"And now we think they're after us," said Rachel, "and John."

Waterman frowned. "And where is John right now?"

She met his eyes with a solemn expression. "Still in the lab."

66

They returned to Pahrump with Rachel and Henry following Waterman in his Ford pickup truck, painted black and in near-perfect condition, despite its age and the light film of dust that covered it. It turned from the highway and into the same neighborhood Rachel and Henry had driven through earlier, taking a slightly different route to Waterman's house.

They parked the Nissan at the curb as the truck pulled to a stop in Waterman's narrow driveway. The dog who had earlier tried to attack them was now waiting excitedly, wagging his giant black and brown tail.

Waterman opened the gate and reached down to unclasp the dog's thick collar. He called out, "Where's your ball?" prompting the animal to disappear inside through a large swinging dog door and return moments later, with it in his mouth.

From a safe distance, Yamada looked sheepish as they watched the dog and his owner play. "Is that even the same dog?"

"Wait here," Waterman called, closing the gate. He entered the house through a side door, after unlocking two dead bolts.

He disappeared inside, leaving the door slightly ajar, while Rachel and Henry waited idly in the hot sun. The dog was also gone, having followed his owner into the house.

"Now what?" asked Yamada.

She shrugged. "We wait, I guess."

"How about waiting in the car?"

"A few minutes in the sun isn't going to kill us."

"Not us," he whined, "just me. You have Latin blood. I don't."

She turned with folded arms. "What is that supposed to mean?"

"It means you're more used to this weather. Through your genes."

"My parents are from Boston."

"Well, *somewhere* down the line, your ancestors were in hotter weather than mine."

Rachel rolled her eyes. "I think your brain is suffering from heat-stroke. Maybe we *should* wait in the car."

"Great, I'll take it."

No sooner had Yamada turned toward his old Nissan than Waterman reemerged from the house. He was still dressed in his desert fatigues but now carrying a large duffel bag over his shoulder. Relocking the dead bolts behind him, he continued toward the truck after closing the fence's gate behind him. Finally, he noticed Rachel and Yamada staring at him.

"What?"

"What about your dog?"

"I'll call someone to look after him."

Waterman hefted the heavy bag into the truck bed with a muffled clunk, then stepped back and opened the passenger door.

Neither moved.

"Let's go," he said.

Yamada spoke apprehensively. "What about my car?"

"We'll take mine."

"I can't just leave it here."

Waterman shrugged. "I'm not putting John's chances on that piece of junk."

"What are you talking about? It made it out here."

"Consider yourself lucky," replied Waterman. "Now get in." With that, he moved from the door and circled around the front of the truck.

Henry stared at Rachel. "Is he serious?"

"I think so."

"I'm not leaving my car all the way out here. That's nuts."

The Ford's giant engine roared to life, and the truck's backup lights suddenly illuminated.

"Rach?"

From the passenger seat, Rachel noted the truck's clean interior, with an old-style radio installed in the dash. Complete with large twisting chrome knobs on either side.

"Did you put that in yourself?"

Beside her, Waterman accelerated from a stop sign, turning back onto the main highway as he nodded. "I'm anti-digital."

"Does it work?"

The man glowered at her.

His eyes returned to the road, then glanced up to the truck's rear-view mirror, where he noted the gleam of Yamada's old Nissan several hundred feet behind them. "Where'd your friend learn to drive, his grandmother?"

Rachel turned around to look.

"Thought we were in a hurry."

"We are."

"That word must mean something different with your generation, then."

"You sound like my father."

Waterman removed his boonie hat and dropped it onto the seat between them, revealing a nearly bald, lightly perspiring head. "Tell me again about this project of yours."

"What do you want to know?"

"For starters, what exactly are you trying to gain by freezing people?"

Rachel thought about the question. "Immortality, I guess. Someday."

"How does turning someone into an icicle make them immortal?"

"Keeping someone from dying is the first step," she answered. "Until cures can be found and applied."

"That doesn't make you immortal," Waterman retorted. "It just lets you live longer."

"Like I said, it's the first step. Not the only one. Immortality is the long-term goal."

"Well, unless I'm missing something, getting frozen when you're ninety means you're still ninety when you wake up. Even if they stop whatever was killing you."

"That's true. Which is where the other steps come in."

"Like what?"

"Like stem-cell therapy, cellular regeneration . . . Things like that."

"Wait. Are you saying you can actually make a person younger?"

"Ever heard of albumin?"

"No."

"It's a protein that's produced by the liver but declines as we age. A couple decades ago, researchers found that proteins like albumin play a pretty significant role in brain function. And that giving old patients infusions of blood plasma from younger patients, still rich in these proteins, doesn't just slow cognitive decline, it begins to reverse it."

Waterman thoughtfully pursed his lips.

"And not just the brain, other organs are affected, too, depending on the proteins. They can also roll back the clock on skin cells. Using a process called 'maturation phase transient reprogramming.'"

"When the hell did that happen?"

"The research has been going on for a long time. And slowly improving."

"I've never heard of it."

Rachel's gaze remained fixed, staring thoughtfully through the windshield. "Well, the world has been distracted for a while."

"So, what, you need to freeze someone to do all this stuff?" asked Waterman.

"You don't have to, but it's easier. Genetically speaking."

"Why is that?"

Rachel grinned. "When a person is frozen, all the body's functions are effectively paused. If you were a mechanic, would you rather work on an engine when it was off or while it was running?"

Waterman remained quiet for a long time, contemplating, until finally speaking again. "So what is it you think these people are planning to do?"

"I'm not sure, but if Henry and I are right about what we've found, destroying the lab is probably the first step. And soon."

"And you're saying John is what, evidence?"

"Exactly."

Waterman nodded. "And the odds?"

"What?"

"The odds," he repeated. "What are the odds?"

"Odds of what?"

"That you're right?"

Rachel turned forward, confused. "Uh . . ."

"You *have* calculated the odds?"

"How would I do that?"

The older man frowned. "I don't mean mathematically. I mean strategically."

"I don't understand."

"I'm talking about scenarios." He looked at her perplexed expression.

"What *else* could they be planning? What other scenarios are we looking at?"

"What do you mean, scenarios?"

"Things never happen the way you expect. Ever. So we need to think through the other outcomes. Just like playing chess."

When there was no answer, Waterman rolled his eyes. "Jesus, you *do* know what chess is, don't you?"

"Yes" said Rachel. "I know what chess is."

"Good. Then let's start going through them. Beginning with who you think is involved."

67

The searing Arizona sun was well into its afternoon descent, gradually stretching shadows as it shifted toward distant pink-and orange-hued desert mesas beneath the western horizon.

Everything in its path was subject to the same relentless, slow baking within the fumes of the parched afternoon air. Everything that was exposed. Which, in this case, did not include the room Robert Masten was sitting in.

A large ornate study, with floor-to-ceiling black-cherry bookcases, populated with thousands of perfectly arranged volumes. Everything from classics to rare and collectible manuscripts to sets of densely packed medical journals. All positioned in neat rows, spanning the width of the room.

Behind him, the outside wall was made entirely of glass. Thick and insulating. Covered by heavy, automated shades. Blocking and reflecting most of the afternoon heat and light, leaving the inside dark and cool. And quiet.

Almost ominous.

The only figure in the room was Masten himself. Slumped slightly in a high-backed leather chair, facing a desk and, beyond that, one of the room's vast bookcases.

Masten's solemn face was resting heavily against his right hand, supported by an elbow from the arm of the chair. His eyes staring forward as if he was in a trance.

No words. No mumbling. No movement of any kind except for a slow rise and fall of the man's chest as he breathed through his nose.

He had been there for hours.

Eventually, there was a soft knock on the door, which eased open when no answer came. Masten's wife, a petite, woman with perfectly kept blond hair, peeked inside and tried to catch his eye. He gave no response, and after a lengthy silence, she gave him a worried look before stepping back and easing the door closed again.

Masten appeared unaware of anything around him. Neither the richly decorated room nor the sunlight, moving in slow motion, errant rays passing through the shades like thin glowing daggers. Steadily growing dimmer as the hours passed. Along with the room.

The man could have been mistaken for dead had his chest stopped moving long enough. Or his eyes ceased blinking. But Masten was alive. Very much alive.

The room was noticeably darker when he finally moved. His chin rising just enough to let his right hand drop onto the leather arm. Then, from there, to a nearby desk drawer, where Masten briefly fingered the metal handle before opening the drawer in one smooth motion.

Inside were several items. Folders, papers, envelopes, pens, and so on. And to one side, a black nine-millimeter semiautomatic handgun. Loaded and chambered.

68

The mountains of eastern Utah were nothing like the images most people had of the state. Unlike the western half's vast stretches of dry, barren desert, the mountainous regions were much greener and lush, bursting with wildflowers throughout the spring, coloring giant swaths of the towering canyon walls. It gave the highlands a strikingly different feel. In fact, the farther east one traveled, the greener the world became, until one eventually reached Colorado and the famed Rocky Mountains.

Still in Utah, however, and just north of Ashley National Forest, lay a long and private open canyon, with moderately high ridgelines sheltering the valley on either side, the canyon floor, and within it a small, quaint lake. It was almost entirely isolated from the outside world, with the only visible signs of access being a single-lane road meandering beneath canopies of dense tree line. The lake was clean and unpolluted, reflecting a soft azure sky off an almost mirrorlike surface. Disturbed only by tiny ripples from the gentle breeze traveling over it.

It was colder than normal, near sixty degrees, when the helicopter appeared over a low point in the canyon's southern ridge before smoothly descending and heading directly toward a lone house constructed within throwing distance of the lake's edge.

The chopper paused its descent a mere hundred feet over the lake, hovering momentarily over the water's edge, before drifting downward and slightly forward over the moist sand, where it lowered itself the last several feet onto the soft ground.

It was a private aircraft. Based on the popular Bell 222, with the top half painted dark blue and its belly and skids a lighter, bluish gray.

Moments later, the passenger door was pushed open from the inside and Liam Duchik stepped out, placing a foot on a skid step before letting himself fall the last few feet onto the sand.

Unconcerned by the spinning rotors above, he continued forward—quickly and purposefully—toward the sprawling house, noting along his approach at least three partially obscured Secret Service agents.

Ascending the dozen or so steps, he stopped when he reached the gray-painted porch. Two people sat in chairs facing him, or more accurately, the pristine landscape behind him. They looked to be relaxing comfortably in patio furniture upholstered with an orange and yellow flower design.

The woman was thin, almost frail, and in her eighties. The slightly older man beside her was well-dressed, and smoking an unfiltered cigarette, casually allowing the smoke to stream from his nostrils as he exhaled.

Together, the couple gave Duchik a once-over before the woman spoke.

"You're late."

"I was delayed."

The woman nodded to a nearby chair, which Duchik pulled toward him and sat in.

"Well?"

He smiled. "We've arrived."

The older couple looked at him with surprise and then at one another.

"Arrived?" repeated the woman.

Duchik nodded.

The woman's eyebrows rose even higher. "Are you sure?"

"Reiff has stabilized. It's time to begin preparations."

The woman's expression filled with excitement, while the man's remained subdued. As though he was only moderately interested, or perhaps skeptical.

His wife noticed and shot him an irritated look—ending with a brief glance of disdain at the smoldering cigarette.

"What about the hallucinations?" she asked.

"They weren't hallucinations. Reiff checks out. It's time to move forward."

Indeed, it was. They were running out of time. And quickly. She looked again at her husband. The irony was almost sickening at times. Her condition was worse than his. And all he could do was sit and suck down those cancer sticks one after another, while she struggled every day to stay clean.

But she *was* clean. At least for the moment. Still in full remission, which made Duchik's news extraordinarily good timing.

She had to force herself to reel her enthusiasm back in. Thinking carefully, she said, "If they weren't hallucinations, what were they?"

There was no easy way to explain it. So he lied. "What he was experiencing . . . was lingering memories. Visions. From before his accident. Nothing of consequence. Or concern."

"You're sure about this?"

"Very."

The woman's excitement was visibly difficult to suppress. That it could finally be happening. After so much time and so much worry that she would not make it, that the cancer would return and consume her before they could be sure it worked.

The first step was to begin the therapy. Gene therapy, to begin modification of their DNA. Not much. Just to mimic what they had done with Reiff after he was pulled from the frozen river.

"It's time to get your things in order."

By "things" Duchik meant proceedings to formally bring their lives to a close, publicly and legally. The wrapping-up of financial and personal matters. Quietly and completely, without tipping anyone off.

After all, they were both high-ranking members of the new government. Their disappearance would be noticed by millions and therefore had to be very carefully orchestrated in the form of a sudden, tragic accident. Late at night, in one of their cars, which had already been mangled and destroyed and was now just waiting to be towed to the scene of the accident.

The accident reports were already written, save for a few last-minute changes to ensure that details were timely and consistent.

She never expected to feel guilt, and she didn't. She was one of the chosen, with power and prestige. Allowing her to understand and accept that some people were simply more meant to live. More important. More valuable to society. To history. To evolution.

It was her responsibility. Her gift—no, her obligation—to continue living in a world that needed her. That needed her skills. Her vision of where the world needed to go. She was one of the brightest and strongest, mentally speaking. And one of the most important.

Because if there was one true constant throughout the world and throughout history, it was the fact that true power was never liable to its abuses.

As an afterthought, her eyes drifted curiously back to Duchik. "And what about Reiff?"

The man shrugged. "You don't have to worry about that."

She nodded approvingly. Everyone had a role to play. And Reiff's contribution to humanity had been made. The last thing any of them needed now was loose ends.

69

John Reiff sat in the dark, quietly on his bed.

The grunts, as he called them, were no longer outside his door, and all the lights were off, even those in the hallway. There had been no more visits from the doctors. Or from Masten or the Lagner woman. All of this told Reiff that something had changed.

They were more interested in Reiff when he was sick and struggling. But why? As he grew healthier, that interest seemed to wane. The only conclusion was that he was not the sole focus of the project. But instead, the means to an end. An end that appeared to have little to do with him. Perhaps the reason Masten and Lagner had lied to him.

Reiff continued deliberating over everything that had happened since he'd first woken up in this room. He played it over and over again, but everything led him back to the same conclusion. That he—for whatever reason—had become expendable.

The irony was that it didn't matter why. In the end, there were far too many details that he didn't know. All he had was what he'd been told and dozens of scattered images in his brain. Not enough to make sense of it all. Nor enough to keep him trying to guess or understand. The only thing that mattered to him was what to do about it.

70

"Aren't you going to say something?"

Waterman's eyes remained steadfast, glued to the open highway in front of them. Baked and cracked asphalt disappearing in a blur beneath the hood of his truck as they sped forward.

He finally turned. "Huh?"

"You haven't said anything in over thirty minutes."

"I didn't know you were counting."

Rachel gave him a hard stare. "Well?"

"Well, what?"

"I've told you everything. What is our plan?"

"To get to Flagstaff."

She looked at him in surprise. "That's it?"

"Sorry, 'as soon as possible,'" added Waterman.

"That's *it*?"

He side-eyed her before focusing back on the road. "What is *your* plan?"

Rachel scoffed. "My plan? My plan was finding you!"

The older man shrugged. "Mission accomplished."

She sighed and shook her head. "When you grabbed your bag and said 'Let's go' I assumed you had a plan. And now all you can say is our plan is to *get there*?"

"Well, unless you have a better idea or a helicopter in your pocket . . ."

She raised a hand to her forehead in frustration. "You do *like* John Reiff, don't you?"

"We served together."

"That's not what I asked. Are you even worried about him?"

Waterman's eyes were narrow, peering thoughtfully ahead. "What exactly do you know about Reiff?"

"I told you, not much."

"Then tell me what you *do* know."

She stopped to think. "Like I said, he was in the army. Stationed—"

"Again, not what I'm asking."

"What are you asking then?"

"Did you actually ask Reiff what he did in the army?"

She blinked, trying to remember. "His file said he was in communications."

"Communications."

"Yes. A communications officer, I think."

"That's all. That's all it said?"

"That's all they told us, at least," said Rachel.

Waterman became quiet for a long minute. When he finally spoke, he simply said, "Then no."

"'Then no,'" Rachel echoed, confused. "Then no, *what?*"

"The answer to your question."

"Which question? Being friends or being worried?"

There was no response.

71

The younger grunt emerged from the men's room one floor above, finding his superior standing in the hall waiting. A phone to his ear.

Exchanging the last of a few words, the man ended the call. "It's time," he said. "They're pulling the plug on Reiff."

The younger man nodded.

His superior put the phone away and pulled a garrote from one of his pockets. Rotating one hand over another, he unwound the long thin wire attached on each end to a small metal handle.

Choking, though violent, was less messy. They had been ordered to keep things as clean as possible. In any possible future investigation, those in charge didn't want any unnecessary links back to them.

And unlike in the movies, a person rarely fought back when being choked. Instead, they focused almost entirely, and frantically, on the object around their neck and the restriction of their airflow—desperate to remove it—before losing consciousness.

Seven to fourteen seconds to lose consciousness. Then two more minutes for it all to be over.

The two men began walking, almost shoulder-to-shoulder. "You go in first," the older grunt said, finishing the unwinding and letting the thin wire fall loose into a U shape. "Keep him occupied, and I'll come in from behind."

The other man nodded. "We taking him out, too?"

"Yeah. The car's upstairs. We'll have to clean up after, so keep an eye out for any fluids."

"Got it."

"The lights in his room are off, so watch yourself."

Together, they emerged from the elevator and moved forward in strong, purposeful strides. Their footsteps grew softer as they approached in the darkened hallway, passing the lab before turning at the end toward Reiff's room. Pausing briefly outside the door, the older grunt allowed one end of the wire to dangle while he turned the handle. He then nodded and mouthed the words "One . . . two . . . three!" And pushed it open.

They rushed into the room, now illuminated in a faint ambient glow. They moved first toward the bed, where Reiff appeared to be sleeping. But only a few steps in, they knew it was a ruse. Pillows and blankets arranged beneath the sheets to resemble a body. The oldest trick in the book and almost laughingly amateurish.

They didn't take the bait, and instantly turned, searching for Reiff in the shadows. Most likely behind the door. Both men were fast and efficient. Moving in unison as though having rehearsed the attack. But they didn't have to. It was hardly their first time.

Reiff's diversion gained nothing. A few steps at most, and as many seconds, that was all. While the men now focused their attention behind the large open door.

There was nothing behind the door.

No shadows, no movement. Then they noticed the dim outline of light around the doorframe to the bathroom. And at the floor, a variance in the glowing light. Indicating movement on the other side of the door.

The younger man looked back at the other, who slowly unwound the garrote, gripping both metal handles tightly in each hand.

A confrontation was actually preferred. It kept their target distracted and focused on one attacker while the second came in from behind.

Once the wire was around his neck and cinched, it was effectively over. Complete panic would set it while the iron grip was maintained.

Seven to fourteen seconds.

In a fight, seconds either passed quickly in a blur or in slow motion, almost agonizingly so. It depended on the person. Some minds slowed while some sped up. It was genetic and largely instinctual.

They moved quickly, throwing the door open and rushing in with overwhelming force. But the bathroom was empty. Approximately eight feet by eight feet, with a toilet, sink, and open shower. The shower curtain had been torn from the overhead rod and was layered over the light fixture above. On the floor, a tall house plant, artificial. And propped awkwardly on top of the toilet's tank was an oscillating fan.

Slowly moving back and forth, fanning the plant and its large leaves. Giving the appearance of faint shadowy movement near the floor.

It took only a moment for them to realize what Reiff had done.

Their mistake wasn't just in seconds or steps; it was *instinct*. Not theirs, but his.

John Reiff was weak. There was no question. But not as weak as they thought. Neither Masten, Lagner, nor even the doctors Rachel and Perry. Because they had all failed to consider one possibility. That he was not always sleeping when his lights were off at night.

Instead, he was performing slow, deliberate, and soundless resistance exercises to test his various muscles. Legs, arms, feet, hands. Gauging not just strength but mobility. And speed. How well they could move. How well *he* could move.

Yes, he was weak and still recovering. But weak did not mean helpless.

When the two men turned away from the bed, they made three mistakes simultaneously. First was the assumption that Reiff was still powerless, and second was that he was not in the bed.

It was technically true. Reiff was not *in* the bed. Leaving only one other possibility. An oversight in their rush.

He was *behind it*.

The third mistake was timing. They'd relinquished only seconds to the ploy in the bed. And a few more waiting for their eyes to adjust while checking behind the door. By the time they noticed the movement beneath the bathroom door and rushed in, he had seized the moment.

Fourteen seconds was all the time he needed.

Rising and leaping from the far side of the bed, Reiff attacked the closest man, who was standing in the bathroom doorway and holding a garrote.

He judged his strength at no more than forty percent, which was a significant deficit. Coupled with the men's height, build, and age, it meant the only things Reiff had on his side were surprise and vulnerable areas.

Eyes, throat, groin, and knees. The four most vulnerable places on any person. Big or small, the weak spots were the same. And with men, the groin was a bonus.

Too much mass and it wouldn't matter how hard a person could hit. It simply wouldn't make a difference to a larger, stronger attacker. Hurt them, yes. Stop them, no.

Reiff's first strike was to the back of the man's right knee, causing the joint to bend awkwardly forward then out, taking the man directly to the floor. One end of the strangulation wire flailed from his right hand as he reached to brace his own fall against the hard floor and let out a thunderous howl.

As the man collapsed, Reiff followed him down, grasped the man's hair, and forced him back onto his feet, keeping him upright and wobbling. At the same time, he grabbed the garrote from the wavering left hand, and released the man's head. Snatching both handles, he coiled the wire tightly around the grunt's throat.

In a panic, the man immediately moved his fingers to his neck and grasped at the thin wire, desperate to get his fingertips beneath it to relieve the pressure.

The younger man had his back to the door, still studying the rotating fan, and stifled a laugh when his partner appeared to stumble to the floor. By the time he turned, the older man was already up again and rocking backward onto his feet, with John Reiff's face floating over his left shoulder like a phantom.

The younger man lunged but was stopped short when Reiff used his garrote to yank the older one to his left. Then to the right, using him, clumsily, as a shield while the man continued struggling and gasping for air.

Reaching behind himself, the young grunt drew a knife, military-issue with menacing stainless-steel blade and tip, visibly gleaming beneath the bright overhead bulb.

The man caught in Reiff's grip widened his bulging eyes and pushed out a hand. "Ngh—Ngh—" Sputtering, unable to form words. His free hand tried desperately to signal something.

But the young man was no longer paying attention. Instead, he darted right and left with the knife, barely missing the man's head as it flopped from side to side like a lollipop atop a broken stem.

Frustrated, he whirled, grasping the fan in one hand, and ripped it from the power socket. With the blade still spinning inside its metal cage, he threw it at Reiff, only to have him block it with the other man's head, knocking that man unconscious and causing his large frame to instantly crumple. Watching his superior collapse to the floor caused the young man only a moment's hesitation before he charged again.

Reiff was ready, with the uncoiled wire freed from the unconscious man's neck. Sidestepping, he pulled it taut, then wrapped it around the incoming knife and the hand holding it. Yanking the arm up and over his head to the right side, he forced it back across the man's chest and away from himself. Just as quickly, he let go of the garrote with one hand and thrust a thumb directly into the man's left eye socket.

The shriek was long and intense as the grunt grabbed at his face, the knife clattering on the floor.

Two floors above, the outside door opened, and three men stepped inside. All wore black fatigues and carried matching M4 carbines. They paused at the glass-walled security entrance and turned their weapons toward the building's horrified security guard, who—with mouth agape—promptly raised one shaking hand, while using the other to unlock the reinforced door in front of them.

The men immediately filed through, with the last of the three rushing forward and kicking open the guard's booth. Snaking inside, he forced the man down, then reached forward and ripped the security phone from its wall mount. Then, with one knee digging into the guard's spine, he swiftly raised the butt of his gun and brought it down violently into the back of the man's head.

It wasn't the most elegant of entrances, but it was the most prudent. Duchik was taking no chances, and neither were the men he hired.

He needed things wrapped up quietly and expediently. *Take out the guard and get to Reiff. Then Rachel Souza and Henry Yamada—as soon as they're located.* Other, less critical personnel were already being relieved or eliminated, whichever was necessary to ensure that the project disappeared as though it had never existed.

In the unmistakable words of Duchik himself, no one was to leave the building alive.

The elevator dinged, and the double doors slid open. With rifles raised, they rolled out one by one down the narrow corridor. They passed the larger double doors and continued to the end, where the hallway took a left turn. All three gliding together like a single black serpent.

It was just before the turn that the squad's leader slowed to a stop, becoming motionless less than a foot from the edge of the wall.

Listening.

There was no noise.

Duchik said he'd already sent two men he'd been using for a while. Men who now, according to Duchik, also knew too much, and would have to be eliminated with the others.

But the man listening sensed something wrong. It was too quiet, the hallway filled with dead calm. Inching closer to the corner, he tilted his head, allowing the side of his face and one eye to peer around the edge toward the end of the hall and the target's room.

The lighted hallway was empty and appeared undisturbed. The target's door remained closed. No sound. No sign of activity. No struggle. Nothing.

The merc listened for several more seconds before motioning to the others behind him to follow and quickly rounding the corner.

In smooth, methodical steps, they hugged the left wall, rifles raised and poised beneath each man's right eye until they reached the door, where the two men behind fanned out, filling the width of the hallway like a wall of death.

They stopped briefly in front of the door while the man in front reached out, wrapping a thinly gloved hand around the handle. It barely moved.

Locked.

He stepped back, thinking.

Either Duchik's men had already come and gone, or they hadn't arrived yet, which seemed odd. Duchik said they were already in motion from within the building. So, the likelihood of them not having already dealt with Reiff was low. But if they had, where were they?

The man glanced briefly at the other two over his shoulder and inched back again. Raising his weapon to eye level, he fired two rounds in a short burst, destroying the handle and door latch.

Immediately, he pushed the swinging door open. Mercs two and three covered him while he edged the muzzle of his weapon around the doorframe.

His sights moved up, side to side, then down again. Stopping on a shadowy object on the floor inside. A leg. Motionless.

Even combat perfection had its limitations.

Proficiency and experience practiced relentlessly were still inherently human actions. Subject to unexpected variables. Both mentally and physically. Endless considerations that could never be fully accounted for. Which was one of the brain's greatest assets and greatest liabilities.

No matter how much one practiced, the human brain, by its very nature, had a tendency to focus under stress. To narrow in on a target and tune out the rest. A prioritizing of sorts. Especially in a hallway where there was no place to hide in an emergency, forcing a person to move quickly and purposefully to avoid becoming a sitting duck. Which therefore brought stress . . . and tighter focus.

In their need to reach Reiff's door quickly through an open, vulnerable hallway, the three men had moved very fast, ultimately breaching the room in a matter of seconds. In their haste, what they had *not* noticed was the same thing they had already noticed multiple times. A utility closet, like the others they'd passed on their way in. Closed and locked. Presumably.

Except, in this case, a round knob and tiny keyhole that appeared to be horizontal instead of vertical. Or, to a more discerning eye, a knob that was twisted and being held in place from the inside of the door.

And now, the knob was slowly rotating back.

When the utility door slowly cracked open, it was just enough for a glint of light to enter. Then by another inch, allowing a larger sliver of light through.

In one sudden motion, the door swung outward, striking the closest man along his right arm and weapon. The man fired on reflex as he was knocked counterclockwise, striking the first merc standing in Reiff's open doorway and causing the man in the middle to jump and cover, slamming himself against the opposite wall.

The man firing regained control of his automatic and continued through the stumbling spin, finding his footing while turning to the door that hit him, just in time to see a flash of metal as a solid length of pipe crashed down on his weapon hand, breaking it. Then it swung up, making contact with the man's jaw with a sickening crunch.

The second mercenary, backed against the wall, fired at Reiff, who used the first as a human shield, the body absorbing two of the rounds before Reiff flung the pipe at the shooter's head.

Only seconds had passed and all three attackers were on the floor. Two unconscious, and the third badly hurt, with a gunshot wound to his back. The third man squirmed on the floor, groaning, and trying to right himself into position to aim his rifle.

Finding his target, he raised the M4 and opened fire a split second after Reiff leaped back behind the open metal door, pelting its surface with half a dozen rounds and leaving large indentations on the other side. Reiff stumbled and fell backward into the dark closet, leg outstretched to jam a foot against the door to keep it from slamming shut behind him.

Reiff opened the door just enough to reach out and grab the outstretched hand of the nearest man, pulling first the hand, then the arm, then the shoulder toward his closet. Protected behind the door until he was able to reach the unconscious man's rifle.

When he realized what Reiff was doing, the lead merc opened fire. Blasting several more rounds into the bottom of the door. Trying to pierce a hole through the door in an attempt to hit him before he gained control of the weapon. But it was after the barrage that the man on the floor noticed something else. Something at the end of the hall.

Still half in the closet, Reiff cringed at the second wave of gunfire. With one arm up to protect his head and his left hand grasping the muzzle of the rifle. Again, the metal door held—but it wouldn't take much more.

When the firing ceased, he lowered his arm and examined himself. Finding no blood and feeling no pain, he gripped the rifle with both hands and yanked it free of his unconscious assailant just before the third barrage sent him scurrying back.

But this time, nothing struck the door. Instead, the impacts were heard farther away, at the end of the hall.

Prompting Reiff to lean out and search.

At the end of the hall, the first two rounds pummeled the wall in almost two simultaneous explosions of drywall and dust. The next two bullets were direct hits. Striking their target, Robert Masten, through his right shoulder and chest.

72

Still behind the door for protection, Reiff rotated his carbine and blindly fired around the outside edge. Merely guessing at where the man was lying. He then paused, trying to listen through the deafening echoes reverberating in his ears.

When no shots came, he examined his own rifle and regripped it with his left hand. Mentally calculating how many bullets he had left. Standard M4 magazines held thirty rounds. With two releases of perhaps ten to twelve rounds total, he was at least half empty.

The last of the echoes faded within the walls, leaving behind an eerie silence beyond Reiff's ringing ears. But nothing that sounded like breathing or scraping over tiled flooring.

Slowly he pushed the door farther out, until he saw the third man's boot. He watched it, looking for any movement. Even a twitch. But there was nothing.

He pushed until the door revealed the man's lower body. Legs, waist, stomach, and, finally, a pool of blood. Then the man's rifle. On top of him and pointed down at the floor.

He was motionless. Like the others, but with eyes staring up at the ceiling. One of Reiff's shots had struck him under the left armpit.

Reiff let himself collapse, exhausted and in pain, from somewhere around his left foot. But he was alive.

He rolled and looked back down to the end of the hall, where Robert Masten was slouched and leaning forward. A streak of smeared blood on the wall behind him, following him down to the floor in an arc.

He was still breathing when Reiff managed to stand and stumble to the end of the hall, where he found a gun next to Masten's open hand. Not a single shot had been fired.

He managed to look up at Reiff with difficulty, sputtering and coughing blood as he spoke. "I . . . was coming to get you out."

The elevator dinged, and its doors opened on the ground floor to reveal a wobbling John Reiff supporting Masten beneath the man's outstretched arm. Masten's eyes were half closed and his body was covered in blood from the chest down.

Two people were waiting for them in the lobby.

With his right hand around Masten's waist, Reiff raised the handgun with his left and pointed. Blinking through bright sunlight filtering down through a row of overhead exterior windows, he squinted at the two figures before him. One was standing to the right, in what appeared to be a small booth, attending to something on the floor. The other was taller, facing Reiff and Masten from perhaps thirty feet away. With a gun aimed in their direction.

It took a few moments for Reiff to recognize Dr. Souza. The other person was an older man, tall, with a trimmed beard and mustache beneath a boonie hat—and something about him looked very familiar.

Features within the man's face finally crystallized, and Reiff recognized his old friend, now a much older Devin Waterman. Who was staring grimly at him and Masten.

Slowly, Waterman lowered his weapon and began walking forward. With every step closer, his eyes remained locked on Reiff's face until he came to a stop several feet away and studied Reiff from head to toe.

"I thought you would look better."

73

A smile crept across Reiff's worn face. "Look who's talking."

Behind them, a jittery Rachel Souza tried to control her breathing. Shaking, she turned when Henry Yamada burst through the front door and shouted "Oh my God!" at the scene before him.

Waterman stepped forward and took Masten's other arm over his shoulders, helping the man forward and into the center of the lobby.

"Only one exit wound," said Reiff. "The other must still be inside." He then watched as Rachel scrambled out of the booth and ran across the lobby, calling Yamada forward and ordering him to remove his shirt.

Together Reiff and Waterman eased Masten to the floor while Rachel tore the T-shirt in two pieces. She pressed a ball of cloth against each wound, eliciting loud groans from Masten.

"Robert, listen to me. I need you to stay still. Do you understand?"

He nodded painfully.

"We can't stay here," warned Reiff.

"We have to. We need to get him stabilized."

While she worked, Waterman looked up and over Masten with an inquisitive look, which Reiff answered with a simple nod. The threat belowground was not over.

"How long?" asked Waterman.

"Minutes."

The older man looked at Rachel, who was ripping open Masten's bloody shirt. "We have to go."

"I heard you!" she answered. "But we have to—"

"Lady, you don't understand. We *have to go.*"

She shot him a look. "I said—" But she stopped when she saw his face.

"If we don't, we may all be lying here in a few minutes."

She glanced at Reiff, who nodded in agreement and then examined Masten's bare chest. A sunken chest wound into a lung. "Okay, okay," she replied, trying to think. "Let's get him up carefully. Keep him upright."

She could see blood bubbling around the hole, indicating the air was getting inside, which could collapse the chest.

When the front doors burst open, Reiff's eyes weren't ready for full sun, and he quickly squeezed his eyes shut, while still trying to help carry Masten.

Slowly opening them again and stumbling, he spotted the blurry image of a pickup truck at the curb, with two more now arriving and men jumping out to help.

"Reinforcements," answered Waterman before Reiff could ask.

Two of the four men passed the group and provided cover with rifles aimed at the entrance while the rest rushed Masten to the lead truck, opening one of the doors and sliding him into the vehicle's rear king cab seat.

Rachel climbed in after him and pointed Yamada to the front passenger seat. "Help me get him into a sitting position," she said, trying to carefully lift Masten's frame. Yamada squeezed between the two front seats to help until they had Masten leaning against the opposite door.

Rachel quickly removed the bloody balls of ripped T-shirt and threw them to the floor. Grabbing one of Masten's own hands in the same motion, she flattened it and placed it over his chest wound. "Keep your hand right here; we have to seal it off from any outside air!"

With her hand on top of Masten's, she frantically looked around the inside of the truck. "We need something plastic, like a bag! Something airtight."

Yamada searched the area around himself, then pulled up the front seat's center console. "Nothing."

"Check the glove compartment!"

He dropped the small compartment door, rummaging inside until he found a thin plastic baggie holding what looked like the truck's registration information. "What about this?"

"Yes! Give it to me."

Using her mouth and one free hand, Rachel pulled it open and dumped the contents out. Then she lifted Masten's hand and placed the plastic smoothly over the hole. "Is there anything like tape in there?"

Yamada turned back to check. Finding none, he suddenly peered at the driver's door when it opened, and a large man began to climb in. "We need tape!"

The man, a few years older than Waterman, with long, gray frizzled hair pulled into a ponytail, glanced over the seat at Rachel and Masten. He nodded and disappeared from view, throwing open a lid to one of the truck's rear bed cabinets. He returned with half a roll of duct tape.

"Perfect!" Rachel motioned for the man to give it to Henry. "Rip me off four pieces! About five inches each."

While she waited, Rachel studied Masten's haggard face. His breathing was rapidly becoming more labored. "It's getting harder to breathe."

He nodded.

"Slow breaths, Robert. Slow breaths. And minimal talking."

Again, he nodded.

As Yamada began handing her strips of tape, Rachel worked to seal the plastic over the wound as she spoke aloud to Masten. "You're going to be okay. We need to keep any more air out to allow you to breathe." Two pieces of tape were in place, and she reached for a third. "The open hole is creating liquid in your lung. It shouldn't be fatal if we can keep you upright and keep the liquid at the bottom. Do you understand?"

He nodded.

"The wound to your shoulder isn't as severe. We'll tape some more cloth over it to stem the bleeding. Should give us plenty of time to reach a hospital."

Outside, Waterman led Reiff stumbling to his truck and pushed him inside. Then, finally, the two men squatting before the building stood and retreated to the third vehicle.

In less than ninety seconds, they were gone.

Reiff gripped the panic bar above his head when Waterman made a sharp right turn and accelerated to keep up.

"Where are we?"

"Flagstaff."

"Well, at least that much was true."

They passed through a large intersection, mostly empty, and continued as it narrowed into a two-lane street lined with trees, until slowing and turning again.

Maintaining a firm grip, Reiff looked out his side window, bouncing up and down in his seat while Waterman drove.

All three trucks sped from street to street as Reiff peered out in bewilderment. Studying each block as it raced past. Until finally turning to Waterman.

"Jesus."

74

Reiff gazed back through the window at what could only be described as squalor. Blocks and blocks of run-down buildings. Dingy and in disrepair, with papers and debris scattered along the sidewalks below patches of graffiti. Dozens of large, street-facing windows appeared dirtied and abandoned, with others boarded up. A few infrequent storefronts looked open but bereft of anyone resembling customers.

"What the hell happened?"

The older man squinted as he drove. "They didn't tell you."

"Tell me what?"

Waterman slowed the truck as they approached an area of road construction, where tall, skinny orange pylons littered the street in front of them. Sections of yellow construction tape could be seen, but as they drew nearer, Reiff saw the area more clearly. Much of the upturned pavement appeared abandoned. Discarded. With the pylons haphazardly positioned. Some were on the ground, and all connected to nothing more than tattered remnants of faded construction tape.

"This probably isn't the time."

"Time for what?!"

Waterman frowned. "A lot has happened, John."

"Is all of Flagstaff like this?"

Waterman turned to look at him. "It's not just Flagstaff."

Once out of the city, Waterman's voice came through the walkie-talkie. "How's our injured man doing?"

The driver of the truck grabbed his handheld unit and handed it back to Rachel. "He's okay," she replied. "Struggling to breathe but stable."

"Good. Can he last a couple hours?"

The situation was now manageable, leaving Rachel to look to Masten, who closed his eyes in pain but nodded. "As long as we end up at a hospital."

"Understood. Give me back to Wayne."

She complied and passed the walkie-talkie back over the seat, where her ponytailed driver took it. "Where we headed?"

"Kingman," answered Waterman. "The Blue Door."

"Roger that."

Behind them, Waterman noticed Reiff watching him and handed his old friend the walkie-talkie. "Encrypted with a range of only a mile or two. Perfect for short, confined communication."

"Why do you need 'confined' communication?"

"Arizona is a nontracking state. But it doesn't mean they don't still do it."

"Who?"

At that, Waterman smirked. "You haven't been asleep *that* long." He then turned and looked Reiff over. "You look like you haven't slept in days."

"I'm fine. What do you mean by 'a lot has happened.'"

His focus back on the highway, the older man said, "Tell you what, we've got two hours to Kingman. Get some rest, and then I'll explain everything. Believe me, you're going to want to be well rested."

A single set of footsteps echoed eerily through the long hallway, reverberating off the featureless walls with each step. Slowly. Carefully. Until both shoes came to a stop and remained still.

After several long seconds, a soft ruffling was heard, followed by a series of short electronic tones. *Dialing.* Then another short pause before Nora Lagner spoke.

"Reiff is gone. And he took Masten with him."

She continued to survey the scene in front of her. Two men were alive—dazed, but rising to their feet—while three others appeared dead. The two she had hired, and one of Duchik's mercenaries, lying motionless in the hallway in pool of blood, seeping from a wound she could not see.

"How long?"

"Ten minutes. Maybe less." She turned and looked at the blood-smeared wall at the end of the hallway. "He's hurt."

"How bad?"

"There's a mess on the wall. Like a bullet went through him. He might be dead."

On the other end of the phone, Duchik fell silent as he thought. *They wouldn't have taken Masten if he was dead. But depending on where he was hit, he could be in need of medical attention.*

"How much blood is on the floor?"

In the hallway, Lagner squinted and peered closer. "Not a lot."

Duchik clenched his teeth in frustration. "Get the video footage and bring in the cleaners. Wipe anything that could tie us to Reiff or Masten. Bodies, data, everything."

"And then?"

"Then restage. As planned."

He ended the call.

Duchik had considered the possibility of Masten surviving. But there wasn't a scenario in which the man ended up with Reiff. Fortunately, though, while Masten knew a little, he didn't know enough. It would have been better if he were dead, but in the end, it wouldn't derail anything.

On the other hand, if Masten was alive and Duchik could find him, it would most likely lead him to the others.

75

It was an eerie sight. Dark. Foreboding.

Looking down revealed a massive city. Towering buildings stretched in every direction until they disappeared into the shadows.

He was on a balcony, looking out at the streets below. Far below. Ensconced in total darkness.

The entire city was blacked out.

After he stared long enough, images began to appear. Shapes. Angled rectangles. First on the corners, then more as his eyes adjusted. Until he could see them everywhere.

Billboards. No, signs. Giant and dark. First tens, then hundreds of electronic screens. Resting silently. Featureless, around the bases of the cold, darkened skyscrapers.

And between them, in the streets, something appeared to be moving. Like rolling black waves billowing in various directions.

He squinted, attempting to discern what the movement was. It was too difficult to see through the twilight, but something was down there.

And then it came. Even before his eyes could see it. Like a cacophonic wave.

Yelling.

And screaming.

And crying.

All of it mixed together in a swirling wave of anguish and misery.

The movement his eyes could not make out . . . were crowds of people. Wailing from below, endlessly.

From the blackened city streets of downtown Tokyo.

76

Reiff's head rolled him awake when the truck slowed and made a right-hand turn into a driveway.

Opening his eyes, he spotted a dark sky overhead and a building in front of them, briefly illuminated as the truck's headlights swept over it, that could have been a hundred years old, if not more.

Its shape was wide and rounded, like a Quonset hut, with visible sections of missing stucco. It was connected to a large, squared entrance facing outward toward the street. By all appearances, the place resembled a run-down thrift store, with large blue block letters over a single-doored entrance, reading THE BLUE DOOR.

The appearance wasn't far off. It was an antique store. Less than a mile from Kingman's historic downtown, the oddly shaped building had a small private parking lot on its north side, made from thick, rough gravel, long ago having lost any trace of the original white parking lines. Now strewn with small pieces of rock and debris, the lot was wholly vacant when the first two trucks pulled in and stopped, while the third continued calmly around the corner and disappeared.

Near the back of the lot, Waterman shifted his truck into park and looked at John Reiff sitting up next to him. Marginally rested and staring silently through the dirty windshield.

Reiff glanced solemnly at his friend before opening his own door to climb out. Together he and Waterman moved to the first truck, whose passenger doors opened to reveal Rachel Souza and Henry Yamada as they exited. On the other side, their driver, known only as Wayne, opened the rear cab door to support Masten's upper half as he was lowered down.

Gathering on the driver's side, all five pulled Masten out horizontally and carefully, easing him down and onto his own feet.

"Can you walk?" asked Rachel.

Masten took a tentative step to gauge before nodding.

She and Yamada positioned themselves under each arm and helped him forward while Waterman moved to the side door of the building. A door that looked like it hadn't been painted in half a century.

He rapped on the hard wood and waited.

A few moments later, multiple locks were heard unlatching on the inside and the door opened inward to a darkened interior.

An elderly woman, pudgy with white hair, ushered them inside without hesitation, then quickly closed the door behind them and relocked the bolts.

With a brief glance toward the front of the store, she turned and moved in the opposite direction. Past a generously wide room in the back that resembled an oversized garage. Or a receiving area. Nearly filled from floor to ceiling with old furniture and various decorative pieces, all apparently waiting patiently to be restored.

They navigated through rows of odds and ends until reaching an even darker and narrower hallway leading to another outdated wooden door.

"I thought we were headed to a hospital," said Rachel, but she received only silence while the door was pulled open.

Inside, a narrow staircase descended into darkness until it suddenly lit up in brightness when the woman in front neared the bottom. When they reached the last stair, a giant metal door appeared before them with a sizable matching handle.

Waterman turned to Rachel and finally answered her with a wink. "Looks can be deceiving."

The old woman moved forward and grasped the steel handle, making a short movement with her hands they couldn't see, unlocking the door, and pulling it open, revealing an expansive and very well-lit room.

Once again turning sideways, Rachel led the adjoined Masten and Yamada inside to find an interior that looked very much like a medical facility. Or perhaps something more like a sick bay aboard an older military ship, without the crampedness.

Inside the room, a man and a woman stood waiting, both dressed in scrubs, and quickly assisted in getting Masten to a table.

Bright examination lights were wheeled closer and turned on, allowing them to study the wounds in detail, along with Rachel's plastic baggie stopgap solution to seal the open wound.

Together they pulled masks over their faces and began retrieving supplies from a cabinet beneath the table. The man suddenly turned to the others. "We have to expose the wound. Either sterilize or exit."

Back outside, the large door was closed again, leaving the remaining six standing at the foot of the wooden stairwell.

"Well done, Doctor," said Waterman, looking at Rachel.

She barely responded. "He should be fine," she murmured, "but he needs a needle decompression." Glancing at the others before adding, "A chest tube."

Waterman nodded. "Your friend should be safe here until we get back."

"Back from where?" asked Yamada.

"Someplace else."

Reiff shook his head. "Not yet." When everyone turned to face him, he said, "I'm not going anywhere until I know what the hell is happening."

The others, almost collectively, returned grim expressions but were interrupted by their host, who nodded up the stairway and simply said, "Furniture."

Standing next to Waterman, Wayne peered at Yamada and motioned for him to follow. "Come on, kid, we have some furniture to move."

"What?"

The man motioned again without comment, prompting Henry to turn to Rachel, who, to his surprise, nodded in agreement.

Yamada sighed. "Whatever. How much weirder can things get at this point?" With that, he followed Wayne and the old woman upstairs.

John Reiff watched them go. "Furniture?"

"It's part of the cover," Waterman answered. "Trucks draw far less attention if they're moving something."

"Like furniture."

"Correct." Waterman motioned to the bottom steps. "Why don't you have a seat?"

"I'll stand."

"Fine." The older man shrugged. "Then I'll have a seat." He planted himself on the third stair and eased back, staring at both John Reiff and Rachel Souza. "Where to start?"

"How about the beginning?"

He nodded and exhaled. "Do you remember the bus accident?"

"Pieces."

"At least that proves you were in it." Seeing a look of confusion on Reiff's face, he made a motion as if waving the comment away. "When you disappeared all those years ago, we had no idea what happened to you. Neither myself nor Mike McNamara. Hell, it was months before we even knew you were missing. And even then, it took Mike and me a long time to piece things together. Eventually, we figured out you were on that bus that crashed into the river. At least, that was our theory."

"What do you mean?"

"It wasn't exactly front-page news," said Waterman. "Not nationally anyway. And what news we did find didn't say anything about someone dying in the accident except the driver. Nor was your name mentioned at all. In the end, we discovered that you had simply been wiped from the record."

"Why?"

Waterman shrugged. "No idea. Maybe you can tell me."

"I don't know. I didn't do anything."

The older man seemed to grin to himself. "We've all done something."

"I'm telling you—"

"Relax. It's called humor. Besides, I don't know why you were omitted any more than you do." He then glanced at Rachel. "Maybe you might."

She stared back in a sudden look of surprise. "Me?"

Waterman's face turned back to Reiff, and he continued. "Mike and I eventually bribed someone to break in and get us your banking records and phone data. Once we had that, we placed you at an ATM the day before in Chicago. Then eventually put it together that you'd taken a bus for Sioux Falls. And then there was the convenience store. Remember any of that?"

Reiff tried to remember. "Vaguely."

"Well, the owner remembered you. Said you saved him on the night of the accident from some punk who was about to rob him."

"I don't remember."

Waterman shrugged and leaned onto the step behind him. "Doesn't matter."

"So that's how you found out I was on the bus."

"From the owner? No. He didn't know where you went. And I'm guessing you don't remember who else was in the store."

"No."

"No memory of a woman and her son?"

"No."

"Well, they were the ones who put you on the bus. And in the accident. They said you helped them get out. Before the whole thing sank."

Beside him, Rachel turned in amazement.

"I don't remember that."

"We found the woman and her son from a local news article. One of the only articles we found. She also tried to find out what happened to you, afterwards. At least who you were. But she never got anywhere either. Nice lady, though." Waterman leaned forward and rested his arms on bent knees. "You want to hear the details?"

"Of what, the accident?"

Waterman nodded.

Reiff shook his head. "Not particularly."

"Okay. Suffice it to say, you went down with the ship. And were never found or heard from again." Waterman then returned to Rachel: "Until our good doctor here showed up yesterday in Pahrump."

Both men turned to her. "I came," she said, "because John gave me your name."

"Yeah. After miraculously showing up in your lab twenty years later."

"Twenty-two," corrected Reiff.

"I-I already told you, both of you, I don't know how he got into our program."

"Convenient."

Her eyes widened. "What? No! I mean it. I don't know!"

"She doesn't," said Reiff.

"You sure about that?"

He nodded. "She'd have told us by now."

"Fine," said Waterman. "Then, if she doesn't know how maybe she knows *why*."

Rachel continued staring, slightly confused. "What do you mean?"

"I mean why," repeated Waterman. "Why do *you* think he was kidnapped?"

"I don't know."

"You have no idea?"

"No. I don't," she pleaded. "If I did, I would tell you."

The older man frowned. "No idea at all."

"My guess was that it was—that it had—something to do with his makeup. Some unique genetic traits, or something else." She nodded to the door in front of them. "Robert might know."

A few feet away, Reiff was thinking. "Whoever did this wouldn't have known anything about me, or my genetics, until after the accident. Certainly not nearly in time to begin covering things up."

"Unless it was all retroactive," offered Waterman. "Might explain how that small article was missed."

"But why would someone pull me out of the water—pull my body out—and randomly test it, for God knows what?"

"Maybe they already knew who you were."

"Doesn't make sense."

Waterman was about to reply when he noticed Rachel. Standing quietly with an uncomfortable look on her face.

"Doctor?"

Initially there was no answer, but her face slowly began to soften. With her eyes still wide, she turned to face Reiff.

"It's not you," she whispered.

"Huh?"

She glanced between them. "I don't think it's who he was. I mean who he is," she corrected. "I think it's what happened." She continued thinking. "Whoever did it may not have been after John specifically. They may have been after a particular event. Not event, more like a specific set of circumstances, or conditions."

"What do you mean?"

She went quiet again for several more seconds. "Do you remember our conversation about whether you died?"

Reiff nodded. "How could I forget?"

Rachel turned to Waterman. "It was an anomaly," she explained. "Not the accident. But how it happened. How John happened."

"Sorry, not following."

She brought both hands to her face as though trying to choose her words. "Listen to me. Cryogenics, or more accurately *cryonics*, is about preserving someone after they die. In hopes of bringing them back."

"You already explained that."

"No, no," said Rachel, holding up a finger. "What I'm saying is *after* they die."

"We get it."

"No, listen. Even today, cryonics labs are not allowed to freeze someone until they are pronounced dead. Medically and legally. In other words, you cannot *kill* someone in order to freeze them. You have to wait until they are officially deceased." Rachel took a step forward. "The problem, medically speaking, it that *that* is kind of too late. By then, the body is already in a state of deterioration. The cells, the tissues, the organs, have already gone too long without oxygen, without nutrients, and are already degenerating. Quickly. Even today, the process of freezing someone immediately after they're pronounced dead takes twenty to thirty minutes. Until all activity, all degeneration, stops. That means twenty to thirty minutes of your body beginning the process of breaking down. And twenty years ago, it was longer. Like two to three hours."

Again, she glanced between them. "The absolutely best case is to freeze someone *before* they die. Before the degeneration can begin. This is true now and it was especially true twenty-two years ago. Which is what may have happened to you, John. Like I said before . . . were you dead first, or were you frozen first?"

Reiff stared back at her. "You're saying they weren't after me."

"Maybe not."

"They were after someone who froze before they died."

Rachel nodded.

Several feet away, Waterman rose from the wooden stairs. "So, someone . . . was just waiting? For the right circumstances?"

"Maybe," she replied, "the *exact* right circumstances."

It was after a tense silence that Waterman turned to Reiff and grinned. "Guess you're not so special after all."

77

John Reiff lowered his head. "So again, a guinea pig."

There was no answer from the other two. Only a long, sympathetic calm. Until Waterman finally approached Reiff and dropped a hand on his friend's shoulder. "At least you're alive."

Rachel then reached out and took his hand in hers. "And we're here for you."

Reiff nodded in silence before raising his head again and turning to his friend. "Keep going."

Rachel looked at Waterman nervously. It was what she had wanted to tell John all along, but couldn't, for so many reasons. None of which alleviated the guilt she felt over it. Even the most well-intended reasons were often wrapped in a veil of cowardice.

She began to speak, but Waterman beat her to it.

"This might be tough to hear," he said, "so I'm just going to lay it out. Lord knows you've been through enough already." He paused momentarily before continuing. "After you were frozen the world went through a lot of bad shit. To put it simply. And nothing is what it used to be. Even all these years later." He returned to the steps and sat back down. "It started with the pandemic. Then came the wars. First by Russia, then by China."

"I was here for that."

"Right. What you weren't here for was the aftermath. Warfare has evolved. It's not at all what it used to be."

"What do you mean?"

"What I mean is physical warfare, army against army, on the battlefield. Men, rifles, tanks, planes. It's different now. Over the last few decades, it's morphed into something very different. And in some ways, much worse. Things like cyberwars. And financial wars. Just as devastating but all

happening behind the scenes, unseen by everyone except the governments involved. And they're *all* involved. Especially now."

"Cyber warfare isn't new," said Reiff. "It was going on well before—"

"I know," Waterman nodded. "It started with all the viruses and
state-sponsored hacking. Gradually evolving into things called 'Trojan
horses' and 'bots.' Things very few people understood before, but they
do now. In hindsight. Because once it all went underground and disappeared from public view, the wars not only became invisible, but the
results became even more devasting, and more rapid. In ways we could
not even have fathomed. Ways we couldn't even make sense of. Like a
tsunami you can't see."

Reiff stared back, blinking. "And financial wars?"

"The financial stuff had been going on for a long time, too. Decades,
really. Much longer than anyone realized or appreciated. With all the
countries around the world becoming more and more intertwined.
Not just in things like stock markets but entire economies. Currencies.
Commodities. Everything. Conjoined in millions of different ways
with one another. Virtually all countries, completely interdependent
upon one another." The older man breathed out. "And then came the
pandemic."

Reiff raised an eyebrow. "What did the pandemic have to do with
the financial system?"

"It was the tipping point," said Waterman. "Some say it was the match
that lit the financial tinder. Others say the straw that broke the camel's
back. When all major countries began printing money at once like there
was no tomorrow."

"I remember that, too."

"Then you remember it took time for the effects to arrive."

"You're talking about inflation."

Waterman glanced at Rachel as he continued. "What you don't
know is that the inflation came. And it came. And it came. It continued
coming. Sometimes it would look like it was getting better, but then it
would accelerate."

Reiff's stared at his friend. "What are you saying?"

"What I'm saying," said Waterman, "is that it *never* stopped. It just
kept building and building. Until eventually . . . the whole goddamn
system imploded."

78

Reiff looked puzzled. "What do you mean imploded?"

From the wooden staircase, Waterman rolled his eyes. "What does the word 'implode' mean to you?"

"The *world* imploded?"

The older man leaned forward again onto his knees. "There are smarter people who can explain the details better. But yes, that's the gist of it."

"And it didn't happen all at once," added Rachel.

"That's right. Like I said, in the beginning, most of us didn't know what was happening. But the casualties of the cyberwars slowly began to appear out of nowhere. Parts of the electrical grids shutting down. Water systems going offline. ATMs and credit-card transactions working one day and then failing the next. Then suddenly working again. Communications systems became increasingly more spotty, some days crashing altogether. Sometimes it felt like things were getting better only to have things start falling apart again. Then, eventually, came the financial wars."

The older man met Rachel's eyes through the dim lighting; she frowned and nodded.

"Then money started disappearing. ATMs were already unreliable, so at first, people thought that's all it was. By then, internet access was no better than anything else. But when people did manage to get online, their bank accounts were either not accurate or locked. Parts of the economy started freezing up. And people, even corporations, began going bankrupt in huge numbers. By then store shelves were already mostly empty. And then . . . came the *sovereign wave*."

"Sovereign wave?"

"That's what they call it. Sovereign as in 'countries.' The corporate bankruptcy waves were bad enough, especially with millions losing their jobs. But when entire *nations* began rolling over, it was pure chaos. First small nations. Deep in debt and leveraged. Then progressively larger countries. Until it reached the big ones. Brazil, Argentina, Italy—"

Reiff's eyes widened. "Italy?"

Waterman continued. "Britain . . . Japan . . ."

"Good God."

"Turns out there was a limit to how much money the world could print. And when one country would collapse, it would panic and start selling their bonds from other countries, causing them to collapse, too, and so on and so on, like dominoes. All connected. Some collapses were less severe. But sooner or later, they all went down."

"And no one understood why," added Rachel.

"Because it's hard to learn the truth when everyone is blaming each other. We blamed the Chinese. The Chinese blamed Japan. The Japanese blamed Europe. They blamed Russia. And Russia blamed us."

"When exactly did all this happen?"

A weary Waterman motioned to Rachel, who replied, "The worst of it was just over thirteen years ago. What everyone calls 'the Great Collapse.' Which then gave way to 'the Great Struggle.'"

"The Great Struggle?"

She hesitated. "A lot of people didn't survive the collapse."

Reiff squinted. "What do you mean, like starvation?"

"That was part of it, yes. But other people . . . just . . . couldn't accept what was happening. That everything could be wiped out so completely and so quickly. In a matter of months."

"Or in some cases, days," quipped Waterman.

Reiff looked at him. "When you say they couldn't accept it . . ."

"They popped," he replied simply. "Mentally. They went crazy."

"Some people became depressed," said Rachel, "even suicidal."

Waterman frowned. "Some?"

"A lot."

"Others took another approach," he said, "and got violent. Pillaging and rioting in giant mobs. Going from place to place, stripping it clean. Buildings, stores, farms, of any resources they could find."

"That went on for a long time," sighed Rachel. "Years."

Reiff's eyes widened. "Years?"

Waterman stood back up. "There was no one to stop them."

"What about the police, or the government?"

"The government was in shambles. Every government was. And police officers were more worried about keeping their own families safe than protecting the public, which they couldn't stop anyway." He approached Reiff again. "Like I said, a lot of bad shit went down. A lot of people didn't make it through all of it. For a lot of different reasons. Hell, in a lot of ways 'starvation' meant you at least survived through the worst of it."

Reiff's face grew solemn. Bleak. As he tried to grasp everything they'd said. "So, the Great Struggle—"

"Has been the last several years," answered Waterman. "With all of us trying to dig ourselves out of that damn hole. Back to an existence beyond just living hand to mouth. And let me tell you, it's been one difficult climb."

After several minutes, Reiff took Waterman's spot on the steps. Listless and silent, staring at the old, cracked concrete floor in front of him. With Devin Waterman and Rachel Souza standing before him in silence. Waiting. Watching as he tried to process it all.

To their surprise, Reiff seemed to take it better than they expected. Staring absently while slowly wringing his hands in front of him.

"We *are* recovering," Rachel finally offered.

Reiff nodded without looking up. When he finally did, he asked, "Why am I here?"

The two looked at each other. "Huh?"

"Why . . . am I here?" he said again.

"Didn't we just go over that?"

Reiff shook his head. "If things are so difficult. If the world is such a wreck. Why am I here?"

"Like Rachel said, we've been slowly recovering for years. But things are different. Sound money with lots of bartering. Each country wants real things in trade. Not a bunch of paper promises. Japan wants oil for their microchips. China wants real things for their . . . well, pretty much everything."

"That's my point," said Reiff, looking to Rachel. "If resources are so precious, why did you spend so much of it building the lab, and bringing me back?"

It was a good point. One that prompted Waterman to also stare curiously at Rachel.

"I . . . I didn't have anything to do with that. I just needed a job."
When neither man responded, she grew more emphatic. "I'm serious!"

"What did Masten pay you with," asked Reiff sarcastically, "chick-
ens?"

"Things aren't *that* bad."

He shrugged. "All the resources and the technology needed to build
that lab must have been damn expensive. Money that no doubt could
have been put to better use elsewhere."

"That's true."

"If it's true," said Reiff, taking his question to the next logical step,
"if I *am* a guinea pig . . . then *who* am I a guinea pig for?"

It was a question that seemed to suck the air right out of the small,
dank room. Leaving all three staring at one another. Until, almost in
unison, all three turned and faced the large metal door behind them.

"Something tells me," said Waterman, "that your man in there
knows who."

Returning to the top of the stairs and going back into the crowded
aisles of the antique store, Waterman carefully eased the hidden door
closed and turned to find Henry Yamada approaching.

When the young engineer stopped, he tilted his head sarcastically.
"Well, that was convenient. We're done with the furniture."

Rachel gave a wry grin and imitated Waterman's voice. "It's part of
the ruse."

"What ruse?"

"Forget it," snorted Waterman. "It's time to leave."

"What about Masten?"

"He should be okay with some rest," replied Rachel. "But apparently we're not safe here."

Waterman shook. "I didn't say we're not safe. I said we should get to
a *safer* place."

"Like where?"

"It's about thirty miles from here. We'll come back tomorrow to talk
to your boss."

With little else to say, Yamada watched the others pass by before
falling in behind them. Together they wound their way through the
narrow aisles back to the side entrance, where the elderly woman was
waiting.

She and Waterman exchanged a few quiet words before he opened the door and stuck his head out. Finding his friend Wayne waiting by the trucks, he waited briefly for a signal before ushering the others forward into the warm night air.

79

The hallways were empty again. And clean. Without so much as a bullet hole or discoloration on the tile floor. The four-person team, escorted by Nora Lagner, was nearly finished. They had become exceedingly adept at patching walls and removing bloodstains from virtually any surface, hard or soft.

Dressed head to toe in white jumpsuits with accompanying goggles, gloves, and booties, the team was finishing a rapid cleanse of both laboratory levels, including the cleaning and/or removal of all computerized devices containing any compromising onsite data.

It wasn't foolproof by any means. A rapid cleanse removed only what was visible to the human eye, without using special instrumentation. A forensics team could most certainly find telltale signs of what had happened there, but it would have to do for now until Lagner and Duchik could arrange a more thorough job. But a rapid cleanse should get them past any visits from local authorities.

The dead guard in the lobby had already been disposed of. More than enough time to a arrange a deep clean, before abandoning the facility altogether.

Soon after, the maintenance door at the rear of the building was opened and all four cleaners exited—walking briskly to a nondescript van, into which they loaded their large bags, and then themselves. The entire operation was entirely without comment.

Lagner could not help but be impressed with their efficiency and wondered what other sorts of connections Liam Duchik had up his sleeve.

But her curiosity was fleeting. In the end, she didn't care. Over the years she'd learned that asking lots of questions wasn't wise. A lesson Perry Williams had learned the hard way.

Upon closing and locking the heavy door, she turned and paused. Listening. Satisfied, she remained at the end of the hallway, where she retrieved her phone and called in an update.

"Yes?"

"It's done," reported Lagner. "We're clean."

"Give it one more pass. Especially Masten's office and desk. Take anything that might connect him."

"I will."

Duchik ended the call and returned the phone to his pocket, stepping out of the hallway and redirecting his attention into the brightly lit bedroom. In it, the Hustons were lying side by side on separate beds being attended to by nurses. They reclined with opposing arms extended; a clear plastic IV tubing ran from each wrinkled elbow up to its own infusion pump, and a light pink solution was being carefully monitored.

The first phase was the incubation. Chemical stimulation of the cells to help induce absorption of the upcoming gene therapies. Eight in total, over the course of the next fourteen days. A series of successive genetic Cas9 enzyme payloads, each having to be administered, tested, and verified stable before the next application. Meticulously designed not to interfere with each other in their somatic cell modifications.

Nucleotides and nucleotide clusters had an unfortunate habit of overlapping with one another. Relationships that had taken decades to identify and properly isolate.

From the opposite side of the room, Duchik noticed the woman staring at him from her bed. Her eyes fixed intently upon his. Clear, trusting, and eager.

Arthur and Donna Huston were the perfect candidates. At least, as perfect as Duchik could find. Both members of the New Congress and multiple oversight committees. Powerful and influential enough to get Duchik what he needed over the years. Not just to build the lab, but to fund some of the technological research necessary to finally achieve what they had.

Even more importantly, they were desperate.

Both were in their eighties and suffering from numerous maladies. Representative Donna Huston had endured three battles with cancer, and progressively more difficult chemotherapies. The last one had nearly killed her instead of the cancer.

Now she was in remission. At least for the time being. And she was old enough and wise enough to know that a fourth diagnosis would likely be her last. A true saving grace, because the remission was the only thing allowing her to remain strong enough to tolerate Duchik's gene therapy. Assuming she did survive.

Survivability of the regimen was already a risk factor for someone her age. And if she still had the cancer, the genetic changes would merely hasten her death by turbocharging the disease itself. Creating supercancer cells. It was the reason Donna Huston was truly terrified of the disease returning. Not only would it kill her, but it would destroy any chance she had of benefiting from the private research she had helped fund for so many years.

Contrary to her own battles, the woman's husband could not have been more different. While of similar age, he seemed utterly indifferent to what they were trying to do. At best apathetic, at worst flagrantly contemptuous. And Duchik understood why. The man had lived his life in a way some might characterize as a true politician. Greedy. Narcissistic. A boozer. A womanizer. Living a life of sin beneath a veil of public grace that left many confounded as to how he, and some others, managed to get reelected time and time again. Repeatedly entangled in scandal after scandal, only to reemerge before each election with an outlandish surge of charisma and charm. A bizarre savvy instinct that could simply never be taught. In many ways, a true throwback to the politicians of yore, living large on the backs of constituents that never saw them for who they really were.

Arthur Huston had lived a life of extravagance and grift. Excess and self-gratification few would ever experience. In many respects he had done it all. No, in every respect. Worn and tattered, the man was prepared to finish his life with no regrets. Nothing left to do. No thirst left unquenched.

Fitting, given that his body was now riddled with its own diseases. Liver disease, sky-high blood pressure, cholesterol, chronic inflamation, cataracts, neuropathy. The man was a walking poster boy of abuse to the human body. Or a shining example of how to truly go out with the proverbial bang.

Or maybe it was the thought of spending another eighty years with the woman he'd already endured for so long that left him indifferent to Duchik's *experiment*.

As for Duchik, he didn't care what the man's reasons were. He simply needed a male subject. Arthur Huston might not have been desperate, but his body certainly was.

Because in the end, while John Reiff might have been *their* guinea pig, the Hustons were Duchik's guinea pigs.

80

Rachel sat on a wooden chair, staring a framed watercolor painting of wildflowers and southwestern hillside on the bedroom wall. After everything that had happened since she'd found Perry, it was the first time she'd had a chance to just think.

Below the picture and next to the door stood a waist-high handmade dresser. Likely generations old, judging from the nicks and marring.

There was a knock on the door, snapping Rachel out of her trance.

Her eyes blinked back to attention as she rose from the chair, quickly crossing the room but then opening the door just enough to peek out.

Abruptly, she yanked the door wide and reached forward, grabbing Henry Yamada by the front of his shirt and pulling him inside. The sudden movement caused him to drop the ceramic plate of sandwiches he was holding, while Rachel quickly shut the door again.

"What the hell?" snapped Yamada. He stared down at the food strewn across the floor. "That was for you."

"It took you long enough!"

"What—"

"Listen to me," she interrupted. "We have a problem. A *serious* problem!"

"Good grief, what now?"

She rubbed her hands over her face while turning and crossing the room again. Falling back down into the wooden chair. "We're in trouble, Henry."

He frowned, sarcastically. "You don't say."

She peered up at him, as if momentarily confused, before shaking her head. "Not about being on the run," she said. "I'm talking about John."

Yamada's frown faded and he glanced backward at the closed door. "What is it?"

Rachel bit her bottom lip. "Can you get back into the lab? Remotely?"

"Are you nuts?"

"I mean without anyone knowing."

"Uh, no!"

"You're sure?"

Yamada furrowed his brow. "What the hell's going on, Rach?"

"Remember before all this happened, when I had you run through all your data for me?"

He lowered his head, thinking. "Which data?"

"On the animals!"

"Oh right. Yeah, I remember."

"I need to know what's going on with them."

"What's going on with the animals?"

"Yes."

Yamada stepped back and took a long look at her. "You understand *where* we are, right? And *why* we're here."

Rachel responded by rolling her eyes. "Yes."

"Good, because for a second I thought maybe you hit your head or something."

"I'm not kidding, Henry."

"Neither am I. You're not making any sense."

From the chair, she took another breath, this time exhaling more slowly. "Do you have any idea if the animals are still there?"

"I don't. I thought they were supposed to be transferred."

"They were. Yesterday. But then everything happened."

"Why do you need access to the animals?"

"Because of what was happening," she answered. "Before. Remember?"

He thought it over. "You talking about the mice that died?"

Rachel rose back to her feet. "It wasn't just the mice. Something else was happening. To all of them. Starting with the mice, and then the rabbits." She stared nervously at him. "They were dying, Henry."

"Why were they dying?"

"I don't know. That's what I was trying to figure out. But I didn't have time."

"So, you're worried whether they're still alive?"

Rachel briefly closed her eyes in frustration. "No. Well . . . yes." She sighed. "Something strange was happening to them. At first, I just thought it was coincidence. Mice have short life spans. So it was possible there was some overlap in—" She paused, realizing that bit didn't matter. "But then the rabbits started. And it wasn't just that they were dying. It was *how*."

"What do you mean?"

"They were cold," said Rachel. "Not just a normal dead temperature, but *cold*. Unusually cold."

Yamada shrugged. "What does that mean?"

There was no answer.

"Rach?

Her eyes turned back to him.

"What does 'unusually' cold mean?"

"When something dies, like an animal, its body loses heat. Slowly, until it reaches the ambient temperature. Which is why it feels cold." She shook her head. "This wasn't like that."

"Then what was it?"

"I don't know. But it wasn't normal. Which means neither was their death. That I'm sure of."

"So, what do you think was happening?"

"I don't know." She shook her head nervously. "I'm afraid to guess."

"Okay. So what does this have to do with us right now?"

Rachel closed her eyes again and remained silent. What Yamada didn't know was just how bad her insides were churning. She felt sick to her stomach. Like she was going to throw up.

"Rachel?"

She swallowed hard, trying to suppress the reflex.

Concerned, Yamada put his hands on her shoulders. "Rachel? Are you okay?"

She continued swallowing, managing to stave it off. And after a long pause, she finally said, "An hour ago, when we were in the basement under that shop. Devin and I were talking to John. Explaining things. And to a certain extent, consoling him. I reached out and took his hands." She reached up and pulled Yamada's hands from each shoulder and brought them together. "Like this."

"Okay."

"I held them just like this."

"And?"

The reflex was coming back. And she fought to force it back down. "And they were cold," she finally said. "They were *unusually* cold."

81

Outside, beneath a star-filled sky, John Reiff's hands were wrapped around a large mug of steaming black coffee. He watched the faint vapor trail rise from the dark liquid and slowly disappear in front of him. Reddish dirt riddled with a scattering of bushes and trees stretched off into the darkness beyond the glow of the deck lights. Far in the distance, beneath the last glimmer of receding sunset, the outline of a distant mesa could still be seen.

"She's okay," said Waterman matter-of-factly, finally breaking the silence.

Reiff turned and looked at his friend, who was sitting in a sturdy rocking chair. Then, instinctively, he let his head fall in relief.

"I didn't want to say in front of the others," said Waterman, "but she's in Santa Fe now, and has a family. Married. With a boy and a girl."

Reiff's eyes were closed while he listened.

"And Karen?"

Waterman didn't reply immediately. "She didn't make it."

Reiff nodded and raised his head back up.

"Like a lot of people, she lost everything, and eventually fell in with a bad crowd—and drugs."

Reiff raised a hand. "Don't tell me the rest." Then, after some contemplation, he asked, "Does Elizabeth know?"

"About her mom? Yeah. She tried to help her." Waterman shrugged sympathetically. "But things were hard. At that point everyone was just trying to survive."

Reiff looked out into the darkness. "When was the last time you saw her?"

"Elizabeth? Maybe six months ago. I try to check in when I can. Her husband's a good man."

"Yeah?"

He nodded. "She could have done a lot worse. A hell of a lot worse."

Reiff watched as the last sliver of sunset finally disappeared, darkening the rest of the horizon. "Is she happy?"

"As far as I can tell. I know it hurts her to see me sometimes, but I don't take it personally." After a sip of his coffee, he added, "I was at the funeral."

Reiff turned.

"That's right." His friend nodded, beneath the glow of the porch light. "We had a funeral."

"When?"

"A few years later. It was a big river, and your body was never found. Eventually the state declared you dead." He sipped again.

Reiff gazed down at the coffee cup in his own hands.

"You should probably know something else."

"What's that?"

"I think Elizabeth blamed herself for your accident. At least in part."

Reiff's expression twisted into a mix of surprise and pain. "What? Why?"

"Because you were on your way to see her when it happened. I tried to convince her it wasn't connected but she was young, and she was devastated. I don't think I was successful."

"Jesus."

"I don't think Jesus could have convinced her either," joked Waterman. "I wanted to mention that because you might want to give some thought as to how you contact or approach her."

Reiff looked away, letting the words sink in. Then, eventually, he changed the subject. His eyes focused on the porch and then the sliding glass door to the house. "So, what is this place?"

"Just a friend's house."

"Just a friend?"

"One of many," said Waterman. "A lot has changed, but a lot hasn't. The New Government isn't any better than the last. Always trying to fix things in a way that doesn't interfere with their political agendas, but in the end, they just make things worse. Like someone who breaks your leg and then says, 'Don't you appreciate the crutches I gave you?'"

Reiff grinned. "The more things change, the more they stay the same."

"You can say that again."

"How many 'friends' are out there?"

"It's referred to as 'the Network.' Which is simple enough, and there's a lot of us. No one knows for sure. But there are a hell of a lot of people out there who are tired of the government's bullshit. They just want to be left alone. So, we do what we can to help each other, and keep a low profile."

"With walkie-talkies?"

Waterman nodded. "A lot of the government's spy technology was destroyed during the cyberwars. But they still have some, so we have to be careful." After a moment, he tilted forward and rose from the rocking chair. "Speaking of which . . . there's something else we should talk about." He approached and pointed at Reiff's head.

"What?"

"Rachel told me about those pictures, or drawings, or whatever they are."

Reiff simply stared back at him without speaking.

"She said it's what made her realize she had to get you out of that place. And to find me."

"I don't know what the pictures are. Or what they mean."

Waterman stood a few feet away and leaned casually against the railing. "Oh, I think you do."

"Excuse me?"

Waterman studied Reiff's face. "I've known you a long time, John. At least before the accident. Enough to know your reaction may have fooled Rachel, but it didn't fool me. In that basement."

"Meaning what?"

"Meaning . . . that when we were explaining everything, like what had happened while you were frozen, you didn't seem quite as surprised as one might think. And certainly not shocked."

"I guess I'm getting used to this kind of news."

The older man let out a broad smile. "No doubt. But I know acting when I see it."

There was no answer.

"From what I hear about your drawings, I'm guessing you already knew some of what happened. I have no idea how and neither does Rachel, but my gut tells me that some of what she and I were explaining was not a surprise to you at all."

Again, there was no reaction from Reiff.

"And remember," continued Waterman, "they may not know what

you really did in the army, but I do." His smile became mocking. "Mr. Communications Officer."

Reiff stared at him. "I was a communications officer."

"Yeah, and I was just a soldier." He took another step forward, still studying Reiff. "God only knows what's going through that head of yours, but I don't like being lied to. And believe you me, this is not the time to turn inward."

Reiff continued staring, until after a long silence he said, "Being with me isn't safe, Devin."

"Tell me something I don't know."

"I'm serious," he replied. "I'm a liability to whoever is behind this. And therefore, whoever I'm with."

"And why is that?"

"Because I know things."

82

The building was located eight miles west of downtown Salt Lake City. Four stories tall and standing alone on West Amelia Earhart Drive. Painted in a dark beige hue, it appeared even darker beneath the empty night sky.

Salt Lake's former FBI headquarters was a shell of its former self. As were many other government departments across the country. All were gutted physically and financially from the collapse, leaving the Salt Lake location to now house several different government entities at once. Some familiar and some not.

The main entrance, positioned under a large overhang, was moderately lit, and quiet when the Mercedes approached from one side of the long circular drive. It stopped as the only car in front, and the driver's-side door was hastily flung open.

Dressed in a wool coat and dark pants, Duchik climbed out and slammed the door behind him without looking back. In a forceful stride, he approached and pressed a badge against the glass sensor located to the right of the oversized double glass doors. Just long enough to hear the door's internal locking mechanism disengage.

Once inside, he walked to the elevator and rode it to the fourth floor, where in the same quick stride he passed several offices until reaching an unmarked door near the end of the hall. Once again, he used his badge to enter, stepping into a large, almost empty office space.

Duchik waited until someone rolled their chair back and looked out through an open doorway.

"You Duchik?"

"Yeah."

The other man motioned Duchik forward and rolled back out of sight.

Once inside, the man motioned for Duchik to close the door, and grabbed a thick folder from his desk, but held on to it as he studied the image on Duchik's badge.

"First, you are aware that Arizona is a nontracking state, correct?"

"I am."

"Okay." The man nodded and flipped the folder open. "As long as you know."

Duchik did not care about Arizona's laws. Nor did he like having to outsource some of his intelligence gathering. But the NIH didn't have its own cybersecurity department. Entire departments had been re-shuffled over the years to eliminate administrative overlap, which also had the unfortunate side effect of leaving operational holes in other areas. The more Duchik had to employ services outside of his inner circle, the more risk he assumed as a result by way of exposure.

"I printed out most of the information you wanted on Rachel Souza and Henry Yamada. Home addresses, phone numbers, financial in-formation, and travel habits. Some of which I'm guessing you already have. . . ."

"Did you track their phones?"

"I tried. They're both turned off. Their last recorded locations were together, outside of Las Vegas." The analyst searched for a printed map and, upon finding it, placed it on top to show Duchik. "Both cars have been located. Souza's in an empty parking lot in downtown Flag-staff and Yamada's a couple blocks away from the address you gave me of the lab."

Duchik continued listening with no reaction.

"In addition to their addresses, I've also provided the addresses of Souza's parents near Portland, Maine, and Yamada's mother in San Francisco. Don't think you'll need those, though." The man then spun back around to face his computer screen. "You said you wanted a fix on some trucks."

"Yes."

A window was opened on the screen, and the analyst commenced typing in a flurry of keystrokes. "Well, from the security-camera foot-age I have, it looks like they were onsite when your convoy left."

Inside the window, another image from an overhead satellite ap-peared and, a few moments later, began zooming in. Accelerating as it enlarged the country's southwestern terrain and then gradually slowed as Flagstaff's tiny city streets became visible and filled the screen. Until finally, the zoom slowed to a crawl and began to scroll, moving just outside the downtown area until revealing the location of Duchik's laboratory.

The exterior of the building was now clearly visible, as was the street, including the three large pickup trucks.

Freezing the image onscreen, the analyst pointed. "These are the trucks?"

"Yes."

He nodded and noted the time. "Time is three twelve P.M. and seven seconds. Commencing playback."

Standing in the small office behind the younger man, Duchik watched the scene unfold. Similar to what he'd seen from his own cameras, but this time from overhead. Doors on the trucks opening, and men with rifles jumping out. Rushing forward as Reiff and the others emerged. Souza, Yamada, Masten, and one of the other men, who had previously disappeared inside with Souza.

Together, the group proceeded toward the trucks, followed by their armed escorts, until all three vehicles were boarded and sped away.

"I can't make out a positive ID from overhead, but I believe two of those in the video were Souza and Yamada."

Duchik nodded.

"If true, you're not going to find them in California or Maine."

"What else?"

As though in response, the analyst clicked on each truck as they began moving in the video and the overhead image automatically zoomed back. Shrinking the area slightly while highlighting the three targets in a pale yellow.

Together, both men watched the vehicles turn and move quickly through city streets, making their way through multiple intersections until eventually reaching a freeway on-ramp.

The young man turned in his seat to face Duchik. "This part is a little boring. They stay on Interstate 40 almost the entire time until reaching Kingman a couple hours later."

"And then where?"

"That's where it becomes a problem. Because it gets dark."

Duchik squinted. "What do you mean?"

"Unfortunately, we don't have the same infinite recording capabilities like the old days, and this satellite doesn't have thermal imaging, so it's harder to track objects at night. Especially moving objects. We have to rely on things like headlights and ambient reflections to maintain a target."

"Fine."

The analyst frowned. "That's also where we have trouble."

"Why?"

"Because these three trucks turned off their lights just before reaching Kingman."

Duchik's eyes narrowed.

The analyst sped through the recording before slowing down again near the end. In the darkened video, Duchik watched as the bright headlights from all three vehicles disappeared almost at once.

He stared in irritation. "So, what, that's it?!"

"Just for the moment. We can use some AI to compute likelihood from the point we lose them. Basically, a range of possibilities given speed, distance, most likely direction, and possible interaction with other cars. But that takes time as the computer crunches through all the possibilities."

"How much time?"

"I've already started the process, so hopefully not more than a few hours. The good news is that it's pretty accurate and should be able to reduce it down to just a few prospects."

Duchik continued staring at the screen while he crossed his arms. After another few minutes, he said, "Anything else?"

"A few things," the man replied. "For one, while it can be a challenge to figure out where the vehicles went, that doesn't mean we can't still track backward to find out where they came from."

Duchik's eyes suddenly jumped from the computer screen. "Where?"

"Nevada. Just outside Vegas. From three different residences. One in Pahrump and two in Henderson. Along with Henry Yamada's car in tow." The analyst opened another window and another video showing Duchik. "Their first stop was at a small house in Pahrump. Belonging to a Devin Waterman, which matches the name in Rachel Souza's email that you forwarded."

"Who is he?"

The analyst tapped the folder. "I printed his information out. Waterman is retired army, as are the owners of the other two trucks."

What connection would Souza and Yamada have to these retirement-aged vets?

"Did they go to all three houses?"

"Yamada and Souza? No, just the one. The two other trucks met them en route back to Flagstaff."

So they went to Waterman, and Waterman called the others. Duchik continued to think it through. It was Waterman and his friends who helped rescue Reiff. *But why?* What were Souza and Yamada trying to do? What were they trying to gain by protecting the man? *Leverage?* Maybe for their own safety. Safety from Duchik. But they didn't even know who Duchik was. Then again, maybe they didn't have to know, he thought. As long as they knew that someone else was behind it all. And not Masten.

Masten!

Masten had far more reason to get Reiff out, and he was in far more need of leverage if he knew things were about to be shut down. And Nora had said that Masten had figured out Duchik's identity. He could have put enough pieces together.

"I need to know where those trucks went."

The man opened a drawer and withdrew a plain, prepackaged cell phone. "Here. Take this. I'll call you as soon as I know."

He reached out and took the phone.

"If you need something else, call me."

Duchik watched the man straighten the papers and close the thick folder. Securing it with a strap. "It was everything I could find that was relevant."

"Thanks," replied Duchik, taking the case and turning for the door.

"Including some stuff on Reiff."

Duchik's hand was on the handle when he suddenly stopped. "What was that?"

"John Reiff," the analyst answered. "The other name you gave me."

Duchik turned from the door. "I thought there wasn't anything on him."

"There wasn't. Not in the current system. But I was able to retrieve some things from one of the older systems."

"I thought the old data was corrupted. From the cyberwars."

"It is, but not all of it. Some of the old databases still contain pieces of retrievable data, and luckily some information on your friend Reiff."

Duchik lowered his gaze. "Like what?"

"Like divorce papers," the man replied. "And a birth certificate. It appears he has a daughter. Who is still alive."

83

Rachel barely slept, tossing and turning most of the night, until finally waking from a restless slumber to find her room still dark, with the window shade above her bed allowing in only a faint glow of morning light. Her watch told her it was just after 7:00 A.M. when she slowly pushed herself up into a sitting position.

It was stress that had deprived her. Not just about their predicament, but over John. Including her guilt over how he had been treated. Regardless of whether she could have done anything about it. And now, what she feared might be happening to him.

The last thing she wanted to do was to jump to any conclusions, which almost always led to overreaction. But the more she thought through the details, the more concrete it was beginning to feel. And the sicker her stomach became.

After a few minutes of contemplation, she threw the cover off and stood on the carpeted floor, and dressed in the near darkness.

It was a single-story house with what looked to be four small bedrooms on one end of the home. Treading quietly down the long connecting hallway, Rachel emerged into the kitchen area with an adjacent dining room, where three people sat. Waterman, Reiff, and the owner of the house, whom she'd briefly met the night before. *Mick? Nick?* She couldn't remember.

The owner was dressed in a checkered flannel shirt with blue jeans atop a pair of worn, light brown cowboy boots. Waterman was still in his desert-colored fatigues, while Reiff had changed into clothing similar to Mick-or-Nick's.

All three men stopped talking and turned when she approached.

"Morning."

She smiled politely at all three and nodded. Glancing at the fourth chair, she continued past to the sliding glass door, where she looked out at the early-morning sky.

"How'd you sleep?" Mick-or-Nick asked. An older man whom Rachel guessed to be in his early seventies.

"Good," she replied, and turned around. "I'm sorry, was it Mick?"

The old man smiled. "Nick."

Nice, Rachel, it was only a fifty-fifty chance. She glanced at all three before clearing her throat. "I, uh, was hoping to make a phone call."

"To who?"

She rounded the remaining chair and sat down, curtly patting Reiff's outstretched arm as she did so. *Still cold.* "I need to get some information from someone."

Waterman studied her quizzically. "Care to expand on that?"

"Nothing having to do with any of this." Okay, probably more lie than truth, but it was defensible. As long as they didn't ask too many—

"What does it have to do with?"

She wanted to be forthcoming. She really did. But she didn't want to worry everyone unnecessarily. At least not yet. If she was wrong about what was happening to Reiff, it would just be another wrench in the works, while they were just trying to survive. "Just some medical information."

All three men were watching her. Eyes fixed, but without any obvious judgment. Did she look nervous to them? God, she was a terrible poker player.

"Information about what?" pressed Waterman.

She tried to think of something. But instead folded, raising both hands and covering her face in a sign of exhaustion. "I can't do this."

The men looked at each other. "You okay?" asked Nick.

Behind her hands, Rachel shook her head from side to side, eventually dropping them onto the table. "No. No, I'm not." She looked at each man and stopped at Reiff. "I think we have a problem."

"You just realized that?"

She shot Waterman a sarcastic glance before returning to Reiff. "How do you feel?"

"Okay."

She continued staring at him. "Really?"

"Yes."

With a modest grimace, she dropped her right hand, letting it fall onto Reiff's forearm, and squeezed. *"Really?"*

"What's going on?" Waterman asked.

She didn't answer.

"How . . . are you feeling?" she asked again.

John Reiff merely stared back.

Waterman looked back and forth between them. "What is this?"

"Beats me," said Reiff, prompting Rachel to turn to him. Without a word, she grabbed one of Waterman's callused hands and pulled it forward, placing it on top of Reiff's.

Waterman stared in confusion, opening his mouth to speak, but then stopped. Instead, he looked at Reiff, then down at his own hand. The temperature difference would have been noticeable to anyone.

"John?"

"What?"

"You okay?"

"Yep."

Waterman turned back to Rachel, who was watching. "He's not okay," she said.

There was a long silence around the table before Rachel spoke again. "As I said, I have to make a phone call."

"To whom exactly?"

"A doctor named Samantha Reed. At the Association of Zoos and Aquariums."

"What for?"

She was still looking at Reiff when she lowered her hand back down onto his arm. This time for comfort. "There's something you don't know," she said, "about the animals."

"What animals?" asked Waterman.

"Our test animals. That we used to perfect the thawing process."

"They're in her lab," said Reiff.

Rachel shook her head. "Not anymore. At least, they shouldn't be. As of two days ago. The AZA was scheduled to pick them up for transport to the Phoenix Zoo. I need to find out if they were picked up. And if they were, where they are now."

"Because?"

"Because some of them were exhibiting the same issue. The same problem as John." Again, she squeezed his arm reassuringly. "With disturbing outcomes."

Reiff watched the other men's eyes widen in surprise as he replied, "Disturbing how?"

She frowned. "Lethal."

Nothing more was said. Until Nick finally spoke up and motioned with his head. "There's a phone in the den."

Rachel looked questioningly at Waterman.

"If they're expecting the call, it *could* be traced." He then looked at Nick, who suddenly appeared nervous. "What exactly is this phone call supposed to tell you?"

"Hopefully, that the remaining animals are still alive." She turned to Reiff. "Which could suggest that this is not what I think it is."

"And if we don't call?"

Rachel considered the question. "Then we pray that it's something else. Some other slow, lingering side effect."

Reiff cleared his voice. "What exactly happened to the other animals?"

"I'm not sure. I didn't have time to diagnose it. Or even to understand it. But several of the smaller animals died, with body temperatures abnormally low when I found them."

"So they froze to death."

"I don't know how that's possible. Freezing results from exposure to external temperatures that are too low. But my lab was never below sixty-five degrees. It's thermically impossible." She looked around the table. "But if it is happening to the other animals, I need to know, so that I can study the problem while they're alive. And to give me a chance to arrest it."

"But if you make the call," said Nick, "and they find us . . ."

Rachel nodded. "A bigger problem."

Waterman eased back in his chair, folding his arms. Wearing a thoughtful, almost brooding expression. "Arizona *is* a nontracking state," he said with a shrug.

Nick almost spat. "Like that means anything."

"We can't risk it," Reiff said.

Rachel looked at him. "We didn't come this far to lose you now."

"It may not be up to you."

Before she could reply, Waterman put his hands on the table. "Take it easy," he said. "We'll make the call. But not from here."

He pushed himself up out of the chair and towered over the table. "It's time to find out how your man Masten is doing. And what cards he's holding. We'll get a burner phone on the way, and you can make your phone call." He then looked at Reiff. "Let's see if we can keep you alive a little longer."

With that, Rachel was out of her chair, making her way back to the bedroom and her things. On the way she passed Yamada, who had just entered the kitchen.

"What's going on?" he asked.

"We're going to see Masten."

"How about some breakfast first?" Yamada called after her.

"Have a Pop-Tart."

84

Headed north on the two-lane road, John Reiff looked out at the open desert along Highway 40. The flat, barren view seemed to go on forever, extending for miles until reaching distant and shadowy mountains across long patches of beautiful, timeless desert. A view he might expect to find on a postcard. If they still existed.

An old red sedan passed them, covered in a film of dust with a back seat filled with items he could not make out.

He continued studying the vehicle as it gradually pulled away from them. "Haven't seen many new cars on the road."

"There aren't any," replied Yamada from the back seat behind Waterman, prompting Reiff to glance over his shoulder.

"What do you mean?"

The younger man corrected himself. "Sorry, I should say 'not many.'"

"Why is that?"

"When the collapse happened, everything basically stopped. Production of virtually everything ground to a halt. From cars to houses to baby strollers. So did most shipping and technology. Which is only now beginning to come back."

"Technology?"

"Tech got hit especially hard," he answered. "Not just computers and phones, *everything*. Sooner or later, somewhere down the line, technology was at the core of pretty much every industry. Whether in the design, its manufacturing, shipping, personnel. Everything relied on technology. Which made it one of the biggest bubbles of all."

Reiff turned in his seat and gave Yamada his full attention.

"What people didn't realize," he continued, "or think about, was where all that printed money had gone. What people didn't understand was that government-printed money goes everywhere: stocks, bonds, housing, energy, food, and especially technology. Not only did it flow into giant corporations, but it ended up in their research and development departments. Driving huge advancements for decades. Bigger and bigger hard drives. Faster and faster computer chips. Better memory cards. More advanced phones that could do almost anything. Better cameras, better video screens. And in turn, all those advancements flowed into anything that used a CPU or a computer interface."

"How do you know all this?" asked Reiff.

"My dad told me. He was a computer engineer. In the heyday of it all. What he called our gluttonous peak." Yamada grinned. "He said people used to actually line up around city blocks just to buy a new phone on the day it came out. Or to see a new movie. Can you imagine that?"

Reiff looked at Waterman, who raised his eyebrows sarcastically. "As a matter of fact."

"You wouldn't see that these days. My phone," said Yamada, "is twelve years old."

"Really?"

"It's not uncommon," said Rachel, sitting behind him.

"We fix things now instead of just buying a new one. Because a lot of new things either don't exist or they're too expensive—except for the rich."

"The haves," remarked Waterman, "and the have-nots. The collapse turned an awful lot of the former into the latter. In some cases, almost overnight. A lot of people deserved it. But a lot of people didn't."

"So, when all that money vaporized," said Yamada, "it left behind a huge vacuum in its place. My dad called it a 'retrenchment.' In pretty much everything, including things like research and development. He said we became way too dependent on things we didn't understand. Things like artificial intelligence."

"AI?"

Yamada nodded. "My dad hated it. He said AI was where we really lost control. Not just having computers do things, but *decide* things, without us even being able to see or understand how that decision was made. Things were too good to be true for a long time. Almost magical. Until it all came crashing down."

"Literally," said Waterman.

"Yeah. By the time the collapse happened," said Yamada, "AI was part of everything. Self-driving cars, autopilots on planes, phones, watches, even financial markets. It was *huge* in the financial markets. Computers trading with each other instead of with people. Using computerized models that not only created giant financial bubbles, but allowed them to grow to impossible sizes."

Rachel leaned forward. "A lot of people like to say we screwed ourselves, but AI was the piledriver."

"Wow."

"I was too young to really understand it when it happened. But my dad did. And he said we had it coming."

Reiff turned to look at him again.

"He said it was *engineering hubris run amok.*"

Waterman glanced over from the driver's seat. "Not the most uplifting topic of conversation."

"Did *anything* survive?"

"Yeah," he answered, "but with a hell of a lot of pain."

85

"Hello?"

"Samantha! Hi, this is Dr. Souza."

"Who?"

"Dr. Souza. Rachel Souza. I'm calling about my animals."

It took a moment to make the connection. "Oh, Rachel. Yes! How are you?"

"I'm fine, thanks. Did you make the pickup?"

"Yes, we did. And I'm glad you called. I'm afraid we're having some issues. Some rather serious issues."

"Like what?"

"Dr. Souza, it appears some of the animals are suffering from an as-yet-unknown condition."

"What symptoms are you seeing?"

"Your pig, dog, and chimpanzee are experiencing symptoms consistent with hypothermia. But we're not sure that's what it actually is. Is there anything you know about what might be causing this?"

The sound of percolating coffee began to fade as the last of the dark liquid filled the small glass pot. The old coffee maker was decades old but still working. Faithfully pumping out caffeinated energy day in and day out.

The pot was then lifted, and a third of its vital contents poured into a ceramic mug, before it returned to the hot plate. From there, the mug was carried out of a small, barren kitchenette and back across a carpeted office floor. And upon reentering the office, raised and sipped from by the man holding it.

Something caught the analyst's attention. Not from the mug but from the opposite side of his office. A small flashing icon in the bottom right-hand corner of his large monitor. An exclamation point, flashing on and off in bright red.

Curious, the analyst continued across the room, where he set the coffee down and lowered himself back into the faded chair.

He double-clicked the icon, then selected the short alphanumeric code displayed, which opened another window, revealing multiple phone numbers. Next to them were listed the date, time, and duration of each call in seconds. And ultimately, a location.

The man immediately called the number of the new cell phone he'd given to Liam Duchik.

The analyst listened quietly as it began ringing, wondering if the man had bothered to turn it on yet, but his question was answered when Duchik picked up. "What is it?"

"It's me."

"You have the location of the trucks?"

"Not yet. But I may have something better."

The analyst copied the coordinates and pasted them into an online map. Watching as it automatically zoomed in and scrolled to the exact location.

"You requested, among other things, to have all phone numbers in and out of your building's location for the last two weeks marked."

"Correct."

"I think we just got a hit." The analyst began scanning a window of log data. "One of the numbers that recently called in to your lab has just been contacted by an untraceable phone. It may be nothing, but . . ."

"Who did they call?"

There was a pause while he looked it up. "The marked number belongs to the Association of Zoos and Aquariums."

"What the hell is that?"

"I'm looking." The analyst brought up their website and began reading. "Says it's a nonprofit dedicated to the advancement of zoos and aquariums in the areas of conservation, education, science, and recreation. Lots of locations around the country." He continued reading. "Says they also help facilitate the transporting of animals . . ."

"Say again?"

"Which part?"

"The last line."

The analyst read again. ". . . 'assists in the safe transportation of animals between various entities, both private and public' . . ."

Duchik's voice growled, "Who called them?"

"No idea. As I said, it looks like another burner phone."

"Can you locate its position?"

"I think so. The signal seems to be stationary. As in not moving."

Still on the phone and standing in an empty parking lot, Rachel wavered at Samantha Reed's veiled accusation. How could she possibly explain? That the animals had been part of an experiment, frozen solid, and then revived. Brought back to life in order to study biological effects on them.

She went with the most expedient answer. She lied. "No, nothing that would explain hypothermia or anything like it. Can you tell me exactly what symptoms you're seeing?"

"The standard things," replied Reed. "Shivering, shaking limbs, confusion. But the weird thing is . . ."

"What?" said Rachel when the woman's voice momentarily faded. "What is weird?"

"It's their body temperature. We cannot get their core temperatures up, even with heating blankets. No matter what we try. It's almost . . . like their thermogenesis is simply not working."

Thermogenesis was the fundamental molecular process responsible for generating a body's internal combustion. In essence, its metabolism. Otherwise known as body heat. By way of the system's constant cellular operations, from things like muscles, or organs, or the brain.

"We're doing what we can," said Reed. "But it's not encouraging."

Rachel pictured Bella and felt sick all over again. The small white dog that couldn't wait to see her every morning. And Lester. And Otis—

"Wait," she suddenly said. "You said the dog, the pig, and the chimpanzee."

"That's right."

"What about the capuchin?" *Dallas.*

"So far, the capuchin seems fine. He hasn't shown any of the signs."

Rachel's brain began racing. Rewinding. Trying to remember all the details of the testing. And more specifically, the timeline. Dallas, the capuchin, was tested before Otis, the larger chimpanzee. But by how much? At that point, they knew the Machine worked. They were then just searching for issues as they moved to larger and larger animals. More biologically complex animals.

"Dr. Souza, are you there?"

"Yes. I am. Sorry. I was just . . ." She continued thinking. "Where are they now?"

"At the Phoenix Zoo. We have a full medical facility there. If there's anyone who can—"

"I can be there in three hours." Rachel looked up from her conversation at Waterman, Reiff, and Yamada, all standing and waiting near the truck, and remembered where they were headed. "Make that four hours."

"Uh, sure, if you think you can help."

"I'm sure I can," she lied again. "Just keep them alive until I get there."

"Dr. Souza, we're doing all we can."

She did not hear Reed's final words. Instead, she hung up and stared absently at the men. Before walking forward to rejoin them.

"Well?" asked Waterman.

"They're at the Phoenix Zoo," she said. "And alive. But first, Masten."

The analyst had a live satellite feed onscreen. Using GPS coordinates to locate the parking lot. "I have them," he announced. "The call just ended, but I have a visual on one of the trucks." He then watched quietly as the dark vehicle began moving, making a small circle before exiting the lot. Heading back toward the highway, where it veered onto an on-ramp.

He relayed to Duchik. "They're headed north, back toward Kingman."

"Good. Don't lose them."

Duchik pulled the phone away from his ear and muted the call. Simultaneously extracting his other phone and dialing. A voice answered immediately.

"Head for Kingman."

86

Robert Masten's eyes opened slowly. Drearily. As if trying to see through a fog.

"Be patient," said a nearby voice. "He's under some strong medication."

Still flickering, his eyes struggled to remain open. To focus on anything within the bright and blurry cloud before him. Someone was in the room. Not just in the room, in front of him. Gradually crystallizing. One, then two, until he could make out four separate people.

He blinked. Trying to work the extra moisture from his eyes. Until things began to focus, visually and mentally.

He made out Rachel first, then Henry, and then Reiff. The fourth man he did not recognize.

"Can you hear us, Robert?"

Masten nodded while still blinking. He then attempted to clear his voice. He could remember . . . furniture. A maze of furniture and a flight of stairs. Then entering the room, they were in. And after that, nothing. Until now.

He twisted his head and spotted a doctor standing next to him. A woman. With her hand gently on Masten's shoulder.

"How are you feeling?"

Moving his mouth took some effort. "Like something rolled over me."

She grinned. "I'm not sure which would be worse. But the good news is you're going to be fine."

He managed a nod.

"Are you up to talking a little?"

"Sure."

Masten's eyes then turned toward the others, examining them one by one and stopping on Reiff.

"You saved me."

"Now we're even."

His reply was a faint chuckle while he watched Rachel take a small step forward.

"Hi, Robert."

His eyes lingered on her before speaking. "You're fired."

"What?!"

Masten's lips worked their way into a grin.

"Very funny."

"You all saved me," he acknowledged, looking at each one of them. But when he reached the fourth person, his brow furrowed. "Who are you?"

"An innocent victim," quipped Waterman.

"Robert," said Rachel, "we need to ask you some questions."

He took a deep breath and forced his eyes open wider. "Okay."

"Who was it you were working with?" she started softly. "At the lab?"

Masten mulled the question for a moment before calmly replying, "Nora. And the NIH."

"Why the NIH?"

"They were the ones who provided the funding. Most of it."

"No, I meant, why would the NIH be involved in our project?"

Masten shrugged. "They're involved in everything."

"But what would they be hoping to gain with us?"

"I don't know."

Rachel looked at the others, puzzled. "Who were you working with at the NIH?"

Masten had to think. "A man named Duchik. Liam Duchik."

"And who is that?"

"I don't know. I didn't know his name until recently. He was our handler."

"Handler?"

"The project handler. Our point of contact. At least that's what I thought he was."

"What is he then?"

"I'm not sure. But he has authority . . . probably a lot."

Rachel glanced at the others.

"Now he's taken things over."

"What has he taken over?"

"Everything. The lab. The technology. Everything we've . . ." Masten's eyes moved to Reiff. "He's the one . . . who sent those men to kill you."

Everyone looked at Reiff.

Masten grinned. "Guess it didn't turn out the way he planned."

Now Reiff stepped forward. "Why did he want to kill me?"

Masten thought about it with a curious look. "I'm not sure. Probably because he got what he needed."

"What does that mean? What did he get?"

Masten took another breath. At first, leaving it unclear whether he'd heard the question. Until finally he answered. "He has everything he needs now. All the data. The Machine. And a successful outcome: you." His eyes turned to Rachel. "He knows how it all works. He doesn't need us anymore. Any of us."

"So, he just wants to clean the slate and erase everything?"

"Seems that way."

"But why?"

Masten shook his head. "Probably to avoid culpability."

"Who else is involved?"

"I'm not sure. Duchik was the only one we ever talked to. But there have to be others."

"Why is that?"

"Because the project was too big, too expensive. The technology, procurement of supplies . . ."

Waterman turned to Reiff. "Just what you said."

He nodded and continued studying Masten. "I was their guinea pig?"

The director nodded. "You were. For them, at least." He looked at Rachel. "But not for us." Reading the doubt on the faces, Masten lowered his brow. "You think I was with them."

"Weren't you?"

He stared at her, disappointed. Almost hurt. "I wasn't with them," Masten said. "I didn't care what they were after. I only cared what I was after."

"Money and fame?" suggested Rachel.

"Not money," he said, rolling his head from side to side. "Fame, maybe. But not why you think."

"And why is that?" she asked.

His eyes stared forward for a moment. "Publicity."

"It's the same thing."

"No." Masten rolled his head a second time before appearing to change gears. Returning to Reiff. "You've been outside now."

"I have."

"You've seen it. How the world is."

"Some of it."

"They explained what happened?"

"A little," said Reiff.

Masten took a deep breath. "The world . . . is a terrible place. So much pain and misery. Suffering. And it will be like that for a long time."

Reiff turned to Waterman, who said nothing.

"So much . . . despair. Sadness. Anguish. For generations." He sighed. "That's what I was after."

"You wanted despair?"

Masten glowered. "An *escape* from it."

Rachel looked confused. "I'm not following."

He peered at her affectionately. "You never did look very far ahead. It wasn't just about a longer life." He rolled his eyes. "I may have embellished things a bit. Immortality is only a part of it." He fell quiet for a moment. Thoughtful. "Do you have any idea how many people are suffering? Every day."

"A lot," acknowledge Rachel.

"People everywhere, all over the world, are living hand to mouth. Still. Not knowing where their next meal will come from. Or even if it will. Watching their children suffer. And starve." His eyes began to glaze as he spoke. "We rode too close to the sun. Because of hubris. And greed. And gluttony."

Rachel squinted at him, confused. "Robert, what are you talking about?"

His eyes refocused. "What would people give to escape it all?"

"Escape what, death?"

Masten shook his head. "No. To escape life."

Again, Rachel glanced at the others. "Escape life?"

"To escape *this* life. This misery. This torment. This . . . blight."

"Jesus, what are you talking about, mass extinction?"

Masten suddenly looked at Rachel, perturbed. "I'm talking about another chance. About a reboot. Not a reboot, a new chapter. A better chapter."

"A new chapter of what?"

"In their lives," Reiff suddenly said.

Masten nodded. "A chance to live a better life. At a better time. Like a fast-forward."

Rachel continued staring, incredulous, until it finally hit her. "Fast-forward?" she said. "With cryonics?"

"Yes."

"You want to send people into the future?"

"Far away from this terrible place. To a better time. A time with hope. And beauty. And optimism. And laughter. Like things used to be." He grinned. "You're too young to remember."

Rachel was stunned. Frozen, staring at Masten as he lay in his bed. "*That's* what this was all about?"

"For me, it was always about the future. About hope. And now John," he said, looking at Reiff, "has proven it's possible. Difficult, but possible."

"I think 'difficult' is an understatement."

"It won't happen tomorrow. Just like anything, it will take time. But the technology works, and it will only get better and cheaper."

Rachel could not believe her ears. It was all about some mass exodus. A mass exodus into the future.

"What did *you* think it was?" Masten asked.

She was dumbfounded. "I don't know. The medical achievement of a lifetime."

"Exactly. But an achievement to do what?"

"To help people."

"Precisely what I'm talking about."

"No, it's not the same. . . . God, do you even know how long that would take? How many people you're talking about?"

"Every journey begins with a single step."

"Oh, please."

"Rachel, *any* use of our technology would include sending someone into the future. Regardless of the reason. It doesn't matter. In the end, it's the same thing. And someday, they'll remember I was the one who made it possible."

All she could do was shake her head. "Well, you're missing one thing. A big thing."

"Like what?"

She turned to Reiff. "John." When Masten didn't answer, she added, "He's still one in a million, remember?"

At that, Reiff turned and winked sarcastically at Waterman.

"Or at least, one in a thousand," she said.

Waterman then smiled back at him. Watching Reiff turn back around. Noticing trembling in his friend's hands.

"What are you talking about?"

Yamada, who had remained silent, spoke up. "She's talking about the cryoprotectants."

Rachel nodded in agreement. "We still don't know why the ice crystals didn't form in Reiff's blood like all the others. Which means we're still a long way from declaring victory."

Masten stared at both of them for a long moment before shocking them with a single sentence: "Of course we know why."

87

A dark yellow van glowed in the early-morning sun, with remnants of some of its original red pinstriping. The logo itself had been completely removed.

The vehicle from a courier company, long since out of business, provided the perfect cover. Old enough not to attract attention yet familiar and reminiscent enough for no one to wonder where it was going. And windowless, save for a single driver visible through the front windshield.

They had the address. Forwarded by Duchik. An old antique store, of all places. Most likely part of some underground network, where the truck was now parked, according to the live satellite feed.

In the back of the van, two more men remained standing. Gripping overhead straps to steady themselves and their cargo. One hand through a strap and one hand securing the long wooden boxes in front of them. In one, an M134 Minigun, with Gatling-style rotating barrels and rapid-fire capability. Below that, a much larger and wider box for the ammunition.

With spread legs, the two leaned slightly as the van left the freeway and veered onto the Andy Devine off-ramp. Gradually slowing as it descended and approached a set of bright traffic lights.

They were four minutes away.

88

Rachel and Yamada were stunned.

"Come again?"

Masten raised his eyebrows. "You didn't figure that out?"

"Figure *what* out?"

"John's antifreeze."

Rachel looked at Reiff.

"How . . . did you do it?"

"I didn't do anything," replied Masten. "But I know what *they* did."

Rachel was breathless.

"The NIH did it. After pulling you from that river, John. They were the ones who kept you. For years."

Reiff's reply seemed unfazed. "Of course."

"Back then, they wanted someone who was frozen before death. Not after. A body was arrested in its functioning state."

Reiff looked at Rachel.

"Where did they take him?" she asked.

Masten shook his head. "I don't know. That was way before my time. But they were the ones able to keep the crystals out of his cells by changing his DNA."

"How?"

"Ever hear of the crucian carp?"

"No."

"It's a fish that freezes in the winter and comes back to life. Apparently, the NIH had identified the carp's unique genetic compounds, and by the time John was in his accident, were ready to try splicing it into a human genome."

Rachel stared at him, astonished. While Waterman grinned and leaned forward to say into Reiff's ear, "If it's any consolation, that probably puts you back in the one-in-a-million club again."

"Wait," Rachel said, shaking her head. "That's not possible. If he was frozen, his system was suspended. The virus couldn't circulate through the systems. Through his blood or tissues."

"My understanding is that they found a temperature cold enough to keep his system suspended while still allowing viral load absorption. Very slow, but still able to spread." Masten looked at Reiff. "You were their test subject."

"To see whether it would prevent the ice crystals from destroying his cells."

"Correct," he replied, then looked at John. "Your visions were a total surprise."

Rachel shook her head and covered her mouth with a hand.

Masten was still focused on Reiff. "I want you to know I had nothing to do with any of that. I just wanted to bring you back. I swear."

"That doesn't make us any less complicit," said Rachel.

"That may be," sighed Masten, "but for the record, I never fully understood Duchik or his motivation. Cryonics is not immortality. It doesn't roll back the clock."

"Then what *is* Duchik after?" Reiff asked.

"I have no idea."

The van calmly passed historic Williams Park and turned onto Grandview Avenue. Where it accelerated and passed through multiple intersections until reaching Copper Street, then slowed and turned again.

Once outside the room, Waterman turned with a dubious expression. "That didn't feel overly helpful."

Rachel nodded. "I know, it still doesn't answer what Duchik is up to. Or why he wants us dead so badly."

"No ties," Reiff replied simply. "The man wants no ties. We're evidence that he wants to get rid of."

Waterman nodded and began climbing the wooden steps. "He obviously doesn't want anything connecting you three to him. At this point, the reason why is irrelevant."

On the street in front of the antique store, the yellow van pulled to a controlled stop, and its large side door was pulled open from the inside, revealing the two men. One facing out, with a heavy leather harness around his chest, supporting the Minigun at waist level. Aiming directly at the store, he gripped his hand around the thick trigger handle and squeezed.

89

It could only be described as pure hellfire. The unleashing of thousands of rounds of 7.62 × 51 mm rounds in a whirring, thunderous column of utter destruction.

Erupting from the spinning barrels, the near-invisible stream of carnage began at the building's old casement window and moved across its face as though it were simply being erased through exploding chunks of stone and cement, in a roar that was beyond deafening.

In less than a minute, five thousand shells littered the asphalt, after the steady uninterrupted attack of reverberating chaos. The entire antique store was destroyed, it and everything within torn to pieces like bits of paper. Shards of wood, metal, and glass littered the surroundings.

An incomprehensible sight. Ending as quickly as it had begun, in a sudden absence of sound. The fiery, spinning barrels whirring to a stop.

Smoke and debris were everywhere. A cloud of gray dust lingered over what used to be the building's entrance—eerie in its silence—before part of the roof collapsed in a thunderous implosion.

90

There was nothing but darkness. And silence.

Thousands of rounds of unrelenting carnage had reduced everything in its path to rubble, including large sections of wall, now lying in ruins along with much of the arched roof they had supported, causing portions of the flooring to buckle and collapse into the basement. Burying everyone in a cascade of wood, metal, and glass.

There was no sound except the ringing still in their ears. Gradually fading as though time had stopped—until someone sputtered and coughed.

It was Reiff, as he managed to slowly push a large chunk of wood off onto its side and snake out from under it.

He stood and tried to orient himself in the darkness before hearing something else move nearby.

"Can anyone hear me?" he called.

There was another cough. Female. Rachel. Groaning in pain. "Help. Me."

Reiff tried to move toward her but was stopped by a pile of something unseen. Causing him to feel his way around it until he found Rachel's hand. Next to her, Yamada cried out, muffled beneath debris. "Oh my God. Help!"

Behind Reiff, the door to the small clinic was pulled inward, and one of the doctors rushed out, illuminated by red emergency lighting behind him. Inside, everything was on the floor, but the walls appeared intact—protected by the room's concrete construction.

The doctor stared at Reiff, who must have looked like hell. "Are you okay?"

He didn't answer. Instead, he took stock of the rubble in front of him. The remains of what appeared to be an antique desk. He pulled it off and grabbed Rachel's arm. Joined by the doctor, who began moving debris off Yamada.

"What the hell was that?" cried Yamada.

"An attack."

Reiff pulled the rest of the pieces off Rachel and had begun pulling her to her feet when she cried out. "Ow! Wait!" She tried to rise, but grabbed her left arm and shrank back to her knees. "My shoulder."

"How bad is it?"

"I don't know. I can't move it."

Together, Reiff and the doctor got her up, careful to avoid her arm. Once she was on her feet, they turned to Yamada, whose face was contorted in pain. "I think my leg is broken."

They moved quickly, digging him free, and then Reiff turned to the stairs. The stairwell was completely filled in.

He motioned for the doctor's help and clawed rapidly at the pile. The two of them moved as fast as they could to uncover the first step, then the next, and the next, until they spotted one of Waterman's boots.

They moved faster. "Devin! Can you hear me?"

There was no answer.

Reiff pulled off part of the door of a small antique Coke machine, throwing it aside and exposing the older man's waist and chest. "*Devin!*"

Together he and the doctor lifted another large section of splintered wood, and suddenly they saw Waterman's head and face. Bloodied on one side with eyes staring up. Motionless.

After several long seconds, the eyes blinked. Then looked directly at Reiff.

"What the hell did you *do* to these people?"

It took nearly thirty minutes to free Waterman and finish clearing what was left of the narrow stairwell. Several wooden steps were gone, and only pieces of the original doorway were left standing. The door itself looked like Swiss cheese, twisted and mangled, hanging precariously by a single remaining hinge. Their only exit, blocked by something on the other side.

It was then that a voice could be heard from above. "Devin! You down there?"

Waterman limped to one of the holes above him and peered up through the smoke and dust, searching. "Wayne, over here!"

Part of his friend's face appeared. "Good God! Are you okay?"

"More or less."

Wayne looked up and surveyed the damage around him before peering back down. "Who in the hell did you piss off?"

Without waiting for a response, Wayne disappeared. He could be heard climbing over and through the wreckage before he returned a few minutes later. His face was forlorn. "Victoria's dead."

The old woman. Waterman's expression fell, and he nodded.

"Give me a few minutes to try to move some things."

Reiff struggled up the damaged stairs and banged against the remnants of the door to give Wayne an idea of where to start. At the bottom, one of the doctors was helping Rachel get her bandaged arm into a sling, adjusting the strap up and around her neck.

Why had their attackers fled? Why didn't they stay to make sure the job was done? Reiff had no idea, and frankly, he didn't care. All that mattered at the moment was that both doctors were unhurt, as well as Masten. And they all had to leave as quickly as possible.

91

The greatest saltwater lake in the Western Hemisphere spanned nearly seventeen hundred square miles and hosted almost a dozen individual islands. Several of which had their own unique ecosystems. A seemingly endless stretch of deep blue water from the view of the penthouse suite of one of the city's few remaining hotels. Towering dozens of stories high, it provided the unobstructed and mesmerizing view of the lake, glistening under a late-autumn afternoon sun. And beyond that, desert as far as the eye could see.

The scene would have been striking to almost anyone else, provided they were not Liam Duchik, who now stood in front of the floor-to-ceiling window, gazing absently over the vista.

Behind him, Nora Lagner was in a plush red fabric chair, studying Duchik's motionless outline.

It was after the second call from the analyst that he had grown completely reticent. The man had witnessed, through satellite footage, several people emerging from the remains of the antique store.

It was inconceivable. No, not inconceivable. Unthinkable that they could have survived.

He was beyond angry. Beyond irate. He was fuming. Over all of it. Everything that was happening.

"Is it really necessary?" asked Lagner delicately.

The question caused Duchik to turn from the window and stare at her. He was too incensed to be objective. But he tried to control his rage and inject some level of detachment into his veins.

Was Reiff really that important?

There were limits. Duchik knew it and so did Lagner. Self-imposed, perhaps, but still limits. Which, in some ways, was the mother of all ironies.

Duchik had enough clout, enough political leverage, to mobilize half the armed forces if he had to. But the catch was that there were only so many people he could afford to use. That he could afford to let in. Only so many he could risk knowing about his secret. And the more resources he spent trying to stop Reiff, the more outside attention he ultimately brought upon himself.

That was the crux of it all. Of the anger and frustration. He had worked for so long to reach this point, and he simply could not afford to risk losing control now. Which, even in his enraged state, begrudgingly brought him back to Nora's question. Was Reiff really that important?

The fact was, Duchik didn't know.

He didn't know what the man knew, or what he didn't know. All he had to go on were Reiff's pictures. Drawings. While he was in the process of recovering. Pictures that had no scientific explanation at all. And yet could not be dismissed either.

Dozens of scenes were simply too close to be coincidence. Like Reiff's picture of the torching of the ECB's headquarters. Or the different riots across the country. Or the tanks.

The truth was that there was no way to know exactly how dangerous Reiff was to Duchik's operation. Maybe the man just wanted to be left alone. To disappear. Or maybe he didn't know enough to obstruct a damn thing.

But maybe he did.

Even a small risk over a long enough timeline could become an enormous problem. A problem that could derail everything Duchik had worked for. Everything he was still working for.

The long-term risk simply wasn't worth it. Because Duchik's end goal was still decades away. Which was a long time to leave a cancer to fester. And Reiff was very much a cancer. Whether he knew it or not.

Duchik was facing the window again. Contemplating. Calculating. Before finally answering Lagner with a shake of his head. "There's still too many loose ends," he said. "But we're done chasing. Time for him to come to us."

92

Leaving the main street, Waterman turned his truck in to a large parking lot and headed for a three-story parking garage, entering on the bottom level.

Daylight immediately darkened, and Rachel watched from the back seat as they slowed and began passing dozens of parked cars.

Waterman made a turn and continued down the next aisle, slowing even further as he and Reiff studied the vehicles.

"What are we doing?"

"Swapping vehicles."

"Why?"

"We're most likely being tracked by satellite," answered Waterman, still scanning. "There's enough traffic in and out of this garage that it should make it hard to follow us from here."

He stopped when they spotted an aged green Jeep Grand Cherokee and motioned Reiff to the glove compartment, where he found and withdrew a square piece of metal resembling an old car part, along with an oversized screwdriver.

Rachel held up a hand. "Wait a minute, we're *stealing* a car?"

"I'm not in the mood for an ethics debate. Besides, Wayne and Henry should be doing the same thing about now."

Reiff opened the door and climbed out while Waterman scanned for witnesses. Reiff peered through the Jeep's driver's-side window, checking for an alarm, before smashing the glass with the base of the screwdriver. He opened the Jeep's door and quickly ducked inside, reaching under the dash and popping the hood. He then moved forward and raised it, leaning in over the engine.

"What's he doing?"

"Didn't we just establish that?"

She frowned. "That's not what I mean."

"He's replacing something called the engine control module."

"The thing from the glove compartment?"

He nodded. "Compatible with a lot of similar makes and models."

Together they watched Reiff drop the hood, then move back and slide into the driver's seat.

"Now he just needs to break the ignition switch and—"

The Jeep's engine suddenly roared to life.

Waterman quickly leaned over and pulled the truck's passenger door closed, then straightened and immediately accelerated, speeding down the aisle and turning, watching as Reiff followed. It took a minute to find an open space in a far corner of the garage before pulling into it.

"Let's go!" he barked, jumping out and opening the door directly behind him. He grabbed his large duffel bag and motioned for her to follow. As soon as they were both in the Jeep, Reiff accelerated toward the exit.

When they were back on the highway, Rachel leaned forward with a wince from her shoulder. "So where exactly are we going?"

"Running an errand."

"I see." She leaned back and continued staring at the men from the back seat. After a few minutes of silence, except for the whirling wind through Reiff's broken window, she leaned forward again and raised her voice. "By the way, I think I know what Duchik is up to."

Reiff's eyes looked at her in the rearview mirror while Waterman spun around. "What?"

"I said—"

"I heard what you said. *What* is he up to?"

"It was something Robert said. Before the attack. About John's DNA being changed to prevent ice crystals in his system. When he was frozen, and then when he pointed out that cryonics is not some path to immortality. Even though a lot of patients think that. That someday they will be reawakened, and their problems will be cured. Or their diseases. And for the record, aging *could* be classified as a disease."

"But you just said it doesn't give you immortality."

"It's doesn't. Anyone revived will find themselves in the same body. The same age, the same condition. Maybe their cancer has been cured, or their pulmonary disease, or Alzheimer's. But their body is still the same age it was when they were frozen."

Reiff was still watching her in the mirror. "Yeah, we heard that part."

"But there may be a way around that," she said, meeting his eyes in the rearview mirror. "What they did to you may be the key. Not the ice crystals per se, but *how* they did it. Robert," she continued, "said they found a temperature that kept your system suspended but still allowed the virus with the genome changes to gradually propagate through your system. And that may be the key.

"You see, the common practice in cryonics is to freeze the person's body at somewhere between minus two hundred and three hundred degrees Fahrenheit. Which basically turns the body into a frozen block." She grinned at Reiff. "No offense."

"None taken."

"The problem, though, is that at that temperature there is no cellular activity at all. Nothing. Everything is like ice. Hence the ice crystals. But, if Robert is right, and whether Duchik or one of his predecessors found a way for frozen cells to still be manipulated, that could change things dramatically."

"What would it change?" asked Waterman.

"Manipulating DNA is a regular occurrence now. It has been for a long time. We even made some subtle changes to John after he was revived, to help speed up the healing process. But they were very subtle and extremely targeted. We were stimulating cells to help natural processes. Therapies that have been around for a while now, like fasting, which releases large amounts of growth hormone and in turn builds and repairs a whole host of things. By affecting DNA we can maximize the cellular responses to some therapies, which are natural and safe. *But,*" she added, "the important point here is that we had to wait until he was revived. Until his temperature was back to normal."

"And you're saying that's what Duchik found a way around?"

"It sounds like it. Whether it was Duchik or someone else, it sounds like they may actually possess the ability to make live DNA changes *while* the person is suspended. And that is a very big deal."

"How big?"

"Huge," she replied. "There are a whole host of *regenerative* therapies these days. Profound therapies, like turning skin cells into stem cells then back into skin cells. Which results in cells that are effectively much younger. Or liver cells. Or heart cells. A lot of these practices can literally *reverse* the age of our cells. The problem, though, is that they take time. But what if those therapies could all be done at the same time, *while* the body was near-frozen? Time would no longer be an impediment."

"Wait a minute. So, you're saying someone *could* wake up in a younger body?"

"Maybe. The process would likely be much slower at low temperatures, but you would have decades to wait it out. And to the frozen patient, it would seem like the blink of an eye."

Reiff looked at Waterman. "I can attest."

"And there's more," Rachel continued. "If the new timeline for rejuvenating cells is now twenty, thirty, or even fifty years, there's another possibility. A very exciting one, medically speaking."

"I can't wait."

"Like I said, a lot of these regenerative advances have been around for a long time, targeting specific types of cells. But there was also a discovery made a long time ago that could potentially apply to all cells, especially given enough time. Have you ever heard of something called telomeres?"

"No."

"Telomeres have been studied for at least fifty years by researchers working to slow or arrest the aging process. Telomeres are little caps at the ends of our chromosomes that scientists believe determine how long a person lives. Kind of like a genetic switch that determines when cells stop reproducing. Each time cells replicate, the telomere or the 'ends' of the cell's chromosomes gets a little shorter. Over and over throughout our lives until finally the telomere gets too short and it tells the cells not to replicate anymore. And that, biologically speaking, is the end of the road. Old cells no longer reproduce, and they just get older, until . . . well, you know."

"Okay."

"Here's the interesting part. Instead of trying to come up with therapies that target individual systems or tissue types, you might be able to affect all of them by targeting telomeres instead. I think it was back around 2020 that a research team discovered something big. Teams had been working on telomeres for a long time, but this team discovered something truly extraordinary. And surprisingly simple. Much simpler than having to change complicated DNA chains. This team figured out not only a way to stop the repeated shortening of telomeres, but to *reverse* them. As in relengthening them again. And they did it by using oxygen."

"Oxygen?"

"Uh-huh. They found that by putting their subjects in hyperbaric chambers for a period of time every day, or in other words, by flooding their systems with very high levels of oxygen, they were able to re-lengthen telomeres in different cell types by as much as twenty percent."

Waterman turned back around to look at Rachel. "Twenty percent?"

"Yep. And it took only several months. So, imagine if Robert is right and this Duchik guy has found a way for near-frozen cells not just to absorb DNA changes, but in this case high levels of oxygen for years. It at least suggests the possibility that a patient could actually wake up younger, at least biologically, than when they were frozen."

A stunned Waterman continued staring at her, until finally turning back. "Well, color me impressed."

93

What might have been a revelation to Dr. Rachel Souza was little more than common knowledge to Liam Duchik. Even as close as she was, Rachel would have been astonished to learn just how far ahead of her hypothesis Duchik's technology now was.

Nor was it one or the other—specific DNA targeting versus oxygen-induced telomere lengthening. Duchik's therapy could do both, and then some. Targeting dozens of the body's systems *along* with telomere DNA.

The process was far more expansive and far more complicated than what she had deduced. Which was why Duchik needed new test subjects. Human subjects. In a very real sense, John Reiff was simply one of the last pieces of the puzzle. Making sure a patient could not just be suspended "ice free" for years but could also be successfully revived when the time came.

Yet, Duchik's influence came with a price. He remained as obscure a figure as possible, always trying to stay in the background and out of the public view. But to acquire the resources he needed, the funding, the technology, the experts, he often had to exercise the very power he worked so hard to conceal. Presenting an extraordinarily difficult line to walk. Use too much and risk the limelight, or remain in the shadows and fail to achieve the unachievable. On top of that, his inescapable notoriety also presented another problem. The ability to disappear. Not just now, but forever.

After all, one could not simply reappear decades later, and younger, without someone noticing, and asking questions.

Which was where the Hustons came in. Duchik was back at the ranch house, watching the couple receive their second injections. His test subjects, not unlike the animals Masten and his team had used.

And the Hustons were receiving the full treatment. The full concoction of genome changes. For their role was not only to prove that the complete therapy worked, but that people as distinguished and well-known as they were could vanish . . . and stay vanished. A test case for Duchik. To help him learn how best to protect his secrets and his wealth. And the wealth of the nine other people he trusted to join him.

After all, what was the point of immortality, of true longevity, if everyone else had the same ability?

The simple answer was that there was no point. True unending power was only possible through a timelessness that no one else possessed.

He, and those he trusted, would be the only ones. The only ones immune from the machinations of life and death. The monotony. The pointless and endless repetitions that held no discernible purpose at all.

They would be the leaders. And the rest of the world would be *the led.*

And to keep that secret safe, every possible lingering loose end had to be severed.

94

Awakened from her sleep by a jolt of pain, Rachel opened her eyes and looked around. It was predawn and they were stopped in front of a modest hill, where she had evidently been left to sleep in the car.

Using her good hand, she pulled herself into a sitting position, and groaned. The dislocation hadn't been too severe, but it would still take time to heal. Allowing her to discover new ways in which she used those muscles every day without realizing it.

From the back seat, she yawned, staring through the darkened windshield until spotting two figures outside. Reiff and Waterman, near the top of the hill, silhouetted by the faint glow of an approaching sunrise.

She waited for several minutes, contemplating the climb up to join them, before one of them turned and began to descend.

It was Waterman, who continued heavily down the embankment, heading for the car, where he continued to the driver's side and climbed in behind the wheel.

"Morning," he said.

"Where are we?"

"A bit off the beaten path."

"No kidding. Where?"

Waterman inhaled, staring up at Reiff, and then glancing at his watch. "Not yet."

"What the—" Frustrated, she looked out at Reiff's silhouette. With a sigh, she finally turned. "Are you ever going to tell me?"

"Tell you what?"

"About *him*," she retorted. "What we're doing here, who he really is, what he did in the army? Anything!"

Gazing through the windshield, Waterman smirked. "He was in communications."

"I'm not kidding."

The smirk spread into a grin. "John Reiff," he said, "is a rare breed, Rachel. Not like anyone else you've met. Or that I've met. And I've met a lot of people." He shook his head. "But none like him."

"What does that mean?"

He sighed. "We met in Ranger School. We were both part of the 101st Airborne. A tough group of guys." Waterman paused for several moments. "It's funny, John wasn't the fastest, or the strongest. Probably wasn't even the toughest. But he may have been the smartest."

"I can believe that."

"I don't mean in the way you probably think. He's smart, sure. But there's a lot of smart people in the world. With John, it's different. Something deeper. More instinctual maybe. Not really sure how to explain it. But the guy is just not like anyone else."

"In what way?"

"Intuition. Instinct. An ability to somehow know what no one else does. Maybe just *before* anyone else does."

"For example?"

"Let's put it this way, if I was in a bad situation, I mean really bad, like life or death, there's probably no one else I would want with me than him."

"He's a good fighter?"

Waterman almost laughed. "To say John Reiff is a good fighter is like saying water is wet."

"I see."

"No. You don't." He looked over his shoulder at Rachel. "You ever been in a fight? I mean a real, physical, knock-down drag-out kind of fight?"

"No."

"There's something that happens to a person in those kinds of situations. In fights where dying is a real possibility. In those situations, a lot goes on all at once. A lot of adrenaline, a lot of fear. Anger. Panic. Emotions all commingle and surge through your veins faster than you can make sense of it. Flooding your system and impairing your senses while your body is trying to react to what's happening. Trying to survive. Trying to win. It's like a fog of war on an individual level. Something every military tries to train *out* of its soldiers. By teaching them to block things out and focus on what matters most. What will allow you to persevere. To prevail."

Rachel opened her mouth to speak, but Waterman continued.

"And then . . . there's John Reiff. Someone who doesn't have to be trained at all. Not for fighting. Because somehow, he just knows."

"Knows what?"

"What to do. How to move. What the other person is going to do. Not intellectually, but instinctively. And not just what but when." He shook his head, still peering out the window. "In all my years, I still haven't seen anything like it."

Rachel slowly slid back into her seat.

"Like I said, he's not the biggest, or the strongest. But he doesn't need it. No one in our regiment could beat him. Not in any combat training. And in a real fight . . . I've never seen him lose."

"Never?"

"Never. That instinct inside of him is just . . . I don't know . . . exceptional." Waterman glanced again over his shoulder. "This Duchik guy really has no idea who he had frozen as a block of ice. And he sure as hell doesn't know who or *what* he reawakened."

There was a long silence inside the car. "So that's what he did in the military."

Waterman smiled. "That's actually the funny part, believe it or not. After leaving the 101st, John was, in fact, a 'communications officer.' In a manner of speaking. He was part of the army's psyops group."

"What's a psyop?"

"It stands for 'psychological operations.'"

"And what's that?"

"'The careful creation and dissemination of product message.' That was the official description," said Waterman. "What it basically means is subterfuge. Propaganda. Psychological manipulation of the enemy, by whatever means necessary. Military intelligence, interrogation, and a host of other things. My point is that John's not only deadly, but he's also seen it all."

Rachel stopped asking questions, still processing everything she'd been told . . . when Waterman's phone suddenly rang.

He answered with a simple "Yep?" Then, after listening briefly, replied with "Roger that" and hung up.

He grabbed the large screwdriver from the seat next to him and used it to turn the broken ignition switch, starting the Jeep. Then dropped it again and pulled the gear shift back into drive.

Rachel looked around, wondering what was happening, and then looked up the hill as they pulled way.

John Reiff was gone.

95

The sunrise was extraordinary as the pink and orange morning sky slowly stretched up and over the open desert. Quiet and desolate, in a beauty all its own.

Several miles outside of the larger urban sprawl, a modern adobe-styled house rested alone in a slight depression between two bluffs. The distant sound of a diesel engine broke the peaceful ambience of the morning. Rumbling as it gently accelerated over a long stretch of single-lane dirt road.

Almost an eighth of a mile from the house came the soft crunching from beneath three sets of shoes. A mother and her two children, walking in unison over a soft incline toward the road.

"Are you picking us up today?"

"Yep. We need to go to the nursery. I have some things coming in."

The boy playfully skipped over a small hole has he walked. "Another tree?"

His mother smiled and nodded. "Mm-hmm."

A young girl, a couple of years older than the boy, peered up. Her hand was still wrapped inside her mother's. "Can we visit Daddy?"

"If we have time."

"Why wouldn't we have time?"

"It's going to be long day, honey. We'll see."

Satisfied, the children continued walking. Short strides trying to keep up with their mother, while the yellow bus emerged from behind a group of white firs.

Reaching the road, they waited as the engine's growl continued before abruptly beginning to slacken as it drew near, the giant vehicle downshifting and slowing until it managed to roll to a stop several feet in front of them.

The vertical door at the front of the bus folded inward to one side while both children hopped cheerfully aboard. The mother, watching them scamper up the steps, smiled at the driver, an older woman with dark shoulder-length hair. "Morning, Diana."

The woman returned the smile with a slight look of weariness, while glancing back at the rowdy children. "Morning, Elizabeth. Care to come along?"

The mother laughed. "No, thanks!"

With a quick wink, the driver closed the door and moved her foot to the accelerator, leaving behind a faint dust cloud as they roared away.

A few minutes later, walking back toward her house, the woman, dressed in light blue jeans and a long-sleeved shirt, heard something behind her. Something subtler. She turned to find a dark SUV in the distance. Approaching, rapidly, leaving a much larger trail of dust in its wake.

She kept an eye on the vehicle as she walked back home. There were other houses on the same road. It didn't mean—

The SUV then began to slow, until turning in to and beginning the ascent up her long driveway. Prompting the woman to stop and turn in curiosity.

As it neared, her eyes narrowed. Focusing on the windshield. Curiousness turned to uncertainty. And then . . . to unease.

With the morning sun behind the vehicle, she could make out people inside what looked like a government car. Approaching faster than normal.

It was then that her unease became fear. And then she turned and began running.

"What are we doing?"

Waterman continued accelerating. "I'll tell you in a minute." With hands wrapped tightly around the wheel, he dodged back and forth between potholes.

Behind him, Rachel grabbed the overhead handle. Glancing up through the window, she could see a small plane overhead.

The woman was now in a full sprint. Running for the house. Panicked when the vehicle sped past her, suddenly sliding to a stop over an open patch of gravel, sending a wave of pebbles scattering over the same walkway the woman was racing for.

Doors were flung open from the passenger side, and two men leaped from the SUV, running to intercept. They grabbed her as she began screaming.

"Whoa, whoa! Where do you think you're going?"

"Let me go!" she cried out, trying to break free. "*Let me go!*"

"Shut up!" One man slapped her hard across the face, then grabbed her hands and growled, "I said *be quiet!*"

He hit the woman again, knocking her off her feet and onto her knees before the second man yanked her back up from her waist.

The first man grabbed her by the hair. "Who else is here?"

The woman sputtered.

"I *said* who else is here?" He raised his hand to strike again.

"No one."

"Where's your husband?"

She could taste blood in her mouth. "Gone. At work."

"Kids?"

She winced as he yanked on her hair. "School."

"Good. Do what we say, and you won't get hurt . . . at least any more."

"What do you want?" she cried, still struggling. "We don't have anything!"

The man almost laughed, still clutching her hair in his fist. He opened his mouth to speak, but suddenly stopped as he looked over her shoulder.

Another car was approaching.

The assailant spun, pulling her toward him, and along with his partner scurried behind the SUV and squatted down. They peered through the car windows at the second vehicle as it slowed at the entrance of the driveway and came to a stop.

"Who is that?"

"I don't know!" she cried.

Rachel leaned forward to get a better view out the windshield. "Oh my God, what's happening?"

There was no reply from Waterman. Instead, he calmly put the Jeep into park and opened his door. Climbing out, he moved to the rear and opened the tailgate, then reached inside for his bag.

Rachel followed him out and suddenly realized that she and Waterman were directly in their path. "Uh, what if they try to get out?"

Waterman returned with an AR-15 in his hand, with two small bipod legs affixed to the bottom. He brought the rifle up and, resting it comfortably on the top of the Jeep, said, "No one's coming out this way."

She gasped and quickly retreated, lowering herself and ducking behind the rear of the vehicle. Watching nervously, before she heard something. She looked up in time to see the small plane tip its wing as it passed overhead, then changed direction, banking away.

Waterman followed her gaze up. "If you can't beat 'em, join 'em."

The two men watched from a distance as a man took his place behind the Jeep, rifle in hand—and pointed at them.

One of men banged on the SUV's side window, causing the driver to lower it from the inside. "What the hell do we do now?"

They were the same three who destroyed the antique store in Kingman, and the driver had no intention of giving the man behind the Jeep a clear shot. He quickly scrambled over the center console, opening and pushing the passenger door out. "Get in the house!"

Through his scope, Waterman watched the men run for the front door, the last man dragging the woman behind them as a shield. Within seconds, all three disappeared inside and the door slammed shut.

Silence returned, and after several long seconds Waterman shook his head and looked down at his shirt pocket. Fishing out a stick of gum, he muttered, "They were safer outside," and popped it in his mouth.

96

Inside, the men fanned out. Two of them drew their guns and, staying low, took positions on opposite sides of the living room window. They peered outside and down the long driveway at the Jeep. Behind them, the third man continued to the other side of the room, still struggling with the woman, who screamed and managed to claw one of his cheeks.

In a rage, he twisted and struck her hard with his right elbow, stunning her. "Shut the hell up!" He kept her in front of him and looked at the others. "Now what?"

At the window, the driver tried to think. They had cover for the moment. Staying out of sight would keep the prick outside from trying to take a shot.

He waved the third man in closer, along with the woman, motioning him to keep out of view. When they neared, he looked at woman's disheveled face. "You got a car?"

With her assailant's hand around her neck for control, she shook her head.

"Great. Is there another way off this property? Another road?"

She nodded. Struggling to breathe, she said, "Out back."

The driver looked toward the back window. Another route wouldn't matter if they couldn't get the car. And the terrain outside was likely too flat to provide any meaningful cover. They would be picked off trying to get off the property on foot.

He motioned to the man behind her. "Get back there and check it out."

The man nodded and pulled the woman with him, stumbling backward. Continuing through the meagerly decorated living room and around the corner. Knocking pictures and then a lamp onto the floor as the woman tried to grab on to something. In the kitchen, he held her in front of him and looked over her shoulder and out the window. The land outside was as barren as the front.

He opened his mouth to call back but was stopped by a surge of pain as the woman got her mouth onto his hand and bit down hard.

"Ahhh, God dammit!" he cried as she woman bit down on his hand. He spun her around and threw her violently into a shoulder-high china cabinet, breaking the glass as she fell to the floor. He grabbed her again by her hair and yanked her to her feet, clenched his right hand, and swung his fist at her head.

His arm seemed to freeze in midair.

Behind him, John Reiff grabbed the man's hair and violently jerked his head back. Forcing something in the man's gaping mouth, he raised his boot and smashed the man's knee sideways with a deep, sickening crunch.

The man's eyes bulged in pain. Silenced by the object forcing his jaw open, he began to crumple forward, and felt his right arm break as he fell. Reiff was already on top of him by the time he hit floor, immediately raising the man's head and smashing it face-first into the hard linoleum, and felt the body instantly go limp.

The scuffle was easily heard from the living room. But not alarming. The woman was frantic and had to be silenced. Even if it meant damaging the goods. But when everything in the other room suddenly went quiet, the two others turned from the window.

They called out, "Anton?"

There was no reply. Just the sound of scuffling and something being moved.

"Anton?! What's going on?"

Still nothing.

The driver motioned for the second man to investigate. He leaped from his position and moved toward a short hallway on the opposite side. Gun raised and cautious.

When he entered the kitchen, he noted the counters and center island, pantry, refrigerator, utensils, a fruit basket, and on the other side, a dining room table, where Anton was sitting facing away from him. Leaning forward as if looking at something on the table.

"What the hell are you doing?" the second man exclaimed, approaching while looking for the woman. "I said what are you—"

He suddenly stopped. Just a few feet from the table. He could see something just past Anton's shoulder. It looked like . . . a giant bowl turned upside down.

He inched closer and could see something strange about Anton's position. His jaw seemingly outstretched, with his face and chin resting on top of the bowl . . . with a bloody apple stuffed in his mouth.

"Holy sh—"

It was all it took. A temporary distraction. Seconds, for the man to face away from the pantry, unaware that the door had opened behind him. And Reiff had stepped out, with Waterman's .40-caliber Smith & Wesson gripped firmly in both hands.

The driver at the window jumped at the two shots. Whirling and pointing his own gun.

"Anton! . . . Ivan!"

Confusion instantly gave way to fear. *Someone else was in the house!*

Then came rage.

The driver opened fire, shooting through the wall dividing the two rooms. He fired systematically. Low, waist-high, and every couple of feet. Each shot punched giant, exploding holes through the drywall. *"Come on, you son of a bitch!"*

One line across. Reload. And then another, back in the opposite direction, lower this time. When he finished, he withdrew a third magazine and reloaded again. Rechambering and rising from his position.

Reiff lay flat on the floor and moved only slightly to check the pantry door. *No holes.*

He turned back. Remaining perfectly still. Waiting. And listening.

As the ringing faded, he could hear the other man's breathing on the other side of the wall. Labored. Fearful. Unsure what to do. Trapped between Waterman outside and Reiff inside. Desperately trying to think of a plan. A way to escape.

The man's only hope was that he hit Reiff in his barrage. It was a bad guess. But the longer Reiff remained quiet, the more hopeful the man would become. And the more desperate, as he grasped the fact that his men were already dead.

It took over a minute. A very long minute until Reiff sensed movement. Soft, slow steps, but not entirely silent. Boots were like that.

He knew which way the man was coming. One careful step at a time. And as soon as the first foot was visible, he fired.

It was some time before Waterman entered the house. Carefully. With his rifle high and cheek pressed firmly against the stock. Sweeping and moving. Around the far side of the kitchen. One by one, spotting all three men. Dead.

And in the pantry, squatting on the floor, was John Reiff, still holding his sobbing daughter.

97

Outside, behind the house, Waterman stood next to Rachel, listening to her on the phone.

"Henry's texting me what he found," she said, hanging up.

"Good."

Together they looked out over the expanse of open dirt and weeds where Reiff and his daughter, Elizabeth, were sitting on large rocks, facing one other, talking and holding hands.

"How the hell does he explain all this?" Waterman wondered aloud.

Rachel shook her head. "I can't even imagine."

"She blamed herself for her father's death."

Rachel frowned, still harboring remnants of her own guilt over how they deceived Reiff.

As if reading her mind, Waterman said, "You know you can't blame yourself for any of this, right?"

"What I know and what I feel are two different things."

"They usually are."

He suddenly turned, noting the distant wisps of a rising dust cloud a good half mile away. Elizabeth's husband. Rushing home.

A couple of minutes later, a white Subaru rounded one side of the house and skidded to a stop. Her husband, just over six feet with dark hair, jumped from the vehicle and began running.

He came to a halt several feet from John and Elizabeth, staring at his wife, who rose to embrace him. And after several moments, pointed to Reiff, who stood up to shake his hand.

Waterman waited patiently. They had a little time, but not much. They had to get the bodies out of the house and find a way to dispose of them, including the SUV.

But for now, introductions were more important.

98

The Phoenix Zoo was only a fraction of what it had been. But it survived when many others had not. Neither private nor public.

It was much smaller now, with more than half of its grounds closed. Comprised now of the main entrance and several habitats, with just two of its original four trails still operational. And less than half of its animal residents. A testament to the efforts of the still-operational Phoenix Zoo Auxiliary in their undying struggle to keep things running, no matter what.

The earth-toned entrance with a slatted overhead roof was where Dr. Samantha Reed greeted them, dressed in the zoo's old zebra-striped vests.

"Thank you for coming," she said to Rachel, her face somber. "But I'm afraid I don't have very good news." Intertwining her fingers, she lowered her hands. "I'm sorry to say we've lost them."

Rachel's heart sank. She was losing what little optimism she still had. Not just for her animals but for the man standing behind her. His whole body was now shuddering.

After everything they had gone through. Everything they'd managed to ensure. Was it all for nothing?

She could feel the hopelessness welling inside of her. That it was now all for naught. She stood there, wavering, in silence.

Until she felt a hand on her shoulder. And John Reiff leaning in to whisper, "It's okay, Rachel."

No, it wasn't! A surge of emotion suddenly rose within her. Of anger and defiance. "Where are they?"

Dr. Reed was taken aback by the force of her question, but quickly motioned them forward. "Come with me."

She led them to one of their smaller facilities. A room not more than a few hundred square feet, where rows of metal counters and shelves lined one wall, filled with supplies, and in the middle, two three-foot-by-six-foot chrome-colored examination tables positioned side by side. Along the far wall were several metal cages. All empty except three.

Rachel continued to the cages, staring at the lifeless animals inside. First at Lester, the Duroc pig. And then Otis, the chimpanzee. And finally Bella. The small white Chihuahua-terrier she had come to love. Jumping up and down every morning when she saw Rachel. Now lying rigid and unmoving.

Tears formed in Rachel's eyes as she opened the clasped door and reached inside, stroking Bella's tiny head, before moving to her belly. Her body was colder than normal but gradually returning to room temperature.

Something occurred to her, and she looked around, checking the other cages, before turning to Dr. Reed. "Where's the capuchin?"

The doctor sighed. "We don't know."

Rachel raised her eyebrows. "What?"

"We don't know," repeated Reed.

"What do you mean, you don't know?"

"We're still looking."

"Looking?"

"Both primates were kept in different habitats. When we found the chimpanzee, the small capuchin had already escaped."

Rachel suddenly stood up. "Escaped?"

Dr. Reed cleared her throat. "It managed to cut a hole through the netting."

"How?"

"By sharpening a rock."

Rachel stared at her, dumbfounded. *"Sharpening a rock?"*

Outside, Dr. Reed led them to the outdoor habitat, covered on all sides by a vast sage-green netting. Beneath it, one end of the habitat was sectioned off into a smaller area, where on the far side some of the netting appeared to be stitched back together with black nylon cord.

"It was a surprise to us, too," she said. "We've never seen anything like that before. But we're sure he's still on the premises. He was most likely looking for a quiet place to die. We'll find him."

Rachel thought for a moment. "On the phone, you said the capuchin wasn't showing any signs yet."

"He wasn't. Not like the others. But it was just a matter of time."

"Did you ever observe symptoms in him?"

"I'll have to check. The rest succumbed very quickly, though. Within days, so . . ."

It was then that Rachel stared at Yamada. Then Waterman. And finally, Reiff.

Something in her gut told her Dallas was still alive.

99

Less than two hours later, Henry Yamada plopped down with a thud in front of the round table, setting his laptop on it and immediately flipping up the screen. The table was large and old, covered in a light brown laminate dotted with a smattering of tiny nicks and scratches. Just like everywhere else in the world, the downtown Phoenix library was a shell of its former self. Still wall-to-wall with bookcases and books, but almost entirely devoid of actual people.

"Are you sure this is going to work?"

"No." He began typing without looking back at Rachel. "But I've seen programs that do this."

Rachel looked over as Waterman and Reiff both approached and sat down. Together, they dropped several old geographical magazines on the table and began leafing through them, stopping to study maps of the surrounding area.

Turning back to Yamada, she said, "So what do these programs do?"

"Ever hear of image stitching?"

"No."

Henry paused and looked at the others. "It became big about forty years ago, based on something called 'projective geometry.'"

"Kid," said Waterman, "if you're trying to get us to understand something, you're going in the wrong direction."

Yamada nodded. "The general concept is not as complicated as it sounds. It has to do with computer pixels, tiny dots that make up any given image or picture. Ranging from hundreds of thousands to several million. Millions of dots that together create an image and dots that can also act like tiny digital fingerprints. Especially when you group them! Because if you group enough, their colors and hues can create a combination of unique digital values. Unique enough that you can then use a mathematical algorithm to 'search' for that particular combination."

"I didn't understand any of that," said Rachel.

Yamada grinned. "Let me try again. The pixels are not just unique in their colors and hues but also in what they are displaying. Say, for example, a building or piece of architecture. All the details of its shape; its edges, its lines, various shading, and angles. When you include everything, even the most boring object becomes unique. And you may not need the whole object to fingerprint it; a lot of times, you just need a piece of it. Nor does it even have to be an actual picture; it just needs enough detail for the computer to create that fingerprint when we scan it." He returned to his keyboard and resumed typing. "A lot of data was lost from the internet, but there's still a lot of stuff out there."

Rachel was not following. "So, what then, this all comes down to what we can find?"

Yamada stopped again and shook his head. He then grinned and looked at Reiff. "No, it comes down to how well *John* can *draw*."

100

The road was old, littered with gravel-filled potholes, winding beneath a massive grove of bare maple trees. The ground was awash in a sea of orange-and red-colored leaves.

The narrow valley, located in southeastern Utah, was now barren and forgotten. Dotted by deserted structures as the gray Mercedes passed through with only a muffled rumble beneath its tires.

It crossed the open expanse until reaching another outcropping of buildings. Old and scattered over a few acres, with only one appearing to be even remotely usable. Situated at the base of a small hill.

The car stopped in front, where Liam Duchik pushed his door open and stepped into the cold westerly breeze. Pushing it shut, he proceeded forward, climbing three deteriorating concrete steps to enter the building.

Much of the original visitors' center was still in place. Including most of its original contents, now covered in a thick layer of dust. Shelves of books, calendars, toys, and on the top shelves, branded mugs and sets of wineglasses. All facing a long glass countertop, supporting an aged and rusted cash register.

All of which Duchik ignored. Passing everything as though the room were empty as he headed for a set of large metal doors on the far wall. Stopping only briefly to withdraw a key and unlock one. When he reached the bottom of the concrete steps, he flipped on the overhead lighting, illuminating a giant and almost empty room. Save for the ten identical and yet unused white objects lining the far side. Tall, cylindrical hibernation tanks.

And somewhere on the opposing side of the wall could be heard the smooth audible hum of a two-ton diesel generator.

It had been over twenty-four hours with no word from his men.

Which meant they were most likely dead. Throwing yet another wrench in an otherwise perfect plan. At least, it *had* been perfect.

Not only did the loose ends still exist, but they had now frayed so badly that Duchik had to rethink everything. They were still out there, making the erasure of the project difficult, if not impossible.

No. Nothing was impossible. It would just take more time. And more energy. Both of which Duchik had in ample amounts.

Even if the details got out, they would still be limited in scope. The lab itself had been wiped clean, and the data destroyed. At worst, confessions from Masten, Souza, and Yamada could prove disruptive. And, at best, they would be viewed as unsubstantiated claims and ignored. Misdirection was one of Duchik's specialties.

And he *would* find Reiff. Eventually.

He would have to be patient. And diligent. But in time, he would find him. Just as he would find the others.

As he stood there, alone, in the quietness of the room, staring at the cryo tanks, he pondered just how long it would take—

Duchik suddenly turned when he heard something above him. Faint, but nearby. And repeating. Something that sounded like . . . footsteps.

The shock was genuine when the footsteps began descending the concrete steps behind him. Slowly. Delicately. Until boots appeared, followed by pants, a checkered shirt, and finally, a face.

John Reiff.

Duchik was stunned. Trying to comprehend several things at once. But he recovered quickly.

"I . . . don't know whether I should be surprised or relieved."

Reiff's expression was hard. "I'd say the former."

The older man's face morphed into acceptance, and he grinned. "We have a lot to talk about."

"I'm not so sure."

Duchik examined him. Noting the trembling throughout his body. "You don't look well."

"Who does?"

Duchik sighed. "I must say, you've been quite the thorn." He clasped his hands behind his back. "I suspected you were going to be a problem when I saw a few of those drawings. Especially the burning of the European Central Bank."

Reiff did not respond.

"I suppose I should have dealt with you sooner."

Duchik continued watching Reiff, subtly shifting his weight while reaching up to withdraw a four-inch blade from a small belt sheath. Bringing it down in his right hand and gripping it firmly.

Reiff calmly peered at the knife before turning and noting the room's heavy door propped open near the steps. Without a word, he moved to it and eased it closed.

It was some time before Reiff emerged. Through the visitors' center and back outside into the open air. Where the other three were waiting by the Jeep.

"Where's Duchik?"

"Where I found him."

Waterman nodded in understanding, and then studied Reiff while speaking aloud to Rachel.

"Tell him."

There was no reply.

Waterman turned and looked at her. "I said *tell* him."

"Tell me what?"

"You don't have a lot of time left," said Waterman, "but she thinks there may be another option."

Reiff, visibly shaking, waited for her to speak.

Rachel swallowed nervously.

"It's extreme," she said. "And we'd have to hurry."

101

Reiff could barely concentrate. The shaking was now accompanied by bouts of intense pain throughout his body. Making any position difficult, even sitting.

He glanced through his window at the giant side mirror, vibrating from the rumble of the truck's loud engine, but not enough to prevent him from seeing the bright headlights of Yamada's Nissan behind them. The rest of the small car was obscured behind a swirling cloud of snowflakes as they drove along a dark and empty two-lane road.

When they arrived, a strange feeling came over him as Waterman pulled off onto the frozen dirt before stopping and throwing the hulking vehicle into reverse. Backing up and stopping within twenty feet of the edge.

In the Nissan, Yamada and Rachel circled around the front and came to a stop on the other side. They hopped out and moved to the truck to help Reiff down.

The freezing wind cut through him like a knife. A welcome, if only momentary, distraction from the pain. Together they led him away from the truck, which Waterman had turned off, leaving only the external generator running in the back.

Waterman took Yamada's place under one of Reiff's arms and motioned him back to the Nissan before looking to his friend.

"You sure about this, John?"

He winced and peered up through the falling snow. "Got a better idea?"

Waterman glanced at Rachel, wearing a heavy coat with one side left

open for her folded arm and sling. Giving Reiff whatever support she
could, her expression was a mix of apprehension and fear. "Are you
sure you don't want Elizabeth to be here?"

Reiff shook his head. "She doesn't need to see this."

"John, I . . ." Rachel shuddered. "I have no idea if this will work."

"We don't exactly have a lot to lose."

She nodded reluctantly. "I don't know if there was something special
about this river. The temperature, the depth, some special composition
of who knows what. But it's the only thing I can think of. I just can't—"

"I get it, Rachel."

She stared into his eyes. "And if there is any possible way, any way
at all, to bring you back, I swear I will."

"I know." With that, he looked past her at the iron bridge covered in
snow. Long since repaired, but nowhere in his memories.

Yamada returned with his arms full, handing everything to Waterman, who held up the rubber dry suit to search for the large metal pull
tab and then began unzipping it.

One leg at a time, he climbed in, assisted by Yamada, who brought
up each arm when ready. Waterman then grinned at Reiff. "Don't
make me do this for nothing."

His only reply was to reach out and shake his friend's hand. Then
Yamada's.

On the bridge, Reiff faced the railing, unable to tell how much of the
shaking was from the cold or his own body. His trembling hands were
now upon the icy guardrail, with Rachel standing next to him.

She turned and checked with Yamada on the opposite side of the
bridge, who looked down at Waterman, suited up and standing surrounded by ice chunks to his knees.

Back on the embankment, their large truck's cargo hold was open
with its industrial freezer running, along with a waiting stretcher and
monitoring equipment inside.

Reiff unzipped his jacket and removed it, dropping it onto the frozen
ground.

"What are you doing?"

"I wasn't wearing a jacket on the bus," he said. He turned and lifted
one leg onto the railing.

"Wait!" she cried, grabbing him with her good hand and pulling
him back. She hugged him and said, "I'm sorry. For everything."

"Don't be. You gave me a second chance." He turned back to the rail and grinned. "Besides, it's not the worst way to go."

With that, he climbed up, placed a foot on top of the guardrail, and jumped.

102

The funeral was lovely. Pleasant and simple against the backdrop of Sedona's beautifully red-tinted mountains. Small and rugged with meandering patches of rich green valleys providing a breathtaking contrast of nature. Perfect for their gathering to honor Perry Williams's life.

His children were there, his grandchildren, and even one great-grandchild. A small boy, perhaps three or four, standing quietly and gripping his crying mother's hand.

It was a modest gathering, which was more common now, but the atmosphere was warm and happy, just as Perry would have wanted.

His children spoke of a wonderful father. A man focused not just on appreciation of life but the gift and duty of trying to make it better—for everyone. To remember that it wasn't just about savoring our time here but about helping someone else savor theirs, too. And hopefully to contribute to the world around us in whatever way we could.

It was to this that Rachel also spoke. Sharing how she had first met him in Denver and the countless ways he had helped people while they worked together at St. Luke's. And to know that he had indeed made the world better. That he was a wonderful man and one they could all be proud to call their father and grandfather.

When the service ended, Rachel stood solemnly to the side, Henry beside her, watching people slowly file away over an endless carpet of thick green grass.

"Perry told me an interesting story once," he said. "He said that many years ago, he was working on a project that required him to look up old articles from something called microfilm. He said just for fun, he looked up a newspaper from the day he was born." Henry slowly grinned to himself. "He said, 'You know what people were arguing and fighting about back then, Henry? The same crap we are now.'"

Henry turned to her. "He said the names and words were different, but it was the same arguments. The same bickering that's been going on for ten thousand years and will go on for another ten thousand. One constant and never-ending argument, going on and on, about who is better and who is worse. Most of which never actually matters."

Rachel gave Henry a warm smile. "He told me the same story."

"The funny thing is . . . I don't think he was telling me a story as much as giving me a lesson."

"Yeah?"

He watched with Rachel as the last of the people reached their cars. "So, what now?"

"What do you mean?"

"I mean, what do we do now?"

Rachel frowned, not answering for a long time. Until she finally said, "I think maybe you should go home. And find a nice comfortable job. A safe job. And focus on what matters, like Perry said."

"Maybe," he replied, staring forward. "Or . . ."

"Or?"

"Or maybe we continue. Making a difference."

Rachel smiled again, this time wider. "I was hoping you would say that."

"Now that John is stabilized . . . I say we go find that monkey."